THE
TEXAN'S
TOUCH

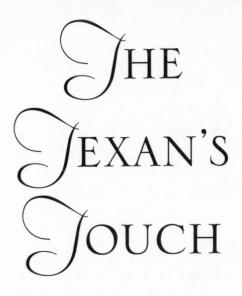

THE TEXAN'S TOUCH

JODI THOMAS

JOVE BOOKS, NEW YORK

THE TEXAN'S TOUCH

A Jove Book / published by arrangement with
the author

ISBN: 1-56865-868-0

A JOVE BOOK®
Jove Books are published by The Berkley Publishing Group, a
member
of Penguin Putnam Inc.,
200 Madison Avenue, New York, New York 10016.
JOVE and the "J" design are trademarks belonging to
Jove Publications, Inc.

PRINTED IN THE UNITED STATES OF AMERICA

This book is dedicated to
my editor,
Gail Fortune,
with great love and respect.

ONE

THE CROP-BARREN HILLS ECHOED WITH RUMBLES OF MAN-MADE thunder, scattering it like death's breeze through the cluster of hospital tents and worn, muddy transport wagons. Dr. Adam McLain pulled off his bloody coat and tossed it atop the mountain of dirty laundry beside the opening of the surgery tent.

He fought the constant churning in his stomach from a combination of bad food and unbearable working conditions as he slipped into his double-breasted wool uniform. He didn't bother to button it to meet the proper Union dress code.

After working almost thirty hours straight, a numbness had settled over him like damp flannel, covering even the creases of his mind, blocking out all dreams, all hopes, and most of his senses. His hands were badly chapped from hours of being cold and wet with blood.

They'll scab over while I sleep, he thought as he moved through the shadows between tents. The smell of boiling coffee blended in the cool mist of early spring. There had been another time, another place in his life, but after four years of war, the memories were odorless, tasteless, and almost invisible.

He could feel his body shutting down with each step toward his quarters. For a few hours he would close his eyes and escape in sleep. He no longer wished for a touch of beauty in his life, silence seemed enough. Living seemed a luxury, survival the only necessity.

The chief surgeon's words still rang in his ears. "Work faster, McLain! For every moment you hesitate to consider, another soldier dies waiting."

So, at twenty-five, Adam's dreams of becoming a great physician were shattered, splattering his hopes like soldier's after soldier's blood in the dirt. He wasn't saving lives, or healing. He was only digging bullets out. If he was successful, the man would live on to fight, to shoot rounds into men in gray for some other doctor to worry about. Adam had thought he'd be a knight in this game of war, but he was only a pawn, cutting away like a butcher until he no longer saw faces, but only blood over blackened flesh.

As Adam lifted the flap of his tent, he thought he caught a movement in the corner. For a moment, he hoped his older brother might have found him. It was time for one of Wes's one-hour reunions.

But, before more could register, the cold butt of a gun struck him from behind. Pain splintered into total blackness. Adam felt his body falling as he surrendered all feeling.

"You're an idiot, Rafe!" a low, angry man's Southern-accented voice whispered. "When we said bring back a doctor, we meant one in gray, not a damn Yankee."

"I couldn't find no one else!" a higher voice answered in almost a whine. "Docs don't grow on trees, you know. I went by the camp and there weren't one, so I followed the river a few miles and stumbled on another group of hospital tents. I figured a doc's a doc, Tyler."

"I say we kill him now," a third tone, cold with indifference, offered. "He's no good to us. We're so close to the line as it is, one good scream could bring all hell down on us."

"No!" the first man, who'd been referred to as Tyler, answered. "We haven't got time to find another doctor. Nick will be dead by dawn."

Adam McLain slowly opened his eyes, then closed them in dread. Just as he'd guessed, the men before him weren't green recruits, but seasoned fighters who looked born to war. They had no hint of uniform, but the voices and the weapons they carried marked them. One was older, harder. The angry one called Tyler looked to be the leader. He was young and rawhide lean. The third, called Rafe, was little more than a boy.

Opening his eyes once more, Adam looked straight into the face of Tyler.

The leader knelt close without breaking his stare. "You awake, Yank?"

"I'm awake." Adam saw a coldness in the reb's eyes and knew he was alive only because they needed a doctor. He saw a man curled up on a table amid the clutter of an abandoned farmhouse. A thin stream of blood ran across the dusty wood and dripped onto a stool pushed halfway beneath the table.

"Untie me." Adam could hear the dying man's breathing from across the room. If he didn't help fast, the man on the table wouldn't have enough blood left to survive.

Tyler laughed. "Not yet, Doc. I got a proposition for you first. We're part of a group of men known as the Shadows. Ever hear of us?"

Adam nodded. Who hadn't heard of the Shadows? They were men who crossed the lines as if they were playing jump rope. Every soldier who walked the perimeters of camp thought he heard them move in the darkness just beyond the campfires.

Leaning closer, Tyler said, "We got one of our troop down and we need a doctor bad. I risked a fire and brought in water, but none of us know what to do. If you agree to take the bullet out and sew him up, we might just let you live."

"Might," the older man answered from behind the leader. He appeared to be trimming his fingernails with the end of his hunting knife.

"And if I refuse?" Adam pulled at his ropes. The dying man's breathing told him they were wasting precious time.

The young reb smiled again. "Then I turn you over to Henry here. He knows ways to make a man die slow. You'll meet your Maker deaf from listening to your own screaming."

Adam knew he now measured his life by a watch and not a calendar. "I'll help the injured man any way I can, but I won't operate with you breathing down my neck. If you trust me with his life, then I work by my rules. And the first one is, I work alone."

The older man snorted at the request, and the kid laughed as though he'd just asked for the moon.

"All right." Tyler straightened to his feet after he weighed the request. "Everyone out. We'll cover the doors. You do the best you can, Yank." He cut the ropes at Adam's feet. "But if Nick is dead come morning, you can count your remaining heartbeats on your fingers."

As Tyler sliced Adam's hands free, Rafe tossed him his medical saddlebags. "Nick's the little brother of our captain and he won't take kindly to you butchering the boy, so be careful. Your life is tied to his."

Adam hardly noticed as the men slipped from the room. He knew whether he saved the bleeding man or not, he'd be dead by sunrise.

They couldn't afford to let him live after he'd seen their faces. He knew it and so did Tyler.

Slowly, Adam moved to the side of a long table where a thin man, still in coat and boots, rested. "Let's take a look, reb. No use both of us dying."

As Adam gripped the man's shoulder and rolled him over, a Colt, pointed straight at Adam's heart, rolled with the patient.

"You're not touching me!" A low pain-filled voice whispered. "I'd rather die."

Adam watched the youth before him, more frightened by what he saw than by the pistol. Blood pulsed out with each heartbeat from the wound at the man's side.

"Dear God, didn't they apply a pressure wrap?" Adam shoved the gun aside and pulled the man's bloody fingers from the injury.

His patient relaxed, too weak to stand his ground as Adam began pulling away clothes.

He noticed the reb didn't turn loose of the Colt, even when unconscious. The youth wore a thick cotton undershirt that was skintight. With sure hands, Adam grabbed the small scissors in his bag and went to work.

As he cut the cotton away, surprise almost made him cry out, not at the wound, but at the body of a woman.

This Gray Shadow was female. Thin to the point of starvation, pale from lack of sun, but definitely all woman.

Adam smiled. Probably another reason he'd be dead come morning. If the others let him live, she'd kill him for finding out her secret. She'd kept it well by binding her now free, full breasts and her bulky clothes covered any curve of waist or fullness of hip. If Tyler had known she was a woman, Adam knew he'd never have left them alone. And if the woman guarded her secret so carefully, she'd have to see him dead . . . if she lived through the night.

There was no time to worry about tomorrow or her being a woman. With each heartbeat, she was a little closer to death. Right now all he had time to think about was that she was his patient and he had to fight to keep her alive.

TWO

Nichole felt the stranger's hands moving along her side. The wound still throbbed but it no longer burned, and the pounding in her head had eased. She seemed to be floating deep beneath murky waters. Only the skin he touched came alive as his warm fingers moved over her.

Without opening her eyes, she waited, trying to guess what this man in blue might do next. If she'd learned nothing else from her big brother, it had been to anticipate the unexpected from the enemy. Only this Yank wasn't acting like an enemy.

Slowly, she tightened the fingers of her right hand and felt her Colt still in place. The fool hadn't bothered to remove the weapon when he'd had the chance. After years of riding with the Shadows, she'd learned to keep her grip tight even in sleep.

Warm water dripped across her waist just before a cloth gently stroked her flesh. Long strong hands moved to her back and lifted her slightly from the table. She felt his fingers spread along her skin as he began wrapping a soft bandage around her.

Nichole tensed. She'd never encountered a man who so boldly touched so much of her body. In fact touching anyone, or being touched, was not a part of her life.

"Easy now," he whispered as he worked. "I'll have you all bandaged up in a minute."

She tried to relax, as if still in sleep, while his fingers slid along the bandage, checking his work. The warmth of his caress penetrated the material in healing strokes. She'd always thought a lover's hands would feel like this—strong, and sure, and kind.

He lifted her carefully from the table and rested her head on his shoulder as he pulled her shirt down over her injury. She felt his heart pounding next to hers and smelled the hint of shaving soap and wool. Nichole pushed the memory of a blue uniform from her mind and gave herself over to the sanctuary of his arms.

"You're going to be all right," he whispered against her cheek. "No matter what happens to me come morning, you're going to live. Who knows, maybe you'll even allow the world to know what a beautiful woman you are hidden beneath these dirty clothes."

He cradled her against him and moved to the half-crumbled fireplace. Very gently, he knelt and sat with his back against the brick. He sat her between his chest and knee as she stretched her legs toward the warmth of a dying fire. She could feel his heart beating as his knee braced her back and his outstretched leg rested against hers.

She fell asleep with his hand gently brushing over her short hair and the warmth of his body barring any cold from her back. For the first time in years, her fingers uncoiled from her weapon. Her hand moved against the wall of his chest. His embrace seemed to welcome her safely home.

It was almost dawn when she awakened. Without moving, she slowly opened her eyes. The man, only inches away, slept soundly, his warm breath brushing her forehead. One of his arms draped across her shoulder, the other lay along her leg, his hand resting just above her knee.

Nichole shifted slightly, watching his face. As her hand found the gun, she couldn't stop staring at the man. His hair was chestnut brown, his face tan and handsome. Tiny worry lines ran along his forehead. Light brown stubble covered a strong chin. Nothing seemed hard or cold about him, unlike every man she'd known. There was a strength about him, a quiet strength.

Slowly, she raised the Colt.

He reacted to her movement and opened his eyes.

Sleepy, brown eyes, filled with worry, stared at her for a moment before he smiled with what she thought was pride.

" 'Morning," he whispered as his hand moved along her leg and across her hip to gently rest against her side. "Feeling better?"

Nichole straightened. He'd touched her so easily, so naturally, as if he'd done so for a lifetime. "I'm fine," she lied. In truth she wasn't sure she had the energy to stand. "And I thank you for taking that bullet out of me last night."

The man chuckled. "I somehow guessed your voice would have a slow low drawl to it, but I never thought your eyes would be green. So green. Like full summer just after it rains."

He looked away, thinking he was making a fool of himself. She was his patient, his enemy. "I checked the stitches I had to make in your side about an hour ago. They were holding, but you'll have to take it easy for a few days."

His voice died suddenly as she brought the barrel of her weapon to his throat.

"Did you touch me last night?" Nichole had to know how much liberty this Yankee took while she was unconscious.

"I did," he answered as if he didn't know he'd just signed his death sentence. "Doctors usually do touch their patients."

"How much?"

He closed his eyes and leaned his head back against the wall. "No more than was necessary during the operation. Afterward, I did my best to clean away all the blood around the wound." He let out a long breath. "But when you were bandaged and sleeping." His confession came slowly. "It's been so long since I've seen anything but war. I couldn't stop myself from . . ."

Nichole forgot about the throbbing in her head and the pain in her side. Her finger tightened slightly on the trigger. This man had to be telling the truth. Why would he lie about such a thing? Unless he had a death wish. She'd heard of men just looking for a reason to die and be done with the war. She was torn between killing him for what he'd done and letting him live just to ruin his plans.

"Where?" she demanded. "Where'd you touch me?"

The man stared at her with gentle brown eyes. "I assure you, miss, it was nowhere improper. No more than we'd have touched if dancing."

Now it was Nichole's turn to laugh. She'd never danced in her life, and probably never would. She was in the company of men enough to hear how they talked, and she'd be willing to bet most of her comrades would have fondled her plenty if they had the chance and knew she was a woman.

Pushing the gun against his throat, she whispered, "I have to kill you, Yank."

He didn't look surprised. "I know," he answered as he swallowed. "I thought about it last night. If you don't, one of your friends will at dawn. They're all just beyond the door. But if you kill me first, they'll never learn you're a woman. It's the only way you can be sure of your secret."

The man closed his eyes as though waiting for the end.

When she didn't pull the trigger, he whispered, "It's Adam, Adam McLain. My home address is engraved on my medical bag. If you're able, let someone know I'm dead. If you don't, I have these two brothers who'll never stop looking for me.''

''You're the chattiest corpse I've ever met.'' Nichole saw no fear in his face. Either he was the North's biggest fool, or he'd seen enough killing to be hardened to even his own death.

Adam looked down at her. ''Maybe I'm just tired of all the killing. Until I touched your cheek last night, I'd forgotten what a woman felt like. I'd forgotten there was anything soft and beautiful in this world.''

''I know,'' she mumbled, wishing she'd shot him before they talked. His words scraped against her heart, causing more pain than the bullet lodged at her rib. When her parents had died three years ago, her big brother had done the only thing he could do. He'd taken her with him. She hadn't slept in a bed, or bathed with soft soap, or had a man so much as hold her hand. She'd grown from a girl to a woman without anyone knowing.

He moved slowly, not toward the gun at his throat, but to brush his fingers along her jawline. ''Is it Nichole?''

''Yes,'' she answered. ''But I've been called Nick for so long I probably wouldn't answer to anything else. Once upon a time, a lifetime ago, it was Nichole Casey Hayward. But now, it's just Nick.''

She knew she should end this discussion. The proper thing to do would be to shoot him and be done with it. But his touch was so light, so caring. Without lowering the Colt, she turned her head slightly so that his fingers trailed along the length of her throat.

Nichole was starving, color-blind in a war that was never ending. They'd both been robbed of years of youth and discovery. And for one moment, one timeless moment, she stepped away from reality and responsibility. For just a blink in time she wanted someone to see her as a woman and not a fighting Shadow. She wanted there to be more in her life than running and hiding. She wanted there to be this man.

Moving his long fingers over her chin, Adam lifted her head slightly as though he'd read her mind.

She let the gun slip away as he lowered his lips to hers. A hunger sparked in her as his mouth gently covered hers. She felt his hand slide into her hair as she tasted the warmth of his lips.

The shattering of the door echoed through the room like a cannon shot. Adam instinctively tightened his grip around Nichole's shoulder. She reached for her gun.

''Nick!'' a bear of a man shouted. ''Nick!''

To Adam's surprise, she lowered her weapon as a huge, wild half animal of a man stormed forward. He stood well over six feet with coal-colored hair to his shoulders and a beard of curly hair that stood out in every direction.

"Wolf!" she answered. "Wolf, over here!"

The giant shoved the bloody table aside and knelt to one knee. "I sent the others on ahead. I figured if you were dead, I wanted to kill the doc with my own hands. If you were alive, I'd let you do it, then we'd be on our way."

The huge man stared at them, as if he were seeing a two-headed cow. His gaze narrowed to Adam's arm resting protectively across his sister's shoulder and a Union jacket covering her legs.

"What's going on, Nick?"

"Nothing." She looked at Adam. "I was just kissing the Yank."

The big man slowly stood, drawing in air as if he planned to use half the room's supply in one breath. "You kissed him?"

"Actually, I was kissing her," Adam answered, seeing no need to lie or hide behind her.

"Shut up!" Wolf growled. "You're a talking dead man."

Nichole leaned away from Adam. "You can't kill him, big brother, I kissed him."

Wolf rubbed his face with a beefy hand, as if he could rub away what his eyes were seeing. "You kissed a damn Yankee?"

"I kissed a very kind man who saved my life."

Wolf sobered and looked straight at Adam. "I thank you for that, Doc, and I'll see you're buried proper for it."

"You're not killing him, Wolf. He saved my life. I'm the one who kissed him, and I'll be the one who shoots him."

Wolf seemed to relax slightly, as if concluding that his little sister had finally come to her senses. He turned and moved toward the remains of the door. "I'll saddle your horse," he mumbled as he shoved wood out of his way. "But don't go around kissing no one else. I can't be limiting the number of Yanks I shoot."

As the door fell back in place, Nichole pushed away from Adam with a groan. "Go!" she whispered. "If you stand on the table, you should be able to jump to the loft. From there, go out the place where the roof has fallen in. I'll give you to the count of thirty, then I'll fire. You should be in the woods by the time Wolf opens the door and finds you gone."

"But—"

"There's no time." She pushed him away.

He leaned forward and kissed her cheek as his fingers moved over the soft curls of her midnight hair.

"One," she whispered. "Two."

"God, you have beautiful eyes."

"Three."

"Thanks." He jumped on the table and pulled himself into the loft.

"Four," she forced the words out in a hurried breath. "When this war is over, I'll find you, Adam McLain, and finish that kiss."

"I'll plan on it, Nichole Hayward," he said, and smiled down at her a moment before turning toward the opening in the roof.

"Five," she whispered as she shoved away a tear with her free hand. "Six."

Adam was several yards into the blackness of the woods before he slowed. As he moved through the undergrowth at the creek's edge, he heard a single shot shatter the cool dawn air. A bullet—meant to end his life. The solitary blast brought him back to the reality of hell.

Silently, he slipped into the cold water and began moving upstream. If the kid, called Rafe, had followed the stream up to find Adam's camp, it made sense that if he followed the water's guide, he'd eventually reach the Union hospital tents.

The stream widened, growing deeper and slippery, but he didn't dare move ashore and leave a trail Wolf could follow. Nichole might not want him dead, but her brother had no such weakness. He'd track Adam down if he had the time.

The wool uniform was soaked to the shoulders, but still, Adam moved. Dawn light slid between the branches in slivers of silver, reflecting off the water in diamond brightness, but bringing no warmth. The smell of spring was thick in the air, but fear pulsed through Adam, muting all else.

Twice, he fell, losing ground to the rushing water, but he didn't dare slow his pace. If Wolf was on horseback, it wouldn't take the reb long to overtake him.

Rushing water drowned out most sounds, but Adam could hear the low thunder of a horse's hooves coming toward him. When he tried to increase his speed, the stream fought him for progress.

Just as he leaned to dive beneath the water, he heard someone shout, "Adam!"

Suddenly, Captain Wes McLain, dressed in his cavalry uniform and riding a powerful roan, was splashing through the stream toward Adam.

Wes didn't pull the reins when he offered his arm to his brother. As he'd done a hundred times in childhood, Adam locked his hand at his brother's elbow and Wes did the same. With one mighty pull, Adam swung up behind Wes, and the roan turned to reverse his track.

They sliced the stream with wings of sparkling silver. The huge animal spanned the distance to the camp in thundering seconds. When Wes turned the horse toward land and headed for the hospital tents, he slowed enough to shout, "Trying to get yourself killed, little brother? I thought you had more sense!"

Adam ignored the teasing. "I was managing fine. How'd you find me?"

"It took me about a minute to figure out what had happened in your tent. Whoever kidnapped you left a trail even Daniel could follow. When the tracks hit the water, I knew they wouldn't be heading north."

He slowed at Adam's tent and gave his brother a hand down. "I decided the rebs weren't looking for soldiers to kill, so they must have needed a doctor. And if they crossed the line to get one, they were desperate and you probably wouldn't be coming back."

Adam moved into his tent with his brother following. "You guessed right."

"And you helped them, of course." Wes reached beneath the straw mattress and pulled out Adam's total supply of liquor—a half bottle of whiskey. "Your war's with the angel of death, brother, and no one else. I was just hoping you had time to make them believe that before they shot you."

After a long drink, Wes made a face. "This is terrible."

Adam laughed as he pulled off his wet uniform. "It's what you left here last month." He tossed his shirt aside. "And you're right, I did what I could for the injured Gray Shadow."

Wes stopped in midgulp. "You saw Shadows? No one sees Shadows."

"I did." Nodding, Adam ordered, "You'd better get into dry clothes, too."

Wes took another swig of whiskey. "Stop mothering me, Adam. I've lived in mud and rain for half this war. Could you find the Shadow camp again? I'd love to get my hands on a few of them."

Adam shook his head. He thought of telling Wes about the black-haired, green-eyed woman, but somehow that seemed a betrayal. She'd saved his life, just as he'd saved hers, and they were bound by that even if they stood on different sides of a line. "They were riding out when I escaped. They're too far south by now."

Leaning back on his elbows, Wes ignored the mud on his boots as he relaxed on the cot. "For once, you may have an interesting story to tell, but I've no time. I'm just riding through toward a little place in Virginia called Appomattox. Word is Lee's going to surrender. I saw the first of this war at Bull Run, and I figure to see the last."

He finished the whiskey.

Wes's words took a few minutes to register. "The war may be over?" Adam let out a long breath.

"It may." Wes stood and looked at himself in the shaving mirror hanging by the bed. "Daniel is north already with a leg injury. May's at his side. He'll be home months before we can get there." Wes touched a thin scar running across his left cheek, then turned away from his reflection. "But if this war ends, start home as soon as you can. I'll catch up."

Adam knew he'd be moving at a snail's pace with the wounded. Wes would have no trouble finding him. Adam nodded as his brother stepped to the opening.

"Stay safe," Wes mumbled. "Keep an angel on your shoulder." He repeated the phrase their mother always told them.

Wes had said the same words since they'd been boys running half-wild. Then he added, as he always did, his own ending. "And your fist drawn until your brother is there to cover your back."

The older brother disappeared into the maze of tents. For four years, he'd been the best fighter the Union had produced, but if the war was ending, Adam could only guess how Wes would survive. War pulsed through his veins as strongly as peace pumped through their younger brother, Daniel's.

Adam would be going home to a fiancée, Daniel to a wife, but Wes . . .

"Bergette!" Adam slapped his forehead. How could he have forgotten about her? He'd kissed another woman without one thought of his fiancée waiting at home. Sweet little shy Bergette who'd promised him she'd wait.

He should be feeling guilty or calling himself every name of the fool he was. But Adam could still taste Nichole's kiss on his lips. The warm feel of her body sleeping against his chest was still with him. Bergette was a faraway memory, no more than a tintype in his mind, but Nichole had been flesh and blood. He'd almost risk running into her brother if he thought he could find her again.

This war better end fast, Adam thought, or he'd go mad.

Perhaps he already was. He was daydreaming about a Shadow . . . in every sense. A woman who slipped back and forth across enemy lines. A woman who, if he ever found her again, would probably slip just as easily in and out of his life.

THREE

WES MCLAIN GUIDED HIS HORSE AHEAD AS ADAM SPOTTED THE FIRST sight of their farm near Corydon, Indiana. The morning air felt cool, but everything around them was green with the summer of July 1865. Their parents' home looked like a painting framed in nature's fullness. The small white two-story house, the old barn in need of repair, the few apple trees their mother always called the orchard, the garden out back big enough to enable them to lay up winter supplies, all spoke of a peace Adam hadn't known in four years.

"We're home!" Adam shouted as he started racing his brother down the road.

Suddenly they weren't soldiers hardened in war, but boys again, racing to their mother's porch at full gallop. Only a year in age separated Wes from Adam. The two men were within an inch of the same height and with the same coloring, no one doubted they were brothers. But there was a hardness about Wes and a thin white scar on his left cheek that made him seem ages older. He was born to soldiering and it showed in his carriage.

They rounded the corral at full speed and laughed when dust flew to roof high as they reined.

"I beat you as always," Wes bragged.

"I got out of practice the past few years," Adam defended as he swung down. "If Mom were alive, she'd be out of her kitchen yelling at us by now."

Both men glanced at the kitchen door as if expecting her, even though she'd passed on the same winter as her husband. He'd been wounded when Morgan led a raid into Indiana in 1863. Though their father was up there in years, his Irish blood had demanded that he serve in the home guard. Corydon was one of the few towns hit hard by the Southerner's raid. He'd turned his horses loose at dawn and rode to fight. By nightfall the rebs had taken his entire stock of supplies and left him dying with no one to care for him except their mother.

Adam missed her, but he often thought of the pain she must have felt losing her husband while her sons were far from home fighting.

"And Dad would be running from the barn yelling that we almost rode over Daniel again." Wes's words brought Adam back to the present. "Or that we woke Danny boy from a nap and now we'd have to watch him till supper. I don't remember a day from the time the kid was born that they didn't accuse us of trying to kill him." Wes laughed.

"And you almost did!" a voice shouted from the house a moment before Daniel appeared.

Unlike his brothers, Daniel McLain was blond and still thin with youth. Even though he was twenty and had been married for two years, Adam thought of him as "the kid brother." Not even the leg Dan nursed as he moved down the steps made him seem old enough to have fought in a war.

The McLain men became children once more, roughhousing and hugging one another. A bystander might have had trouble telling whether the brothers were greeting each other or fighting. They didn't stop until May appeared on the porch. One look at Daniel's petite wife's new girth stopped Adam and Wes in midlaugh.

Daniel straightened with pride at their sudden shock. "I guess my letters didn't reach you two. You'll both be uncles before the month is out."

Wes looked uncomfortable, mumbling his congratulations as he moved to the horses. But Adam couldn't hold back his delight. He hurried up the steps and gave his sister-in-law a careful hug.

Waiting for her nod of approval, he spread his hand over the rounded ball at her middle. She was a tiny woman, not pretty at first sight, but her gentleness softened her imperfections better than any paint and powder could have. The McLain boys had always treated her like a treasure since the day she followed Daniel home from school.

"I'm so glad you made it home before time." May covered Adam's hand with her own. "Dan and I want you to deliver our baby."

"But," Adam was flattered, and a little frightened, "I haven't delivered a baby since medical school."

"Doc Wilson said he'd be near to act as second in case the new uncle faints." Daniel joined them, slipping his arm lovingly around May's shoulder. "But with the war over you'll be birthing plenty of babies now. You might as well start by bringing a new McLain into the world."

They moved into the kitchen with Wes mumbling about how he hoped he wasn't going to be asked to do anything. Children had never liked him, he claimed. And now with the scar, most were afraid of him. In fact, he went so far as to comment that babies were like cats—a man wasn't meant to hold them, but he ought to avoid stepping on them.

Adam stopped just inside the kitchen, closed his eyes and took a deep breath. Nothing had an aroma like his mother's kitchen. The stove, the hint of soap, the years of baked cinnamon bread and apple pie.

"The smell of home," Wes echoed Adam's thoughts.

"Nowhere else in the world," Adam added.

May moved to the stove to stir a pot of stew while Daniel poured his brothers coffee.

"We've been living here for about three months," he said as he handed them each a cup. "I thought of getting my own place, but I had to wait for the leg to heal, and I didn't like seeing this house empty. I'm preaching at a little church near Twin Rivers, but I'm here with May the rest of the time. We've planted a big garden and the orchard's almost ripe. I've taken care of the horses Dad had left, but the few the rebs didn't manage to round up have about gone wild from lack of riding."

"I'll help you break any horses you need to sell before winter," Wes volunteered.

"Thanks, I've been waiting for you to make it back home." Dan rubbed his leg. "There's also—"

Dan would have added more to be done, but Wes interrupted. "I'll help while I'm here, but as far as I'm concerned, this place is yours now, Daniel, not mine," Wes said calmly as he gave away his inheritance. "Yours and May's and your children to come."

"But . . ." Daniel began shaking his head.

"Wes is right," Adam added. "The farm should belong to you. You can't raise a family on what a preacher makes on Sunday. I'll need a house in town with my practice. I'd never make a farmer. And though I enjoy riding, I've never been good with animals like you are, Danny. I think Mom would like the idea of you and May filling that second floor with children."

Wes looked up over the rim of his cup. "I've had offers in Texas. With my back pay, I can make a great deal of money moving cattle to market. A friend of mine said you can round up cattle, or pay a dollar a head for them in Texas, then move them north and sell them for twenty, maybe twenty-five in Kansas. I could never stay out of the saddle long enough to see roots grow."

The brothers respected each other enough not to argue. The farmhouse would be Daniel's. Adam would live with them until he found a place in town. Wes said, none too convincingly, that he'd like to stay until the baby came, but he had to get to Texas as soon as he rested a few days.

They ate breakfast, all talking and questioning at the same time. A silent bond was still between them, but Adam felt them pulling apart as he had when they'd left for war. No matter where he was, or how far away they were, they were his brothers, his blood. He guessed he'd always carry both their joy and their pain inside him.

An hour later, as Adam climbed the stairs to what had always been his room, he relaxed. It would feel good to sleep the day away and wake to another one of May's meals. She might be a quiet little lady, but she could sure cook a meal worth shouting about. The war seemed a lifetime away as he stretched out atop the quilt covering his bed and slowly closed his eyes.

A moment before he fell asleep, sudden insight flashed across his tired mind. No one had mentioned Bergette.

Adam tried to push worry from his thoughts, but he couldn't. Daniel and May lived in the same town with her. She was Adam's fiancée. Wouldn't they have mentioned Bergette's name once? Or sent word that he was home? Why hadn't he thought of going to her first?

He didn't bother to pull on his boots. He ran down the stairs in search of May or Danny.

May was sitting at the kitchen table with her sewing in her lap as he entered. She smiled, telling Adam without words that he'd always be welcome in what was now her home. Adam could see why Danny had loved her since childhood. She had a kindness about her that made everyone want to try harder. Daniel called her his touch of heaven, his private angel.

"May?" Adam pulled a chair across from her and forced himself to be calm even though he was in a hurry to know. "Is something wrong with Bergette? Has she been killed? Did she tire of waiting and marry someone else?" When May looked at him with doe-round eyes, he added, "I have to know." She didn't smile as he'd hoped she would, telling Adam something *was* wrong.

"No," she whispered. "When I saw her in church last Sunday she was well and still unmarried. As far as I know, she still waits for you, Adam."

Her words should have calmed his worry, but they didn't. "What is it?" He hated pushing May, but he had to know.

"Bergette is a lady, a grand lady now," May's voice was without judgment or emotion. "Her father made a great deal of money during the war, making her quite wealthy."

"There are worse things I can think of than coming home to a rich fiancée." Adam grinned. "Are you sure she still wants to marry me?"

May didn't return his smile. "She still wears your ring. And Nellie Wilson said she sent all the way to Paris for a wedding dress as soon as she heard talk of the war ending." May didn't look at him as she spoke. The sewing seemed to demand her attention.

He couldn't push her more. Whatever it was about Bergette that saddened May, he'd find out soon enough for himself. Maybe the two women simply weren't fond of one another. Adam grimaced. If that was true, he wasn't sure he could marry Bergette. A woman who didn't like May surely wouldn't be able to live with any McLain.

"I think I'll ride into town and pay her a call." He stood. "I'll be back by supper time."

He couldn't shake the feeling that something was wrong. Maybe it had nothing to do with Bergette. Maybe it was him. Maybe he wasn't as interested in getting married as he thought. For the past few months whenever he tried to sleep, it was green eyes he saw and not Bergette's crystal blue . . . it was short midnight black hair he reached for and not sunny blond.

But Bergette had been the only future he'd let himself believe in for so many years. The plan of coming home and living a normal life someday had been the only dream that had pulled him through the years of night. He wouldn't give up that dream, even if he had to court Bergette all over again.

One hour later as Adam stood outside her door, he thought himself a fool. Of course he loved Bergette and she loved him! He'd loved her since they'd danced that summer he'd come home from medical school. Just because he'd kissed a woman one night in the middle of a war didn't matter. Bergette and he were alike. They'd both come from hardworking, stable families. They were alike in their values and beliefs. Four years couldn't change the core of a man, or a woman. Nichole had just been a shadow that passed over his thoughts, nothing more. Bergette was his future.

An aging lady Adam didn't recognize answered the door. When he asked about his fiancée, she pointed, "Go past the state capitol building one block. It's the largest house on the left."

Adam knew the square two-story building she referred to hadn't been the state capital in forty years, but to her it probably always would be, for she'd never make the trip north to Indianapolis. Corydon had been the capital in the old woman's youth.

"Thank you," he said as she closed the door without another word.

Adam walked down the street and up the steps of a home twice the size of Bergette's former house. When he rang the bell, a butler showed him in with great hesitation. Almost before Adam was through the door, the man closed it as though fearing more trash might blow in.

Squaring his shoulders, Adam fought down a few choice comments that came to mind. He might not be rich, or high ranking, but as far as he knew the McLains had always been welcome in any home in town. Their father had been a foreman when the canals were built and even years later, most folks remembered.

About the time he'd decided he was in the wrong place, Bergette came down the stairs in a cloud of satin. Adam could only stare. She was far more beautiful than he remembered. Perfection. Absolute perfection.

When she saw him, her face lit with the delight of a child. She hurried to his outstretched arms, but stopped just before he could hold her. With a hand on each of his arms, she held him away as she stood on her tiptoes and kissed his cheek.

"Darling!" she cried. "I can't believe you're home."

When he reached for her, she stepped away. "But sweetheart, you're dirty!"

Adam looked down at his uniform. It had several days of trail dust on it, but compared to what he'd lived in of late, the uniform didn't look all that bad. Yet, compared to Bergette, he looked filthy. She was a brilliant butterfly standing next to a mud dauber.

"I didn't take the time to change," he mumbled in half apology, half explanation.

"Well, don't worry," She waved at the butler to bring tea and moved into a room larger than most officers' barracks Adam had seen. "You'll have time to dress before tonight. Even though father is in the capital, I must have a party to welcome you home." She clapped her hands and danced around like a figure on top of a music box. "We'll have the most delightful dinner."

"Then you're glad to see me home?" Adam smiled. It wasn't the greeting he'd hoped for, but she certainly looked happy. He had to slow down and remember she was a lady, sheltered from the war, protected from hard times. She was the same as when he'd left, only more mature, more beautiful. It would take time for them to feel comfortable around one another again. But she was every ounce as perfect as he remembered.

"Oh, yes, I'm glad you're home. I've planned for years, and I've kept the servants ready since the war ended. We'll have a small dinner party tonight, then a grand ball in a few weeks. An ever so grand ball!"

"After we're married?" Adam added. Every man in town would be jealous when he walked with her on his arm. "I'll dance with my wife at the ball."

"Oh, no." Bergette's bottom lip came out in a pout that broke any defense he might have built. "I'd planned on marrying in early spring. It's too late to wear my dress now. It will be fall before I could dream of putting a wedding together. When the war ended in April, I thought you'd be home by May. When you weren't, I stored the grown."

"I had to help the wounded make it back. The hospitals needed doctors for a few months longer." Adam saw from her bored expression that his explanation mattered little. "It took time for some to be well enough to travel, and sometimes weeks to find hospital space for those who hadn't recovered." He was wasting his breath.

"It doesn't matter." Adam tried to hide his disappointment in both the wait to be married and her reaction to his reasons. "I can wait till spring. It'll probably take me that long to find a house here in town and set up an office." He couldn't stop looking at her. Her hair was the color of sunshine. "I thought I'd get a place where I could have my office in part of the house, that way I could be close to you." He could almost picture her smiling as he dropped in to check on her when she was as rounded as May with his child. He'd want his office close enough where she could call him if she needed anything.

Bergette shook her head as if he weren't being logical. The young girl before him had grown to be an independent woman. She spoke her mind, saying that she had already started planning for their new house, and that they would talk of it later.

He admired her for having her own ideas, but felt uneasy with what her plans might be. Adam told himself he'd have to give her time. His life with her might have been his only dream for four years, but she'd had her own dreams. Only he found it interesting that during the hour he stayed at her house she showed no interest in even hearing his ideas.

His admiration slipped another notch later when he came down all dressed and ready to go to his welcome-home party and found his brothers still in their work clothes.

"Aren't we eating at Bergette's tonight?" Adam asked.

"Nope," Wes answered without further explanation.

Daniel suddenly grew busy hauling water for May.

Only his meek little sister-in-law faced him. "It wouldn't be proper for me to go anyway this far along in my condition. And Daniel would never go without me."

"What about you, Wes?" Adam could feel the tension in the room. Tension that had never been there before.

"I saw that fine fiancée of yours in town an hour ago. She said she was real sorry she didn't invite us, but the guest list was full." He took a long drink from his cup. "Don't know if I'd go anyway," he mumbled. "I'm really looking forward to May's supper."

Adam couldn't believe Bergette had forgotten to invite his family to a homecoming party. It made no sense. The one dream of the future he'd let himself believe in because it had been tucked away back home was beginning to crumble.

"Go, Adam." May tried to smile, but it didn't reach her eyes. "Have a good time. We're all tired and want to get to bed early anyway. All your friends in town will be happy to see you again. And after all, Bergette has a right to ask for a little of your time. She'll be in the family soon enough and have to put up with all of us."

Adam reluctantly left, but when he arrived at the party, he was more unhappy than ever. The people Bergette had invited were the most important people in town, but none were his friends. Most he'd only heard of and had never talked with past a howdy. By the third course, he realized this was Bergette's party, not his. He only provided the excuse. She was the center of attention. All the stories were about her hard time while Adam was gone. The hardest one seemed to have been her battle to remove an old lady from this house so she could buy the place.

By the time the men moved to have their cigars in the library, Adam was feeling completely out of place. He hadn't been able to say a single word alone to Bergette. When she slipped into the study and motioned for him, Adam thought he'd finally have his chance. She must be as anxious to be alone with him as he was with her. They had a thousand things to talk about, a lifetime to plan.

"Darling," she whispered as she pulled him into the hallway and held him at arms' length when he would have moved closer. "There's a man who wants to see you."

Adam thought she looked a little frightened, but he couldn't tell if it was from fear of some man or from the possibility that someone might ruin her evening.

"A man?"

"Actually, there are two. One came right up to the front door and said your brother told him he'd find you here. I tried to send them away, but the man at the door said you treated him for a wound and you had to take a look at the healing. The other, waiting in the shadows, was twice the size of Charles, my butler. I told them to go around to the kitchen and left orders to let them come no further into the house than the butler's pantry."

Adam raised an eyebrow. He'd treated hundreds, but couldn't remember one being from anywhere near his home. Rarely had there been time to ask.

"Send them away, darling!" she cried. "I can't have people like them ruining my party. I swear, one looked more like a bear than a human. You'd think those kind of people would have sense enough to come to the back door."

"But what if one of them is in pain?" Adam started down the hall to the dining room.

"Then let Dr. Wilson take care of him. I can't have this kind of thing happening." She followed Adam. "If you let them come to our home, before you know it they'll be bleeding all over the rugs."

Adam wasn't listening. He wasn't sure he wanted to hear anything she was saying. "Which way to the kitchen?" he snapped at her. Perfection was crumbling before his eyes.

She waved in the direction of a closed door at the back of the dining area. "I hope Charles managed to hold them back. I couldn't very well have the strangers mingling with the guests."

"No," Adam fought down his anger as he stared at her. Her hair wasn't sunshine, it was gold, cold hard gold. "We wouldn't want them dying past the butler's pantry, would we, Bergette?"

She look disgusted. "You don't think he's dying, do you?"

Adam moved down the row of dining chairs pushed back from a huge mahogany table. "Did these men give a name?"

Bergette's full skirts kept her from following him. "I heard the thin one call the huge one Wolf. Wolf, what a name."

He reached for his gun, but no holster was about his waist. It must be two of the Shadows! If Nichole's brother had followed him for four months to kill him, one gun might not be enough. Besides, the war was over. Hadn't this Shadow rider gotten the word?

"Stay with the guests!" he ordered. "I'll be back in a few minutes."

He moved through the dining room thankful that Bergette hadn't argued. As he approached the far exit, a tall form pivoted slowly around the doorjamb, opening the door as he moved.

"Evening, little brother." Wes grinned. "I thought I might just drop in for a few minutes. Hope I didn't spoil Bergette's party." His tone left no doubt that he cared little for Bergette's feelings.

"You saw the two men?" Adam met his brother's gaze.

"I saw them." Wes brushed his gun handle. "The big one almost frightened May to death when she stepped out on the porch and found him standing in the middle of the yard like he grew there at sundown."

"You know who they are?" Adam stood only inches away from his brother. Silently, Wes slipped him a derringer and Adam folded it into his coat.

"I've seen too many men not to be able to size them up. They're shabby and underfed, but both ride like the wind. And the thin one carried your medical bag. A bag you lost right about the time the war ended."

Wes didn't need to say more. Adam knew he'd filled in the blanks.

"Only thing I can't figure"—Wes moved toward the closed doors of the room called the butler's pantry—"is . . . are they here to thank you, or kill you?"

"There's only one way to find out." Adam gripped the knob and opened the door.

FOUR

NICHOLE REMOVED HER JACKET, FOLDED HER ARMS, AND LEANED against the spotless counter. All she'd wanted to do was see Adam McLain again . . . prove to herself that he was more a daydream and less a reality. No man could have been as kind, or good, or tender as she remembered. She must have lost a great deal of blood to conjure up such a fantasy. All the men she'd known were hard and measured their worth by their ability to fight. All but the doctor, it seemed.

But getting to see Adam McLain again had turned into a traveling minstrel show. Wolf, always protective, insisted on coming with her. She'd spent the war crossing back and forth along the line, outrunning bullets most of the time. Now he thought she needed a bodyguard to travel by train to this little town at the southernmost tip of Indiana. Standing in a fine house, Wolf, puffed up like the bear he resembled, was pacing the polished floor of a room not three strides long.

"I don't see why you wanted to come here," Wolf mumbled in a low roar as he scratched his beard.

"I told you," Nichole answered for what felt like the hundredth time. "I owe him my life, the least I can do is bring back his bag."

Wolf looked around. "He can afford another one." He bumped against a cabinet, causing glasses to tinkle like church bells. "All hell's going to break loose back home. I haven't got time to ride a train north just to see some doctor."

"I could have come alone."

"No, sir." Wolf shook his head so hard she could almost see some of his fur fly. "If you're crazy enough to want this, Nick, I'll be close in case there's trouble." He shook one beefy finger at her.

"Always have someone you can trust to watch your back. You never know when you'll have to retreat."

Nichole frowned. The only trouble she could think of would probably come from her brother. He was uncomfortable about her being a woman. Everything had been fine between them when she rode as one of the men. But since the morning he found her kissing the Yankee, he'd been uneasy. Even with the war over, he still called her Nick and referred to her as "he" most of the time.

When the door opened, she forgot all about Wolf. The man who had held her so gently and kissed her so tenderly appeared before her looking far more handsome than she remembered. His brown hair was combed neatly and the peace had eased the worry lines along his forehead.

He was dressed in a black suit that fit him like it had been tailored just for him, and a shirt so white it deepened his tan. Nichole could never remember a man looking so spotlessly clean. His warm brown eyes stared only at her, as if she were somebody special.

For a long moment, he just stared at her as though he were drinking in the sight of her with one long draw.

"Wes," he said slowly as he smiled at Nichole and opened his hand toward her. "I'd like you to meet Nichole Hayward and her brother, Captain Wolf Hayward of the Gray Shadows. Miss Hayward"—Adam moved to the side allowing another man to enter—"my brother, Captain Weston McLain."

The man behind Adam let a smile lift the corner of his mouth as he stepped around his brother. "*Miss* Hayward. Captain Hayward." He nodded at them both. The smile spread until it almost reached a thin white scar along his cheek. His was of the same build as Adam, brown hair, brown eyes, but somehow different, harder.

"This isn't a social call." Wolf's low voice seemed to rumble around the little room like a loose cannonball. "Nick wanted to return the medical bag you left behind and have you check the wound at her side for healing. Then we'll be on our way."

Nichole knew no one in the room except her brother believed the reason.

Adam's brother's smile now infected both corners of his mouth. "Well, Captain Hayward." He turned toward Wolf. "If my brother has got doctoring to do, we best step out of the room."

"What?" Wolf widened his stance. "I ain't leaving her alone with some damn—"

"I'll be all right," Nichole interrupted. "He's a doctor, Wolf.

What do you think he's going to do, kill me right here among the china after he risked his life to save me during the war?''

Wolf didn't look like he planned to be uprooted. "You never know what they're going to do. Keep your gun handy, Nick.''

To prove her point, Nichole handed her Colt to Wes. "I'm not holding a weapon on the man who saved my life. He's under no obligation to check the healing.''

Adam slipped the derringer from his coat and did the same.

Wolf glanced at the doctor as though he'd just proved himself a fool to face Nichole unarmed.

Wes broke the standoff by opening the door. "I passed a crop of pies in the kitchen. I bet we can talk the cook out of one. I'll split it with you, Captain Hayward.'' Wes glanced into the hallway. "And if we run into that bandy rooster of a butler, we can use him for target practice.'' Wes winked. "I've always wanted to test my skill against a Shadow.''

"You wouldn't have a chance, Yank.'' Wolf's laughter rattled the crystal once more. "Plus, he'd be a waste of bullets. How about we just gut him and fry him up for breakfast?''

Wolf moved through the door. He glanced back at Adam, issuing a silent warning to be careful.

"No," Wes said, pulling the reb back to the jest. "He wouldn't make a meal. Probably spoiled meat to the bone. I bet he was bottle fed on vinegar.''

The door closed, suddenly making the little room stone silent. The area, lined with shelves, seemed even smaller than it had when Wolf paced around. Nichole had a sudden urge to call her brother back, but the man she'd traveled days to see stood before her. Now might be the only chance she'd ever have to see him again. The one kind man she'd known was so close she could reach out and touch him and she could think of nothing to say.

Finally, Adam cleared his throat and straightened slightly. "If you'll jump up on the counter, I'll take a look at the wound.''

Nichole didn't move.

He took a step forward and lifted the medical saddlebag from her shoulder. "Thanks for bringing this back, but I won't be needing it soon. A town doc carries a different kind of bag.''

She fought the urge to reach for the pearl-handled knife stuffed inside her left boot. She'd never hurt him, but a weapon in her hand might make conversation easier, for her at least.

"Would you be more comfortable in another room?'' Concern filled his eyes. "I haven't had time to set up an office yet, but I'm sure in this size house there's probably a more appropriate place to conduct an exam.''

Nichole looked around. ''This isn't your house?''

''No,'' he answered. ''I only made it back this morning. I rode with the wounded from the Fourteenth Indiana Regiment as far as Louisville and stayed until they settled in at a hospital. We lost enough men to the war. Even the badly wounded wanted to come home to recover.''

''I guess that would be hard—knowing it was over and not being able to get home. They were probably glad you were with them.''

Adam stood directly in front of her. He pulled off his coat and turned up his sleeves, more from habit than any need to do so. ''How about you? Have you and Wolf been home?''

''We had a place along the Cumberland River right about where Kentucky and Tennessee collide. When your troops, under Bragg, came dancing through in '62 there wasn't much left of our place. I guess all the locals thought us dead because our land was taken over. So we came home to a mess of worry.''

Nichole watched him closely. The starched shirt made his waist slim and his shoulders wider.

''I know.'' His brown eyes were full of understanding. His voice low. ''Corydon was hit in a Southern campaign. When you're away, you think about home being the same when you come back.''

''But it isn't,'' she whispered, not wanting to say more. ''Here's fine,'' she added, forcing herself to look around, ''much better than where you had to operate.''

Adam agreed as his hands touched her waist and lifted her atop the counter. Standing, she'd been shorter than him by a few inches, now she sat slightly above him.

''Would you unbutton your blouse?'' he asked in what he hoped was a professional tone. ''I'll take a look at the wound.''

Nichole smiled. He'd called her shirt a blouse, no one had used that word around her in years. ''Sure,'' she mumbled as she began fumbling with the buttons.

''Have you had any pain? Fever? Infection?'' His voice was so professional, but not cold, never cold.

Swallowing, Nichole fought the urge to tell him that she felt like she had a fever right now. He was looking in his bag, touching all the bottles and instruments she'd examined dozens of times.

She pulled her shirttail out of her pants and shook her head in answer to his question about fever. Gripping the counter on either side of her legs, she waited.

He slowly slid the left side of her shirt open, letting it fall off her shoulder.

Nichole drew in a sharp breath as his hands moved to her waist and lifted her cotton undershirt. She could feel his breath only inches from her throat.

"Are you all right?" he asked as he paused. "Comfortable?"

"Yes," she whispered. "I'm fine." The lie almost blocked her throat to the point of cutting off her air. She wasn't fine. He was touching her again with that gentle touch she remembered. Her face felt afire. She had to turn her knuckles white to keep her hands from shaking, and he asked again if she were all right.

He leaned slightly toward her as his fingers moved the cotton a few inches more to reveal the scar. The clean smell of him filled her senses as she fought to remain still. His abdomen brushed her knee and she moved her legs out of the way.

"It's healed nicely." He touched the thin scar. "Who took the stitches out?"

"I did," she answered.

His hand slid over the wound. His palm warmed her flesh. "I wish I'd been there. I could have made it less painful." His other hand moved to her right side and pulled her an inch toward him. As his body leaned against the counter space between her legs, his voice lowered. "I thought about you in those days after the war. Wondered if you were safe. If you were in pain."

"I was fine," she whispered, completely aware of his nearness and unwilling to lean away. "We headed home almost at once. But folks at home didn't want the war to end. We thought the fighting was over, but we ran into trouble several times. Some thought the Shadows should be tried as spies against the Union."

His hands gently moved along her rib cage. "The war is over, Nichole. It will take a while, but it will come to an end. Eventually, all the hatred and anger will die."

Suddenly, her grip broke from the counter and her arms moved around his neck. She pulled him close. She'd never cried, not even when her mother died. Everyone in her family saw it as a weakness. But now tears rolled down her cheeks, and she felt his hands spread across her back in comfort. She didn't have to tell him she hadn't believed the fighting would ever end, he seemed to know.

"It's over," he whispered against her hair as he pulled her closer. "The hell we've both lived has finally ended. All that's left is the scar."

Nichole moved her damp cheek against his jaw. She lifted her hands and let her fingers glide into the thick warmth of his hair. There had been so few hugs in her life, so little caring. Her movements were jerky with need and fear that he might turn away.

Adam was lost with her wrapped around him. Her arms held him tightly, her cheek against his, her legs on either side of his hips. It didn't matter that he was a doctor and she was his patient, nor that he was in his fiancée's house, or that he knew nothing about Nichole. All that mattered was that she held him the way he wanted and needed to be held.

He pulled her closer, feeling her breasts press against his chest, feeling her breath on his neck, feeling her heart pounding next to his. He was alive for the first time in years. This was the homecoming he'd longed for, and it hadn't come from Bergette but from a stranger he barely knew but hadn't been able to forget.

For a long while, they held one another, afraid to ease their hold lest the feeling end. Slowly their breathing grew in rhythm.

"The examination is over," he whispered against her ear. "You're free to leave." His arms didn't loosen.

"And if I don't?" Her hands spread over the starched crispness of his shirt.

"Then I'll have to finish that kiss we started," he answered.

She didn't give him time to advance. Her lips moved to his. Her mouth was slightly open and willing. This time she was kissing him.

For a moment, he let her lead, making sure that she was a willing partner. Before, he'd surprised her with his kiss. Now her advance surprised him.

She melted against him, wanting to be closer. His kiss was like before, tender. Only now there was a hunger in it that hadn't been there before. He wasn't kissing some woman he'd held one night and called beautiful. He was kissing her. Just her. He was silently telling her that he'd thought of this moment, dreamed of it, wished for it.

Though the kiss ended all too soon for Nichole, she wasn't sure how to ask him to repeat it. She was glad he didn't pull away, but remained close, holding her in his arms as her head rested on his shoulder.

"Thank you," he whispered against her hair.

"For what?" she answered.

"For making me feel alive again." He lightly kissed her cheek. "I was starting to think the memory of you was a dream I had. Thank you for making it real again." He moved his hand along her back, pressing her closer to him.

"Anytime, Yank."

A light tapping sounded at the door and Adam stepped away a moment before Wes looked in. "Sorry to interrupt the exam." Wes raised an eyebrow at Nichole's open shirt. "But Bergette's on her way as soon as she finishes yelling at Wolf for tracking in mud."

Adam reached for his jacket, and Nichole did the same. She'd just buttoned the top button on her shirt, when Bergette stormed through the door. The tiny woman wore more lace and ribbons than Nichole had ever seen in one place before. She looked like an angel, but Nichole didn't miss the devil in her eyes as she stared at the doctor.

"Adam, aren't these people gone yet?" Bergette didn't bother to look Nichole in the face. If she had, she wouldn't have missed the red cheeks and slightly swollen lips.

"We were just leaving," Nichole mumbled with her head low as she'd been taught to disguise her identity. "Thanks for seeing me, Doc."

"You don't have to leave." Adam ignored Bergette. "Stay and have supper at least. You've come a long way."

"What!" Ignoring Bergette was not a safe move. "I believe this is *my* house."

Wes stepped from behind the little lady. With one swift movement, he lifted her off the floor and set her down out of Adam's path. "She's right. This is, and will probably always be 'her' house." Wes smiled as he watched Bergette boil. "Ready to head home, little brother? May will have leftovers and guests have always been welcome in the McLain house."

Adam nodded. Glancing at Nichole, he offered his arm. "Will you join me, Miss Hayward?"

Wes took the battle charge Bergette issued as Adam and Nichole left the room. Smooth as a dance move, Wes covered her pouty mouth as she took in breath to scream and pushed her behind the door. "I wouldn't scream if I were you, dear Bergette. All the guests will come running and see Adam leaving with a woman dressed in a man's clothing. Wouldn't it be better to let him go and make his excuses?"

He could see her mind working, and he guessed she was already planning how her story would make Adam so busy with doctoring that she'd draw everyone's sympathy. Poor girl, he'd even left her on his first evening home. Everyone would comfort Bergette.

"That's better," Wes whispered as he pulled his hand away and wiped it on his pant leg.

"I hate you!" She almost spit the words. "I'll see you dead."

Wes faked a hurt look. "Oh, Bergette! How can you say such a thing? I was just starting to welcome you into the family, dear sister."

"I'm getting Adam away from the likes of you and that preacher brother of yours if it's the last thing I do. The only time I'll be with anyone in your family except Adam is in the family plot when we're all dead."

Wes raised an eyebrow. "Are you suggesting someday we'll lie together, dear sister-in-law-to-be? A corpse of you would be little change from your warmth now."

She slapped him so hard he felt his ears ring. In a tornado of satin, she stormed away before he could focus.

Wes rubbed his jaw. "Or maybe not," he mumbled as he hurried to catch up with Adam and his dinner guests.

FIVE

THE FOUR RIDERS TOOK TO THE NIGHT LIKE BATS, RACING TOWARD the McLain home in silent dare to an evening storm. Strong winds chased their backs and lightning flashed around them. The earth blinked bright as day for an instant, then black again.

Adam needed the pounding ride to challenge his body and ease the frustration he felt toward Bergette. He tried to tell himself that this was only his first day home, and she was under a great deal of stress. Give her time, he reasoned, but his gut feeling told him to ride faster—as far away from her as he could get. She was not the woman he'd dreamed of and planned a life with. All the beauty was still there, but her heart was missing.

When they reined in at the farmyard, splatters of rain smothered their dust. Adam glanced at Nichole. Her smile confirmed that she loved the speed as much as he did. The lightning hadn't frightened her. He wondered what, if anything, would. She was as wild as a spring storm, and it was the wildness that attracted him, nothing more, he decided. The female reb was as far from his world as a woman could be.

But something in her green eyes challenged him to care. Something in her short midnight curls dared him to touch her.

Glancing away from Nichole, Adam realized the storm had followed them in, swirling excitement and rattling the air with summer thunder. He could hear the horses moving in the corral and the windmill speeding around as rain plopped in the already full tank.

Daniel yelled from the porch. "Thank God! You're back." He hurried toward them as fast as his stiff leg would allow.

"What is it?" Wes was off his mount first with Adam just behind.

"It's May." Daniel suddenly looked very young and near panic. Adam grabbed his medical bag. "Has the labor started?"

"No." Daniel shoved his wet hair from his face. "I can't find her! She's disappeared."

His little brother fought to pull himself together enough to force words out. "She was in the kitchen when I left to bring in the horses, but now she's gone." Daniel struggled with each sentence. "I've called and called. She couldn't have just vanished."

Adam touched his brother's shoulder and moved into the kitchen with the others following. For a moment everything looked in place, her sewing on the table, the fireplace bright, supper dishes in a pan by the pump. Touches of May were everywhere, but she was missing.

"We'll split up." Adam tried to make his voice calm and commanding. "Wes, you and Wolf check the barn. Nichole, start on the second floor and call May's name in every room. Daniel, check the outhouse and chicken coops. When anyone finds her, yell loud. She can't be far away."

Everyone moved at once, for they were all used to following orders and knew by Adam's voice there was no time to lose.

When they disappeared, Adam knelt by the table and touched the wet spot on the floor. He brought his fingers to his nose and frowned. The watery liquid was slippery to the touch and smelled of blood. "Her water broke," he whispered to himself.

"Where are you, May?" Fear and frustration banked his sudden demand to an empty room.

Only silence.

He built up the fire and put on as much water to boil as he could find pots to hold it, then he darted to the only downstairs bedroom and stripped the sheets. He laid a soft deerskin pelt on the mattress, then covered it with a thick flannel sheet.

"What did you do that for?" Nichole asked from the doorway.

"It'll catch the fluids." Adam layered the bed with all the sheets he could find. "She wasn't upstairs?"

"No." Nichole helped him. "I can hear your younger brother calling for her in the rain. His voice is full of panic, almost madness."

Adam didn't look at her as he worked. "May's not just his wife, she's his world. They've been best friends since he started school. When Daniel was little, he never talked. My folks feared something was wrong with him until he found May. Seemed he'd saved up all he had to say to tell her. When he got old enough to enlist as a chaplain, they married before he left so she could go with him when he was stationed in a town. He got shot in the leg while visiting an outpost, but she was at his side. When she's near, words come easy for Danny, but when she's not, he dams up inside.''

''I've seen wives go through hard times to stay near their men,'' Nichole whispered. She remembered seeing the small camps of women sometimes only a few miles behind the lines. Their fires and supplies were usually lower than that of the troops, but they didn't complain of wanting to go home as the men did. They were where they had to be.

''It's more than just wanting to be together with those two. She somehow completes his world.'' Adam opened his bag and began laying out what he thought he might need. He'd only delivered three babies during medical school. One was with the help of an instructor, and the other two were women who'd had so many children they lectured him completely through the process. But this was May's first. Her water had already broken. Wasn't that supposed to happen later? He couldn't remember. She wasn't due for days yet. He'd planned to read everything he could find on delivery before then.

Nichole moved until she stood across the small table from him. ''Do you need Wolf and me to stay and help, Doc?''

Adam looked up and guessed from her expression that helping deliver a baby was something quite foreign to both Nichole and her brother. ''No,'' he said, allowing his pride to answer. ''We can manage.''

One thing his mother had taught him, a McLain never asked for help unless he could return the favor. Nichole and he were even, and Adam planned to keep it that way.

She let out a long breath. ''Then we'll be leaving as soon as May's found.''

Adam stared into her dark green eyes and knew there were somehow words left to be said between them that would never have a time. She opened her mouth slightly, her action echoing his thoughts.

''Adam!'' Wes screamed above the storm. ''Adam!''

Adam bolted for the kitchen door with Nichole only a step behind. Wes's tall form materialized through the gray rain. He carried May, covered with his coat. Her forgotten shawl dragged in the mud behind them.

''Adam! Daniel! I found her!''

Wolf ran ahead of Wes and opened the screen door as Dan jumped over the railing at the corner of the porch. When Wes stepped inside, he was dripping wet.

''I found her in the darkness by the barn door.'' He handed her to her husband. ''She wasn't crying or nothing, just curled up in pain.''

Daniel held her close. "She's never been able to open the barn door when the wind's up."

"Get her in the bedroom, Dan!" Adam ordered. "We've got to keep her dry and warm. Nichole, see if you can start the fireplace blazing. I'll bring the water and every lantern I can find."

For an instant brown eyes meet green. He silently asked for the help she'd offered earlier. She nodded slightly and followed Daniel into the bedroom.

Adam turned his attention to Wes. "Get that blood off you and see how fast you can bring Doc Wilson out from town."

Wes looked down. Blood covered the bottom part of his shirt as thick as if he'd been gut shot. May's blood!

Wolf reached out an arm in time to break Wes's fall. Both men crumpled to the floor like timbers falling.

Glancing over his shoulder, Adam saw Wolf rise on one elbow. "Is he all right?" Adam asked as he pointed with his head toward his older brother.

"Out cold." Wolf laughed. "Some soldier. Can't stand the sight of a little birthing blood."

Adam stared at Nichole as she passed with an armload of firewood. "Can you?"

Her gaze met his once more in silent challenge. "I don't know," she answered honestly.

"There's one way to find out." He motioned for her to follow him and yelled back from the other room. "Wake my big brother and ride to town with him, would you, Wolf? We need Doc Wilson as fast as he can get here."

"You bet, Doc." Wolf dropped Wes's head on the floor with a thud and went to get a bucket of cold rainwater from the barrel on the porch. "Come to supper and you join the family around here," he mumbled.

Adam fought down the panic as he moved to May's side. She was cradled in Daniel's arms, holding on to his hand with a tight grip.

"It's too early." Daniel looked up at Adam. "She's too little. What are we going to do?" Tears he wouldn't allow to fall welled in his eyes.

"We're going to do our best," Adam answered, knowing that if he didn't keep Daniel busy, he'd have two brothers as patients, and Wolf wasn't much of a nurse. "Help me get her out of these wet clothes and into a nightgown."

As the room warmed, May relaxed a little. She turned loose of Daniel's arm and tried to smile between contractions. "I couldn't find you when the pains started," she whispered to Daniel. "I thought I lost you. I thought you were hurt somewhere in the dark and I wouldn't be able to find you."

"Never." He kissed her cheek, then shoved curls of hair from her forehead. "Adam's here now. We're going to have our baby soon. We've been through a great deal together and we'll make it through this."

An hour passed. Everyone worked and waited. Nichole kept the fire hot, hauled water in and soiled sheets out. Adam timed the contractions and comforted May. Daniel never left her side, and Adam knew it would be a waste of time to ask him to leave. He could hear Wes and Wolf in the kitchen burning a supper no one would bother to eat.

Dr. Wilson arrived with his usual good cheer, lightening the mood by assuring everyone that having a baby was a natural thing and nothing to worry about. But when he examined May, the lines around his mouth tightened. He glanced up at Adam, silently confirming Adam's fear. Everything was not right. Her womb seemed stretched to the limit, but he could feel no baby aligning to be born.

The night passed, one contraction at a time. May would grip Daniel's hand, seeming to pass the pain to him. And Daniel took it, feeling all she suffered along with his own sorrow of watching her grow paler with each hour.

Adam tried everything he could think of to help her. He shifted her position in the bed, easing her back. He talked Doc Wilson into helping him try and turn the baby. They talked about cutting across May's abdomen, but Daniel wouldn't hear of it. Adam didn't insist. Even if they could get the baby out, there was a good chance she'd bleed to death before they could sew her up.

He gave her honeyed whiskey to ease the contractions. Nothing worked.

As dawn brightened the windows, Adam left the bedroom for the first time. He walked past Wes sleeping in a chair at the kitchen table and stepped outside.

The storm had worn itself out, leaving the morning gray and humid. All the wounded he'd ever treated came rushing back to him. May's suffering seemed to pile atop all the others, until Adam felt his shoulders snap from the load. He dropped on the first step and put his elbows on his knees, wishing he were a boy again and could go back to a time when Mama's words could make everything all right. He wanted the world to make sense. He wanted the suffering to end.

Adam wasn't aware of Nichole until she stood just behind him.

"Wolf left for town to send a telegram home," she said matter-of-factly, handing him a mug of steaming coffee.

"Trouble?"

"The war may not be over so easy for us. We may have to fight for the land we left behind. Wolf and I will have no peaceful farm to go home to or profession like doctoring to fall back on. What becomes of a Shadow when the war ends? It's not exactly a skill that we can continue in peacetime."

Adam felt sorry for her. She'd become an expert in something no longer in demand. "Thank you for helping out tonight. The McLains are in your debt. Name the time and we'll pay you back."

"I don't expect any payment." Her words were sharp. "And I'm not sure I was much help. I could never have the kind of talent you have. You're very gifted."

"No great skill. I don't know if I want to be a doctor anymore," he mumbled more to himself than her. "Maybe I should give the gift back."

"Picked a hell of a time to leave the profession," she answered without sympathy.

Leaning back against the porch railing, he felt her leg pressing lightly against his back. Neither retreated. The warmth of her nearby was reassuring.

"Some doctor. I can't do anything else for May." He straightened slightly, still allowing his back to touch her leg, but letting her know that he wasn't asking for compassion, only understanding.

Nichole let out a long breath. Sympathy wasn't a talent she'd had time to develop. "I guess that takes you out of the running for God, doesn't it?"

Anger sparked in him. She wasn't giving an inch. He'd seen her comfort May again and again. She'd patted Daniel on the shoulder. She'd even brought old Doc Wilson a chair and bullied him until he'd sat for a while. But no kind words for him.

Adam stood, tossing the coffee into the mud. "I'd better get back."

He wanted to yell that he knew he'd let her down. He wasn't the grand doctor she thought him to be. She'd traveled all this way to see a hero, and he was only a man. A man who spoke of his doubt. Something he'd never do in front of her or any woman again.

When he looked at her, she was staring out at the sunrise. She was a hard woman, he'd give her that. Her world had fallen apart, and she hadn't blinked at what might lie ahead. She'd seen things tonight that would have had most women fainting. That was the difference between her and Bergette. Not the dress, or the manners, or even the background—Bergette had no heart, while Nichole's heart had turned to stone over the years of war.

Wilson called Adam. Without a word, he left Nichole's side, thinking that even if he declared himself in her debt, she'd probably die before she asked for help from him.

"It's time!" Wilson shouted again.

Adam crossed the kitchen in three strides as May's scream lacerated the silence and woke Wes. He jumped, toppling the chair backward and almost colliding with Nichole as she raced to the bedroom.

She shoved Wes out of the way. He took a step to follow, but another scream from the bedroom seemed to bar him from entering.

"I'll check the horses!" he yelled to the open doorway, but no one answered.

An hour later, Nichole stood in the shadows watching a second baby crown. May had grown too weak to push, and Daniel looked like he might pass out at any moment. Dr. Wilson put a bloody hand on May's knee as he waited for the next contraction. Sweat dripped off his forehead and into his eyes where it blended with his tears.

The old doctor wiped his face with a towel and glanced in Nichole's direction. "As soon as this one is out, you do what Adam is doing with the first. I've got to help May. You and Adam will have to see these babies get to breathing clear. That's most important, lest all this suffering be for nothing."

Nichole tried to force herself to breathe. She'd seen battlefields covered in blue and gray and blood, but she'd never seen anything like this.

Wilson lifted the baby in the air as it wiggled and screamed in protest. He cut the cord and tied it, then handed the tiny bundle to her. Out of the corner of her eye, she saw the afterbirth begin to emerge and moved quickly away, not sure she could breathe if she witnessed more.

When Nichole reached Adam's side, he took the newborn from her arms and handed her a baby already wrapped in a towel.

"Keep this little lady warm." He smiled at Nichole, as if he thought the messy creature was pretty. "I'll clean up my other niece."

Nichole cradled the wiggling bundle close to her heart as she watched Adam work. He held the tiny baby in one hand and cleaned its mouth and let the lungs drain of fluid. Then he wiped the wrinkled flesh with a warm cloth and checked each limb.

"They're both perfect." He glanced over his shoulder with a smile toward the new parents. "Daniel, you and May have yourselves two fine daughters."

Nichole watched the smile vanish from Adam. His face become a mass of sorrow when there was no answer from anyone near the bed.

"No," he cried.

She followed the direction of his gaze.

"No!"

Dr. Wilson wept openly as he knelt on one knee and slowly raised the sheet over May's face. "I saw her come into this world. Now it's time for her to pass on to the next."

"No!" Daniel's order shook the room. "Don't leave me, May!"

He buried his head in the pillow next to the covered outline of his wife and sobbed. Deep low sobs of a pain too great to bear.

But the sheet separated their tears as death separated them.

SIX

I<small>T WAS LATE AFTERNOON AS</small> N<small>ICHOLE WATCHED THE THREE BROTHERS</small> walk back from the small graveyard. They looked so much alike yet were so different. Wes with his hard exterior, Daniel with his silence, and Adam in his private war within himself. They walked almost shoulder to shoulder, yet each walked alone.

"These babies got to be fed," Wolf mumbled from the kitchen table where he sat staring at the twins nestled in two shoe boxes. "I wish everybody would get back and take over watching these two. I got to ride to town and check on any answer from the men." He talked about those who served under him during the war as if they were still organized. In truth, only Tyler and Rafe stayed with Wolf, more because they had nowhere else to go than out of loyalty to any cause.

"Doc Wilson drove to a farm just north of here to find a wet nurse," Nichole answered her brother. "He should be back soon."

She almost laughed at Wolf. For a man who cared for little in this world, he'd done his share of fretting over the babies. Though the day had been warm, he'd insisted on the stove burning low just to keep any chill from creeping into the room. And he watched them even though he probably had no idea what to do if one cried out.

"Wes offered me his room upstairs for the night. I think we should leave come morning," Nichole mumbled. "It would feel good to have a night's sleep in a bed before we board the train."

There was no reason to stay. She'd done what she planned to, she'd returned the bag and finished the kiss. Anything more had been day-dreams on her part, for Adam had his life here. She wasn't sure what she'd expected, or hoped. But finding Adam engaged to be married and with a sister-in-law delivering babies hadn't crossed her mind. His thoughts were so full of worries, he'd hardly noticed her being in the house.

Wolf spoke to the babies as he answered her. "We've got our own problems at home to worry over, and sorrow don't want company around. Besides, that woman Bergette showed up for the funeral so I reckon she'll stay here with the babies and take over the womanly duties." He took a deep breath. "But we both could use a night's sleep before starting home."

"Don't bank on Bergette's help," Nichole whispered to Wolf as she heard Wes and Adam stomp onto the porch. The McLains entered, both looking exhausted. Nichole didn't know what to say. She knew Adam blamed himself for May's death, and Wes blamed the world, but she wasn't sure how either would react if she tried to comfort them. Wes only needed time and a few more bottles of whiskey to recover. But Adam was a thinker who thought he needed no one. She'd never been around such a man.

Bergette followed the brothers in when Adam held the door for her. She seemed far more concerned with removing her hat and veil without damaging her hair than with anyone's grief or with taking over the care of the infants. She paid no notice to Nichole or anyone else as she walked to the washstand and faced the mirror.

The sharp sound of an ax splintering wood pulsed through the air with a pop.

Everyone paused listening as the sound came again, and again.

"It's Daniel," Wes answered a question no one had voiced as he poured himself a mug of coffee, then laced it with whiskey. "He's chopping down the barn door. Might level the entire barn before he's finished."

No one said a word to hint that the action wasn't totally normal. Nichole listened to the chopping, thinking that in some strange way it sounded like a heart beating. Dan hadn't spoken since May's death. At least the noise proved he was alive.

Nichole watched as Bergette glared first at Adam, then Wes, with the pouty lip of a child. When neither looked in her direction, she stormed, "Aren't you going to make him stop?"

Wes didn't bother to answer her and Adam only mumbled "No" as he looked at the now-sleeping babies.

Bergette seemed to long-sufferingly endure two more blows, then she moved to the doorway in a sudden fit of displeasure. "I must be going," she announced as though her exit were of some great importance. "I'll send a cook over to help you tomorrow. And a housekeeper. Lord knows this place could use a good scrubbing.'' Her gaze darted around the room from the handmade table and chairs to the clothes hanging on pegs along one wall.

"Don't bother," Wes answered. "We can manage."

Bergette looked to Adam for a kinder reply, but he only held the door open for her.

"I will see you tomorrow, won't I?" she asked as she moved to the porch in a rustle of silk.

"I don't know," Adam answered. "Tell your butler to drive you home slowly. The roads can be tricky this time of night." He didn't offer a touch or a kiss and neither did she.

When Adam returned, Nichole didn't miss the hurt in his stare— a kind of pain that made his brown eyes seem stormy. A suffering like that of an animal who might turn on anyone who tried to help. She thought he looked as though something inside him was dying. Or maybe he'd protected and cherished a memory for years only to find it decayed and molded when he finally drew it out. Bergette's lavender perfume suddenly smelled stifling like the smell of too many flowers at a wake.

Wolf stood as soon as Bergette was gone and nodded toward Nichole as he reached for his hat. He'd be to town and back in the time it would take Bergette's buggy to reach home and she wouldn't see him pass her either way.

Nichole closed her eyes, hoping the news he found would be good. Wolf had sensed trouble. The man who'd taken their land during the war would stop at nothing to keep it. She only hoped Tyler and a few of the others could make peace before Wolf and she returned. But the soft rain against the window seemed to wash away her hopes.

Wes poured himself another cup of coffee and took Wolf's place across the table from Adam. No one felt any need for conversation. Nichole curled into the chair by the window and listened to the rhythm of Dan's chopping. Somehow, it was almost a song. A song too sad to have a melody.

Just after dark, the old doctor arrived with a young girl. He'd loaned her his coat, but Nichole noticed her feet were bare and mud covered. The look of her reminded Nichole of the poor folks who lived far back in the Tennessee hills.

Wilson explained quietly, as she looked at the babies, that she'd lost her month-old son three days ago. Apparently she'd never had a husband, and her pa had beat her regularly all during the pregnancy. "She's simpleminded," the doctor whispered. "But as sweet natured as they come. Her baby hadn't been healthy since birth, but she'd taken care of him as well as any mother could. Even walked the four miles to town to bring him to the office several times, knowing her pa would beat her for not finishing her chores.''

Adam knelt by where the woman sat with one of the babies on her lap. She seemed half woman, half child in her homespun dress and faded blue apron. ''Hello.'' He smiled. ''My name's Adam.''

The girl didn't look away from the infant. ''I'm Willow,'' she said. ''I had me a baby, but he died.''

''Would you like to live here and help us take care of these two, Willow?''

The girl giggled and raised her head. Adam noticed bruises spotting her round face and swelling the corner of her bottom lip.

''Doc told me you might ask so I brought my roll of clothes.'' She looked like she was about to cry. ''I'd like to stay, but I'm not much good around the house. I drop things and forget. My pa wallops me but I don't learn. I heard him tell the doc that if you're a-willing to feed me, good riddance to my no-good bones.''

''All we want you to do is take care of the babies. If you do that, you'll earn your keep.'' Adam patted her shoulder. ''And no one here will ever lay a hand on you as long as you're with us. I give you my word.''

''Really?''

''Really.''

''They got names?''

Adam glanced toward the door and the sound of the chopping. ''Dan will get around to naming them in time. We could sure use your help, Willow.''

Willow smiled with pride. ''I got milk. Lots of it.''

Without hesitation, she pulled her blouse open and offered one baby her pink-tipped breast.

Wes shot from the room like a cannon, and Adam couldn't hold his laughter. After a few tries, the baby took to the breast hungrily, making Willow giggle.

''That's good, Willow,'' Adam managed to say before he followed Wes to the parlor. There he broke into a round of chuckles everyone in the kitchen heard.

''Shut up!'' Wes snapped. ''You sound like a fool.''

''I wish you could have seen your face.'' Adam tried to hold down his voice.

''Well, you saw what she did. Pulled that breast out like it was no more than a pitcher, and she was offering drinks.'' Wes paced in a circle around the parlor table.

"That's pretty much it." Adam laughed. "We did need a wet nurse. And with two to feed every few hours, it might be a blessing she's not overly shy."

"Overly shy! I've seen cows with more modesty."

Adam couldn't argue.

"Well, maybe we should look around for someone else," Wes continued. "This Willow couldn't be more than fifteen, and like the doc says, she's simple."

"We don't have time. The infants need to be fed."

Wes paced faster. "Couldn't we let some family take care of them? Just till they're old enough for Daniel to handle."

"You know as well as I do that most families got more than they can feed now. Besides, I doubt Daniel would let them out of his sight. From the look of her face, Willow needs a home as badly as those babies need a nurse."

"Well, I'm not sitting around at the dinner table looking at some woman's breast. Daniel can handle that when he fights through the grief. I'm heading for Texas day after tomorrow, and if you had any sense, you'd go with me and pray Texas is far enough away from Bergette."

Wes stormed out of the parlor, ending the conversation. He almost collided with Nichole standing just outside the door. For a moment, he looked at her, then pointed with his head toward the open parlor door. "My brothers are both crazy, you know."

Nichole didn't argue.

"Between saving the world and healing it, there won't be a sick sinner left within a hundred miles before long," he mumbled.

She smiled.

Wes wagged his finger at her. "I know what you're thinking. It's only a matter of time before they turn on me. Well, I'm not staying around long enough for that."

He grabbed a whiskey bottle and tried to cross the kitchen without looking in the direction of Willow and the table. "I'll be outside watching Danny destroy the barn!" he shouted. "By the time he's finished, I'll have us both too drunk to stand. Then we'll bed down on the porch, it's always too humid in the house after a summer rain." His voice dwindled as he hurried outside.

Nichole moved into the darkened parlor. The room seemed cold and smelled musty, unlike the rest of the house. She should just go, she told herself. Adam had his problems, his family, his life. He didn't need or hadn't asked for her to come to add additional worry. He wouldn't have accepted her help with May, if there had been any way he could have done it alone. When Wolf got back, they'd make plans to leave by dawn.

"Adam?" she whispered as she moved through the shadowy room. "I came to tell you I'll be leaving at first light. Wes offered me his room for tonight and said he'd bunk on the porch."

The air was so still she wasn't sure Adam was there. He could have passed through the door on the other side of the room. He'd shown no interest in talking to Bergette. Why had she thought he would want to talk to her?

She reached a hand out and touched the thick cotton lace cloth that covered a round table in the center of the room. "Adam?" She wanted to say his name one more time even to an empty room. "Adam?"

He moved in the darkness.

She waited. Listening. Her trained senses judging where he stood.

"I thank you and your brother for the help." His words were forced, almost hard. "The McLains are in your debt. If there is ever a way to repay, name the price."

"There's no need—"

"The McLains pay their debts," he interrupted with words laced in anger.

Before she could think of anything to say, he was gone out the far door and taking the stairs three at a time without a word of good-bye.

Nichole returned to the kitchen. She watched Willow with the babies for a while. When both infants were fed and sleeping, Nichole offered the girl a bowl of stew. While Willow ate, Nichole pulled a cot from the downstairs bedroom.

"I think Daniel would want you to sleep here by the babies." Adam and Daniel had moved a cradle by the stove a few hours before the funeral. "Daniel may not be in tonight but he'll know you are watching after the twins. Will you be all right here?"

Willow nodded. "Long as I got water. I get mighty thirsty after they feed."

Nichole checked the pitcher.

"And," Willow turned her head down and to the side as if afraid to ask, "would anyone mind if I ate that bread on the table if the little girls wake me up tonight? This stew is the first meal I've had today. Pa never lets me eat until all my chores are done."

"No one will mind," Nichole answered. "And help yourself to the jam May made."

"May?"

"May was their mother." Nichole couldn't help but smile at the sleeping infants. "I didn't know her well, but I think she'd be pleased if you ate what she made. From what I hear, she was a great cook. Remember to tell the twins that when they're older. And tell them she was brave, very brave to the end."

"I will," Willow answered as she lay down on her cot. "And I'll tell them how their pa chopped down a whole barn the night after they was born."

Nichole lifted her holster from a peg by the door and lowered the lamp's glow before heading upstairs. Halfway up, she realized she hadn't asked Wes which one of the small rooms on the second floor was his.

But when she reached the landing, one door was closed tightly. Somehow she knew that room was Adam's.

He'd closed himself off. If she left at first light, she might never see him again. Nichole stood in the hallway, letting the weight of the day move over her like murky water, pressing against her lungs until she could hardly breathe. She closed her eyes and tried to slow her heart to the rhythm of Dan's chopping. A kind being had passed from this earth only hours ago, and no one might ever speak of her except Willow to say that she could cook. The twins might never know how dearly the three men downstairs had loved their mother and how much their father had cherished her. And how hard they'd all fought to save her. Nichole shook with the pain May's death had caused all in the house.

Suddenly, a hand touched her arm. Nichole jumped, bolting to run as she grabbed for her weapon.

"Nichole?" Adam whispered from only inches away. "Are you all right?" His hand moved gently along her shoulder.

Before she could think that he might not welcome such an action, she wrapped her arms around him and held tightly, preparing to fight if he tried to push her away. The McLains might need no one, but she needed to hold on tight for a few minutes.

But he didn't pull away. He hugged her back with all the hurt and anger and sorrow he had bottled up inside.

For a long while, they just hugged, sharing a weight each was tired of bearing alone. There was so much they didn't know about one another. But it didn't matter at this moment. All that mattered was that her lean body molded so perfectly against his . . . her arms held him grounded to earth . . . and his grip pulled her safely from drowning.

He moved away just enough to brush his cheek against hers. "Stay with me tonight,'' he whispered against her hair. ''Like you did the night we met. Make everything but your warmth go away for a few hours.'' He kissed her cheek lightly. ''Let me hold you.''

Without a word, Nichole followed him through his open doorway. She placed her holster on his bedpost and lowered herself to the bed.

Slowly, he closed the door, circled and slid beside her, pulling her against him as he spread a blanket over them both.

She moved her hand over his chest and felt his heart. Some pains are too great for words. He'd come home, to the place he'd probably dreamed of all during the war, to find his dreams shattered in silence.

Touching him lightly, she tried to smooth away the pain. His body seemed to relax next to her. Within minutes, he was breathing slowly, deeply.

Nichole stretched and kissed his cheek. ''Good night, Yank,'' she whispered.

The chopping continued, blending with the rain. Beating with the rhythm of a clock as the minutes of the night passed.

SEVEN

Deep into the blackness of night, Nichole stretched, moving against Adam for warmth. He rolled slightly toward her. Slowly, the brush of his breath against her throat tickled her awake. She lay in the darkness, feeling his chest rise and fall beside her own.

With fluid movements, she raised her hand and outlined the length of his body from shoulder to hip. He was thin, but she felt his muscles tighten as she traveled over them. The smooth softness of the cotton of his shirt contrasted with the coarse twill of his pants.

Leaning forward, she inhaled deeply. "Adam," she whispered. No man had ever smelled so good. She'd know him anywhere, even in total darkness. The hint of shaving soap, wool, and fireplaces seemed baked, ever so lightly, into his skin.

Before she thought of what she was doing, Nichole leaned closer and ran her tongue along his throat, sampling the slightly salty taste of him.

When he didn't move, she unbuttoned his collar button and tasted again of the warm flesh once hidden beneath his shirt.

She'd never been so close to a man and had no idea how a lady was to behave, nor did she care. In a few hours it would be time for her to go back to her world and she wanted to return with enough memories of Adam to last her a lifetime.

As his easy breathing became a rhythm in her ear, Nichole slipped the next button free and continued her exploration.

With his chest bare, she laid her cheek against the soft hair covering his skin and captured the pounding of his heart in her ear. In some small way, maybe because he'd saved her life, he was hers. If only for a few hours in the darkness of this one night.

Nichole pushed his shirt away and moved her hand over his chest and down to his waist as he slept soundly. He had not been a man who'd trained himself to awaken to the slightest sound or movement as she'd been trained. Now that lack of skill kept him soundly sleeping as she touched him.

She wondered if she was touching him as he'd caressed her the night they'd met. What had he said? *It had been so long since he'd touched anything of beauty.* No one had ever hinted that she might be pretty, much less beautiful. The only time Wolf complimented her was on her abilities as a Shadow.

She began at Adam's face, letting her cheek gently rub against his, lightly tasting his flesh as she moved down. When she reached the plain of his abdomen, she rested her face against the warm softness of his skin. Smiling, she realized she felt very much like an animal nestled deep inside a winter cave with her mate. A hundred cold nights when she'd hugged herself to keep from freezing, she'd wondered how a man would feel beside her.

Adam moved in his sleep, threading his fingers through her hair.

Slowly, Nichole raised her head and straightened to reach his face. His hand continued to stroke.

She tried to see if his eyes were closed, if he was still asleep. But, though her heart was suddenly racing, his breathing was slow and easy. Only the movement of his hand gave away any hint that he might have awakened.

As she lay very still, he rolled to his side and laid his free hand at her waist.

"Adam?" she whispered. "Adam, are you asleep?"

When he didn't answer, she breathed a deep sigh of relief. She hadn't meant her exploration to be quite so bold and had panicked at the thought that she'd been caught.

His closeness now made it difficult to manage, but she moved her fingers between them and again began unbuttoning his shirt. At the second button, she decided to risk one more touch. He slept so soundly, she reasoned, he'd never know.

Her fingers crossed beneath the shirt and spread wide over his chest. The soft curls tickled her fingertips as she explored the hard plain of his chest.

He rolled toward her, trapping her hand over his heart as he buried his face against her hair.

"Adam," she whispered in panic. "Adam, are you awake?"

His arm tightened around her waist, pulling her closer, bowing her back slightly. Her breasts pressed against his chest as his leg weighed heavy atop hers.

"No," he mumbled against her ear. "I'm not awake. I'm dreaming. I'm dreaming a lovely woman is having her way with me."

Before she could deny his claim, his mouth covered her lips.

Nichole thought she knew what a kiss from Adam would be like. After all, she'd kissed him twice. But this kiss was nothing like she'd ever experienced. This wasn't just a kiss on her mouth, but over her entire body. His tongue parted her lips while his hands moved over her with a hunger that warmed her completely. She could feel his body moving above her, pressing, feeling, reacting to her slightest actions.

For a moment, she thought wildly of fighting. But the warm paradise he offered was too great to resist. As she relaxed beneath him, his hold lessened, but not his touch. His fingers seemed starved for the feel of her as he tugged against her clothing.

The kiss continued. She moved with pleasure and felt his body react to each of her shifts. At first, she thought he was controlling her, holding her, but when she pressed against him, she knew the control was hers, not his.

Her arms slid around his neck as her longing to be close met his. She held on tightly as his fingers slowly moved along her back and over her hips. He was erasing all the loneliness she'd silently borne with the years of no one holding her. He was soothing the little girl in her who wanted to be held and drawing out the woman with the warming passion of each stroke.

He broke the kiss and rolled onto his back, pulling her with him. He took deep breaths, holding her to him tightly as though she might evaporate like an image in a cloud. Then, he cupped her face and kissed her so tenderly a tear formed in her eye.

"Do you have any idea what we are doing?" he asked in a voice so low she barely heard him.

"No," she answered honestly. She'd listened to a few of the rough stories the men had bragged about when they'd told of mounting women. None were anything like this. They'd laughed of riding women until they made them scream and of taking all they wanted. They'd never talked of kissing, or holding, or of feeling a heart beat against their own. Whatever they'd done couldn't be the same as this.

"What am I doing?" she whispered as her hand moved beneath his shirt to touch flesh.

His sharp intake of breath told her of his reaction. He kissed her

as his hands grew bolder along her body. The material couldn't bar the warmth of his touch.

Finally, he rolled her gently to her side but didn't move away. She could see his outline in the darkness. She could feel the warmth of him only an inch away, hear the long intakes of his breath, taste the remains of his kiss on her lips.

"Dear God, Nick, you're making it difficult." He combed her hair away from her face with his fingers. "You can't imagine how deeply I want you."

Nichole was growing confused. She wasn't sure how to answer the question. If she said yes did it mean she understood what he was talking about? If she said no, would he think her a fool? She knew of fighting, and riding, and of weapons. She knew nothing of this, except that he felt good by her side and his hands made her feel alive all over.

"I know I want you to kiss me again," she whispered. "I'm not a child, Adam."

He kissed her cheek, then seemed unable to resist moving lower to her throat. His words fanned her skin. "You're not a woman. You've never had a chance to be. It would be unfair of me to—"

She rolled toward him, moving against his side, letting him know she was all female.

Adam took the advance fully, without retreat. She felt his body jerk slightly as her body met his. Without a word, she raised her mouth and silenced any protest. For a second, he hesitated, then accepted her gift.

She wanted him to understand just how fully a woman she was and he'd taken the lesson without complaint.

Dawn crept across the room from the open window as Nichole felt Adam touching her as no one had ever dared. His fingers moved over her clothes as though no material separated them. She was a part of him and he needed to explore. He wanted to know every inch of her.

When she broke the kiss and leaned back her head to breathe, he tasted her neck while his hands cupped her breasts. The fabric did little to mask his bold touch or the heat he stirred with his gentle grip. He closed his fingers around the fullness of her breasts and lowered his mouth to hers. When her lips parted in the sudden wave of pleasure and surprise overwhelming her, his kiss deepened and his grip tightened slightly sending pure delight through her.

Several thuds registered before Nichole's trained senses realized someone was coming up the stairs. The heavy footfalls could belong to only one man.

"Wolf!" she whispered as she shoved away from Adam.

Adam raised his head to listen, then reacted as if she'd yelled fire at the top of her voice. He rolled from the bed and began buttoning his shirt.

"What is it?" she asked as he dressed. "What do we do?"

"Wolf's going to kill me!" he answered. "And I don't blame him."

"Nonsense." Nichole almost laughed. "Why would he kill you?" Adam wasn't making sense. Wolf wouldn't kill him for kissing her. She'd done that before.

"For what I was thinking of doing." Adam moved to the window. "For what I was about to do," he whispered as she followed him. "For what I was doing." He straddled the sill. "All seem just cause for murder."

"Nick!" Wolf called from the landing. "Which room you in?"

Adam leaned forward and kissed her lightly on the lips. "Trust me. If he catches me in here, I'm a dead man."

Without another word, Adam slipped out the window. A shingle clattered to the porch below as he moved away.

"Nick!" Wolf bellowed as he opened the door.

She took a step and lifted her gun belt from the post. "I'm almost ready," she mumbled, hoping she sounded sleepy.

"We're burning daylight." He glanced around the little room. "Don't get lazy just because you got to sleep in a bed last night."

"I'm ready." Nichole left the room ahead of him praying her face would have time to cool before he got a good look at her.

Adam followed the shingle to the porch, dropping within inches of where Wes sat rolling a cigarette.

Wes jerked, spilling the tobacco across his legs and dumped the pack of papers in the mud. "Damn!" he swore.

Adam straightened and tried to act calm. "Sorry. I didn't know you were there."

Wes dusted the tobacco from his pants. "I didn't realize I was standing in a damned crossroads." He met his brother's stare.

Adam was too old to explain anything. "You're up early," he said, trying to sound casual and knowing he was making no sense.

"You're dropping down a little early yourself, Doc."

"Nichole's leaving." Adam tucked his shirt in. "I wanted to say good-bye." He thought about how he'd been saying hello only a minute ago.

"I know. I helped Wolf saddle their horses." Wes shoved the bag of tobacco back in his shirt pocket. "Been thinking of giving up smoking anyway."

As he spoke, Wolf and Nichole tiptoed out of the house.

"Babes are sleeping!" Wolf yelled in what he thought was a whisper. "Daniel's passed out on his bed." He glanced at Wes. "You'll say good-bye to them for us?"

Wes nodded.

Wolf turned to Adam. "And thanks, Doc, for saving my Nick's life. I was sorry I couldn't find you to kill you that day, but now I'm glad I didn't. Like Nick said, you're a fine man even if you did somehow end up on the wrong side."

Adam didn't know what to say. He felt sure Wolf would never utter such a thing if he knew that only a few heartbeats ago Adam had been holding Nichole's breast in his hand.

They moved toward the horses. Wes talked with Wolf, giving him a few directions that would make the way back faster.

Adam had a moment alone with Nichole. He moved behind her and placed his hands around her waist to help her up.

"I don't need any help." She laughed.

"I know," he whispered without removing his hands. "Do you have to go so soon?" His pride wouldn't allow him to say more.

"We've got trouble back home, and I need to stand with Wolf and the others." She had her duty and they both understood.

"About what happened—" Adam began.

She placed her gloved fingers over his lips. "No," she whispered. "Not a word."

If he said he was sorry, it would be worse than a bullet to her heart. If he begged her to stay, they'd both regret it. He belonged here, not with her. She might not know much, but she knew he had turned to her in grief and she'd be a fool if she tried to make it more.

Gripping the saddle horn, she pulled herself up. His hand slid from her waist to her boot, but he didn't try to stop her.

"Until we meet again." He offered his hand.

"We'll never meet again," she answered, knowing she had to cut the wound clean if it would ever heal. "You'll be married soon with your life full helping Daniel raise the twins, and I'll be a world away."

"Let's ride." Wolf kicked his horse.

Nichole covered Adam's hand as it rested on her leg. "I'll never forget you." She smiled and nudged her mount, already dancing to follow.

She was out of hearing distance before Adam answered, "Nor I you."

EIGHT

ADAM WATCHED NICHOLE AND HER BROTHER RIDE AWAY WITH THE feel of her next to him still thick in his mind. Had he really kissed her so completely? He told himself he was an honorable man who was engaged to be married to another, but at this moment, he didn't feel very honorable or very engaged. All he knew was that if they'd had more time, he would have made love to her with a passion he'd never felt toward another or even dreamed he might feel. The logic that had always ruled his mind had somehow been sidestepped this morning.

Wes broke the silence. "Want some coffee before I ride into town with you?"

Adam looked at his brother and raised an eyebrow. "How'd you know I was going to town this morning?"

Moving toward the kitchen, Wes winked. "After the way you looked at Nick, I figure you'll be having a few words with Bergette."

"I plan to, but not because of Nichole. Bergette and I have grown apart these past years. The woman I spent the war planning a future for wasn't waiting for me as I thought. I think I knew it within minutes after I saw her, but I didn't want to admit it to myself. It's obvious we could never marry, and the time to tell her is now. She needs a groom for her wedding, not a husband in her life."

Wes opened the screen door. "Then you'll find Nichole?" he asked.

"No." Adam took a deep breath. "We'll never see one another again. We've said our good-byes." Neither of them had spoken of a future. They both knew it would be impossible. All he wanted was to be a doctor and adventure still ran thick in her blood.

Wes looked like he didn't believe Adam's words, but he didn't question him. Adam considered himself a man who set his life by order and logic. Nichole and he were simply two people who met once and touched one another's lives . . . he would be a fool to think it was more.

An hour later, Adam was wishing he'd let Wolf shoot him at dawn. At least then he would have silence. Bergette's screams were starting to make his eyes cross.

To say the princess had taken the news of their broken engagement dramatically was an understatement. She'd cried, pouted, and finally attacked with a vengeance. When she ordered Charles to throw him out, Adam almost ran from the room. When he glanced back, he wondered how he could have thought her so beautiful.

Adam didn't take a deep breath until he rode within sight of the farmhouse. The loss of the woman he'd thought Bergette was weighed on his heart. The woman he remembered had somehow died while he'd been away, and the replacement was a shallow second to the Bergette he'd kept in his dreams for years. He felt he'd lost someone dearly loved, not to death, but to change.

As he unsaddled his mount, Adam realized he didn't want to stay here and face the rumors she'd start. In one of her ravings, she'd sworn that no person in town would ever seek his medical advice when they learned of how cruelly he'd broken her heart. He wasn't sure he could bear to live here and see the shell of a woman he'd held so dearly in his dreams.

Adam moved toward the house. The sun was setting and he realized he hadn't eaten today. This day had passed in emotions not in hours, leaving him spent and weary.

" 'Evening." Wes fell into step. "You still engaged, little brother?"

"Is the offer to travel to Texas still on?"

"I guess that answers my question." Wes sighed. "But you'll have to get in line. Danny boy told me a few minutes ago that he's going also."

"He found someone to take care of the twins for a while?"

Wes laughed. "Of course, little brother. He found Willow to be wet nurse and two fools named McLain to act as nursemaids. We're all going to Texas."

Three months later, just outside a little settlement known as Fort Worth, Adam looked at his older brother and wondered how they'd made it. He'd thought the war had been hard on them. Fighting the rebs was nothing compared to hauling newborns a thousand miles by train, boat, and wagon.

He'd spent many a night in the saddle with one of the tiny girls sleeping in the fold of his arm. Though Willow had done her best, the brothers all learned to do what was necessary. Daniel loved the caretaking, forgetting his grief only when the babies needed him. Adam also enjoyed the role, finding it fascinating to watch them grow. But Wes grumbled every mile. He'd announced more than once that he'd rather roll through a corral of manure than have another drop of baby spit-up soak through to his shoulder.

Finally, they left Daniel and the girls at a settlement called Parker's Fort near Dallas. Wes lectured Daniel on caring for the twins, though there were several mothers in the small village willing to offer advice.

Adam had heard Daniel talk of the colony named after John Parker and dedicated to religion and Bible study. The folks might look meek, but their settlement had survived thirty years of hardship. With the agreement that Daniel would act as blacksmith, they provided him with a small house and supplies to last through the winter. The community seemed exactly what a young father with twin babies needed: an extended family.

This might be the very place Daniel could find peace, Adam thought. The girl, Willow, smiled more the farther they got from her home. They were a week out before she stopped asking if they were going to send her back to her pa.

The McLains had boarded up the farmhouse on the first of August along with all the memories and left for Texas. Deep within Adam he knew they would never be back. From this point on, like for many of the men from the North and South, Texas would be called home. For Wes and Daniel, it seemed a calling, but Adam was only drifting, more leaving one place than going somewhere else.

Now to the best of his calculation it was the first of November. Adam crossed his leg over the saddle horn and leaned back, looking at the dusty little huddle of shacks that had once been a fort. "What do you think of Fort Worth?"

Wes lit a thin cigar and took his time answering. "I heard this place was never more than a single company post." He stood on his stirrups. The leather he wore creaked with his movements. "Lucky thing Texas wasn't used much as a battlefield during the war. I'd hate to think of this state looking any sorrier. They should let the Indians have it."

"I heard back at the stage station a band of fifteen warriors attacked two men not far from here a month ago. Maybe the Indians will have it yet. They killed one man named Wright. The other, Smith, made it back to a settlement north of here called Denton before he died.''

"Great, another thing to keep a lookout for. I might as well give up sleep while I'm here making my fortune and trying to keep my hair.''

Adam laughed. ''It's not all that bad as long as we're moving fast and well armed. The Butterfield Stage makes it well past Fort Worth without being raided often. If the stage is running regular, how bad could the state be?''

"Are you joking? Besides the Indians, every other man in Texas looks like he's practicing snarling for a picture on a wanted poster. The land, from treetop to soil, is a rainbow of dull brown. And the women, the women are so homely I'm surprised their offspring will take to the breast.''

Wes glanced from side to side and whispered as if someone might overhear them. ''Hell, the friendliest thing I've seen is a rattler waving his tail at me. Everyone hates us. Some because we're Yankees, some because it seems their natural disposition.''

"Still, there's the cows,'' Adam offered.

Wes moved his horse toward the sunset and the town he'd been trying to reach for months. ''I'll give you that. This place is longhorn-rich, but they're wild. It won't be like rounding up the milk cows back home. Going to take some work to be wealthy by summer.''

"It won't be easy.''

Wes agreed. ''Nope. If it was, too many fools besides me would be trying it. Come on along, little brother. I want to make town by sundown. I need a meal, a bottle, and a pretty woman.''

Kicking his horse ahead, Adam added, ''I thought you said there were no pretty women in Texas.''

Wes joined in the race. ''In that case,'' he shouted, ''I'll need two bottles to drink her pretty.''

An hour later, Wes's opinion of Texas had changed. He'd downed a pound of steak and half a bottle of whiskey and managed to rent a room with a real bed.

While Wes struck up a conversation about cattle with men wearing leather and spurs, Adam walked out to the street.

The lodging they'd found was on the edge of town, with mostly remains of what must have been fort building running behind it.

Wes had been right. Texas hadn't been much of what they'd hoped for. It was wilder, more unsettled than they'd thought. But the people seemed friendly enough if given half a chance. They didn't offer a quick smile, but they didn't turn away from questions. The whole state seemed made up of loners. Adam figured none of the McLains were looking for what they left back home.

He walked along the planked boards of what passed as sidewalks in front of the stores. This little frontier post had become the county seat in its less than twenty years of existence. Wes would find his dream here in Texas. He'd organize men and had some already waiting for him further south near Austin, and by spring, they'd be ready to head cattle north to market. There was talk of a half-Scotsman, half-Cherokee scout named Jesse Chisholm being willing to cut a trace all the way to Kansas.

Smiling at himself, Adam realized he didn't even know what "cut a trace" meant a month ago. But here in the West that was how men referred to marking a trail for someone else to follow.

Only Adam had no scout to mark his trail. He had no idea where he was heading. As he passed the stage office, he thought, come morning, he could step on a stage and head farther west. But to where, to what? Wes had his dream. Daniel had his duty. But Adam had nothing. When the war ended, he thought he had his life all planned out. Now six months later he was like so many others, drifting, belonging nowhere.

Since the night he'd told Nichole he wasn't sure about being a doctor, he hadn't allowed himself to think about quitting. She'd cut his doubts off at the knee. Something inside him made him want to be as good a doctor as she thought he already was.

There she was again, he thought. Drifting through his mind like she planned to homestead. Over the past months he'd caught himself talking things out with her in his imagination. Something about the way she'd demanded the best from him made him want to try harder.

"You got a twopenny, mister?" a tiny outline whispered from between two buildings. "It ain't for me, it's for my ma."

Adam knelt down trying to see the child's face. He was thin, deathly thin with hair and eyes the color of rust. His clothes were dirty and worn.

"Is something wrong with your mother, son?"

"She's sick, but for a few pennies the cook will give a plate of leftovers from the kitchen. He's real generous. Sometimes it's enough to feed us all."

Adam fished a twopenny coin from his pocket and handed it to the boy. Then, silently, he watched as the kid climbed the steps to the back door of the small restaurant and asked for a plate.

The cook, who looked like he could be wanted in several states, took the coin and disappeared. After a few minutes, he returned with a plate of mostly beans and potatoes. Atop it, he'd placed a large slice of cornbread.

"Thanks." The boy smiled showing several gaps where baby teeth had been.

The cook grinned back with an equally toothless smile. "Don't tell the boss about the cornbread. It was left over. Ain't no use throwing it out."

The cook touched the boy's shoulder a moment while he stuffed a small package in his coat pocket. "That's for old Terry. Mangy old good-for-nothing dog."

"Much obliged," the beggar whispered as the cook pushed him away in a great pretense of being bothered.

Adam followed as the boy ran into the blackened alley. He could hear the child's footsteps, but had to guide himself by touch.

When Adam finally slowed, deciding to give up the chase, he turned a corner and saw a light. The air was so still in the alley, he could hear himself breathing and smell poverty thick as smoke around him.

Curiosity drew him toward the spot of light.

As his eyes adjusted, Adam found himself boxed in with the backs of two-story buildings on three sides of him. One, judging from the odor and muffled noises, was a saloon, only business didn't seem very lively tonight. The second side of his man-made canyon was some kind of hotel or whorehouse. The third building looked abandoned except for a single candle blinking through a broken window. It was a wide old two-story that could have been officer's quarters in its prime. It looked like it had been converted into a boardinghouse.

Adam moved carefully around abandoned crates as he neared the window. The scene that slowly came into distorted focus through the broken glass made him question his vision.

A woman, pale and fever wet, lay on a small bed. The beggar boy sat on the floor offering her the plate of food.

Taking a step closer, Adam stared at the third person in the room. A nun. Her spotless habit was snow white and raven black in sharp contrast to everything around her. She looked like an aging angel as she wiped the dying woman's brow.

Adam couldn't resist moving closer. As his foot took the first step, a dog the size of a colt jumped up from the shadows and barked an alarm. Adam froze.

After a long pause, the boy opened the door only enough to peer out. "Yes?" he whispered in a brave little voice that said he'd protect those within as best he could.

Adam didn't waste words. "I'm a doctor," he said. "I've come to help if I can."

"I ain't got no money." The boy lifted his chin slightly.

"We'll talk of payment later." Adam smiled. He'd often heard of folks paying in services or chickens, but he'd never practiced medicine except during the war.

The boy hesitated, then opened the door.

When Adam's gaze met the nun's stare, he couldn't move. She had the most knowing eyes he'd ever seen. The kind of eyes an artist would try to paint for a saint. Ageless eyes in a face that shattered into a thousand wrinkles when she smiled.

Without a word, she opened her aging hand and pointed to the woman on the bed. "Please," she whispered. "Help this child of God if you can, Doctor."

Leaning forward, Adam felt the patient's forehead, the side of her throat, then her hand.

"Boy," he snapped. "You know that café where you got the food?"

"Yes, sir."

"Go to the front door and look in. You should see a man about my size with a scar on his left cheek. Tell him Adam said to bring the medical bag."

"But I can't go into that place. Not the front."

Adam smiled, wishing he could see Wes's face when the boy ordered him. "Don't worry. Just tell the man with the scar to hurry. He'll see no harm comes to you."

As soon as the boy left, Adam pulled the covers back. "We've got work to do." He looked up at the elderly nun, knowing she would help. "This woman's fever is dangerously high."

Wes was somewhere into the fog that comes in the bottom of a whiskey bottle. The waitress was starting to look slimmer and less moley. The banging on the piano had almost evolved into a tune when a dirt-covered kid stepped out of nowhere and yelled at him.

Wes shook his head and tried to understand the words as a bartender grabbed the boy up and swung him toward the door.

"Wait! What did you say, boy?" Wes hated it when people seemed to talk in some kind of code leaving out every other word. They tended to do it when he'd had a few too many drinks, but he refused to allow them to get by with it.

"He told me to tell the man with a scar to bring Adam's medical bag." The boy tried to wiggle from the hairy hand that held him captive.

Wes looked around as if expecting to see others with scars. When he turned back, his eyes had sobered slightly. "Let go of the kid," he ordered as he stood and paid his bill. "I'll get the bag. Take me to Adam, son."

NINE

Dawn finally found its way to the alley and brightened the back windows of a building that had once been part of the original fort, Adam guessed, from the wide middle hallway and the square frame. Someone had taken the time a few years ago to add improvements, but now the place needed a fresh coat of paint and a bag of nails.

"Want another cup of coffee, Doctor?" asked the old nun, who'd helped him during the night, as she poured without waiting for a reply.

"Thanks." Adam stretched back in his chair. "I think the boy's mama might have a chance of making it." He looked at the woman who'd been working by his side. "Thanks to you."

She shook her head. "You were the blessing. I sent the boy to seek a doctor two days ago, but he said there was none to be found. I did what I could to help her. Which was a yard short of enough in this case."

Adam watched her closely. She hadn't had any sleep, but she looked the same as she had last night, spotless and efficient. She had a way of guessing what was needed a moment before he asked for it. "Are you with the mission here, Sister?"

She glanced away. "There is no mission near. I travel alone." She straightened as if testifying before a judge. "I belong to a church no longer though I still hold the beliefs. I greatly dishonored my order. I've worn a habit for fifty years. I no longer belong in it, but this is all I have to wear."

Adam clamped his jaw down to keep from asking the dozen questions that came to mind. How could this perfect image of a Sister of

Mercy appear in the middle of nowhere and claim to have committed some great sin?

Before he could think of which question to ask first, she raised her head.

"Thank you for not demanding more of my story, for I can say nothing else." The flavoring of a foreign accent added another unanswered question to his list.

"The boardinghouse belongs to Mrs. Jamison and her son, but I don't know for how much longer." The nun switched the conversation topic. "I'm told she and her husband managed to scrape out a living here before the war. With the war, there was no business. She told me he turned to outlawing.

"In '63, he went to prison and died of a fever within a month. When they sent his clothes back to her, there was not a valuable among them.

"She tried to keep the boardinghouse going, but couldn't. She's not a strong woman and now without enough food or heat she grows sick."

"How long have you been helping them?" Adam found it interesting that she could be so silent about her life, yet so talkative about Mrs. Jamison.

"Two weeks. I came to ask if I could stay a few days for I'd heard of the Jamisons and this house. When I saw how ill she was, I had to help. I've used up what little supplies I had. When the coffee's gone, there will be nothing."

The old nun crossed her hands in front of her and waited. It took Adam several seconds to realize, like a patient teacher, she was waiting for him to give her the answer.

"I'm sorry. I don't have any answers, Sister." He stood and walked to the door. "I'm just passing through. The widow will need good food for weeks to get all her strength back."

The nun didn't move, she only waited.

Adam touched the doorknob. "I don't even know where I'm headed." He reached in his pocket. "I can leave enough—"

He stopped, realizing the little amount he could leave would only delay starvation, not prevent it.

"I'll try to find someone." Even as he said the words, he doubted there would be anyone to help. The entire country was full of widows and children without means.

"I'll think about it," he finally said, and managed to break the invisible hold this nun had on him. "I'll be back later."

He almost ran up the alley to the street. By the time he reached the hotel where he and Wes had taken a room, he was breathing hard and frustrated that he couldn't do more to solve her problem.

When he opened the door to the room he'd rented, a bottle rolled out of the way and Wes's snoring greeted him. Adam unstrapped his gun belt and pulled off his coat, telling himself he needed sleep. He'd worry about the nun's problem in a few hours. Right now, all he wanted to do was relax in the first bed he'd seen in months.

As he pulled off his boots, he looked around the place they'd rented after dark. The room had two beds and an old dresser missing a third drawer. The washstand was grimy and the pitcher empty. Both windows had been nailed closed. It was hard to believe, but this operating hotel was dirtier than the abandoned one the boy's mother lay dying in. Someone had yellowed the wallpaper in one corner to save going to the outhouse. Light, about bullet-hole size, shown through the walls in several places.

Adam closed his eyes in disgust. He didn't like the idea of having to live in a place like this for months, maybe longer, while saving his money to open a practice. He hadn't found a suitable location. Every town needed a doctor, so he guessed anywhere would do. Even Fort Worth.

As he crossed into dreams Nichole was by his side. Only she wasn't sleeping next to him, but waiting for him to help the nun and the widow, and the boy. She seemed to expect it, as though that was the kind of man he was and nothing would change the fact.

Rolling awake, Adam stared at the empty space beside him. He remembered something his mother used to say about not looking for the right person to love, but *being* the right person. It was time he started being the man Nichole had thought he was. He might never see her again, but he'd know.

Three hours later Adam was standing in front of the boy again waiting to be admitted. The huge dog watched him from the corner of the porch, but didn't bark.

"I'm not bringing charity," Adam said for the third time. "I'm here to offer a deal to the man of the house, and I guess that's you."

The boy let the doorway open enough for Adam to enter with bundles dangling from his shoulders.

Adam nodded to the nun as he put the groceries down on the long kitchen table. "How's our patient?"

"Resting, thanks to the medicine." The nun watched him closely, only allowing her gaze to dart momentarily to the bags of supplies.

"I think I've found a solution." Adam saw no hint of surprise in her eyes. He looked at the boy. "I'd like to rent the downstairs rooms of this place from you, sir. Besides this kitchen, I think I noticed four rooms, two small rooms on the side with the kitchen that I could use as living quarters and two larger rooms on the other side of the stairs and front foyer where I could set up a practice. The stairs, foyer, and kitchen would be common ground.''

The child started to shake his head.

"Hear me out. I need a place to stay and work. You and your mother can have all the upstairs. When I walked around last night, I think I noticed six rooms. You can live in them all or rent a few out if you like. This house is so large, you'd hardly notice me.''

Adam faced the nun. "Will you stay with them a little longer? The boy's mother needs care, and I can use help. I can't pay you, but you'll have a roof and food. I'm sure they'd welcome you as their guest.''

"I'll stay as long as I'm needed. I'll accept no pay.'' She folded her arms. "I help when I can, but I work for no man for pay.''

Adam looked back to the boy. "We're not taking over your place, son. We're just asking to be boarders. It's up to you. You can turn us out on the street if you like. For payment, I'll doctor your ma and provide food. Maybe I can pay rent once I open my practice.''

He knew the boy had no choice, but he admired the way the little fellow took his time considering.

"All right, but I help out, too,'' the boy finally answered. "A man who's healthy and don't work shouldn't oughta eat. And don't call me boy or son. My name's Nance, Nance Edward Jamison just like my pa.'' He stood as tall as his five years would allow. "And my dog's named Terry, Terry Jamison. He don't have no middle name cause he's a dog, but he's a Jamison just like me.''

"Fair enough. I'm Dr. Adam McLain, but you can call me Doc, or Adam.'' He looked up at the nun waiting for her introduction.

"I'm Sister . . .'' Sorrow clouded her eyes. "Just call me Sister, Dr. McLain.''

Nodding, Adam moved to the table. He'd spent most of his cash buying food and supplies to be delivered later that day. He'd also sent word for the postmaster in Corydon to send his medical books. He hoped they arrived before his doors opened. He had his worries about treating anything except gunshot wounds.

Adam was so busy the next few days he saw little of Wes. His older brother spent his days sleeping and his nights drinking while Adam used every second of daylight to turn one side of the downstairs into offices and the other into a study and a bedroom.

Wes surprised him one morning when he stopped by to say good-bye. Though his eyes were red and his face dark with a week's growth of beard, Wes still sat the saddle tall and proud just the way the military had molded him.

"Keep an angel on your shoulder!" Wes yelled the familiar farewell with a hint of their father's Irish accent as he turned his horse away.

"And your fist drawn till you brother covers your back," Adam finished the line. He waved, watching Wes ride out. A part of him wanted to go with his brother, but Wes was a loner who guarded his solitude. And Adam liked things settled. Living out of a saddlebag had never appealed to him. He preferred waking every morning and knowing everything would be where he left it the night before.

He returned to his chore of patching the roof. Wes was in as much hurry to start his life as Adam found himself to be. It was time to start catching up on the years they lost.

Once he decided to plant a few roots, there was no stopping Adam. He figured he could have an office open in a few weeks, and by spring would have completely forgotten about Bergette and all the plans he'd dreamed with her. She'd have a fit if she knew he was opening an office between a whorehouse and a saloon. But somehow, he figured, Nick would be proud of him.

Nichole wouldn't be quite as easy to erase from his mind, he realized. Most nights he found himself reaching for her in his sleep, like she'd spent more than two nights in his arms, like he needed her. She was somewhere deep in Tennessee, fighting for her land beside her brother. She wasn't thinking of him, he told himself repeatedly, and he wasn't thinking of her.

The nun offered little help in conversation. She answered no questions, not even that of her name. She also took no orders, but was good at guessing what Adam needed. If he asked her to hand him a hammer, she'd say she didn't have time, but if he left his dirty shirt out, she managed to find an hour to do the wash. She cleaned and cooked and listened.

By the end of November, Adam had told her every thought and dream he'd ever had, and she'd told him how to make potato soup.

He'd spent hours trying to guess what she'd done that was so terrible that she'd left her order and couldn't speak of it. The only thing he'd learned about her was that if cleanliness is next to godliness, she must be heaven's next-door neighbor.

As December blew in bitter cold from the north, two letters came from Daniel. Both were full of facts about the growing twins he still hadn't named, and nothing about him. Adam decided his brother and the nun were bookends.

Slowly, the townfolks started calling to test the new doctor. As he'd expected, they paid in trade, but not in money. Farmers with cuts, housewives with complaints of dizziness, children with colds. One chapter at a time, Adam learned how to treat each ailment. Mrs. Jamison and the boy kept to themselves upstairs most of the day. She was feeling strong enough to come down each afternoon and help the nun cook supper. Though not out of her twenties, the widow Jamison seemed a sad, broken woman with little of life's light in her eyes.

She spoke of her husband sometimes, telling of how dashing he was and how foolish. He and his partner had been carpenters after their enlistment was finished in the frontier army. About the time they settled in Fort Worth, the war came. Her husband and his partner turned their energy less to repairing the house and more to robbing. One day they made plans for rebuilding the street of dilapidated houses, and it seemed the next day they were arrested.

Adam found his work challenging and read far into the night of the new theories in medicine that Doc Wilson kept sending. After a few weeks of burning a lamp late into the midnight hours, people began tapping on the back door. They were the folks who lived in shadows, the drunks, the prostitutes, the beggars. Adam found himself with two practices, one by day, one by night. Though some of the after-dark callers offered to pay in trade, Adam insisted they wait until they could pay him back some other way.

He found himself wishing he could tell Nichole some of their stories. In a way, she was one of them, a creature of the night.

By March of 1866, Adam began to relax and enjoy the challenges of life in Fort Worth. Folks on both sides of the street spoke to him and more books were coming every week for him to study.

Then, on Tuesday, March 22, Nance opened the door and the wind blew in trouble.

"Telegram for you, Doc." The young man from the new telegraph office ran in all excited to have been allowed to bring the doctor something he was sure must be important.

"Thanks for bringing it by, Harry." Adam wiped his hands on a towel and opened the note expecting to hear word from Wes or Dan.

The message read: *Request debt payment. Shipment arriving by stage. Guard with your life until I can pick up. Wolf.*

TEN

Nᴵᴄʜᴏʟᴇ sʟᴀᴍᴍᴇᴅ ʜᴇʀ ꜰɪsᴛ ɪɴᴛᴏ ʜᴇʀ ʙʀᴏᴛʜᴇʀ's ᴄʜᴇsᴛ ᴡɪᴛʜ ᴀʟʟ the fury she could muster. "I'm not going!" she screamed. "You can't make me!"

"Like hell I can't, Nick!" Wolf's voice was so angry it rumbled around the tiny grove like a huge cannon, rattling the air all the way to treetops. "You'll be on that train tonight if I have to lock you in a trunk and have you shipped to Texas."

"But you need me." Nichole paced in front of him, showing no fear of the man twice her width. "I'm the best rider you have. It's my land, too. You think I can stomach the idea of someone stealing it any better than you. Let me stay and fight with you."

"Not this time, Nick." Wolf glanced toward the campfire where two men waited. "Tyler and I have it all planned out. When trouble rolls in, I don't want to have to be worrying about where you are. For my own peace of mind I have to know you're safe. You're all the family I got left, don't you see, Nick?"

"All right. I won't ride with you, but let me go somewhere else. Anywhere else." Adam was probably married by now, and Nichole didn't know if she could face seeing him with that china doll of a woman. "I could camp out in this grove. No one would ever find me. You know I could stay here for months."

"This time we ain't fighting Yanks, we're fighting folks that know these hills as well as we do." Wolf hesitated a moment as if he felt sorry for her. "I know being shipped to Texas and the McLains is a dent in your pride, but better that than getting killed. The McLains are the only men I can trust, Nick. We've no family, and any friends we had before the war won't know us now. Except for Tyler and

Rafe, all the Shadows have gone home to their own problems. I can't fight for my land and worry about you. You're going to Texas.''

Nichole knew it was useless to argue any longer. ''All right, but let me go in my own clothes, not in some dress.'' Before her parents died, when she'd only been a kid, her mother had never minded her living in her brother's hand-me-downs. She could barely remember putting on a dress even as a child.

Wolf wasn't a man who budged easily. ''Dressed as a woman is the only way you'll make it out of the county alive. They'll be watching every man who leaves. Nick Hayward has a price on his head, but Nichole Hayward is unknown. So put on those duds I bought you.''

Nichole stormed off to the stream using every swear word she'd ever heard. She dressed in the ugly olive green skirt and whiskey-colored jacket Wolf had picked out for her at the mercantile. The skirt was too large in the waist and the jacket an inch too tight across the bodice, but she hardly noticed. Her brother, her only kin, was kicking her out of her state. Her own brother was sending her to the hell of Texas with only a prayer of finding one of the McLains. With her luck, they were all dead, or whiny little Bergette had made them turn around and go back to Indiana.

Since Wolf had helped with the delivery of May and Daniel's twins, he'd talked as though the McLains were his family and not just some men he'd met once. Nichole had tried to forget Adam, but Wolf hadn't made it easy. He retold their days in Indiana as though it had been his only trip to the normal world in this lifetime. He bragged about Adam being a great doctor and Wes being one of the only Yankees who knew how to fight.

When she tried to step back in the clearing without falling over her hem, the men froze. Tyler, who'd ridden with her for three years, stood as though a lady had just entered a room. He dusted himself off and smoothed back his curly black hair.

''Nick?'' He tilted his head slightly as if he didn't believe his eyes. ''Is that you?'' His normally emotionless face was twisted with confusion.

''Say a word and I'll gut you like a pig.'' Nichole stared at him in challenge.

Tyler lowered his eyes, slowly—far too slowly for Nichole's way of thinking.

''I . . . I never thought . . . I—''

''Well, you can stop thinking whatever it is you're thinking right now as far as I'm concerned. I'm still Nick, nothing more.'' She'd called Tyler a lot of names over the years, but fool had never been one of them. It came to mind now.

The boy Rafe, not yet out of his teens, slapped Tyler on the shoulder. "She's more, ain't she, Tyler? She's a whole lot more."

"Shut up," Tyler mumbled.

Nichole couldn't stop looking at the way Tyler's eyes had changed. He stared at her so hard it looked as if the firelight was coming from him and not reflecting off the campfire. Suddenly, she knew what he was thinking as truly as if he'd spoken the words out loud.

"Stop it!" she shouted placing her fists on her hips. The effort only tightened the material across her bustline. Nichole greatly missed her bindings and she could see she wasn't the only one who noticed them missing.

"Stop what?" Tyler raised his hands in surrender but couldn't seem to get the smile off his face.

"Stop thinking of me as a woman. I'm Nick. *Nick!* The same person who's been with you for three years. I've bailed you out of more than one scrape and saved your ass more times than I can count. I'm one of you. I'm a Shadow, just like you." How could he think less of her by thinking her a woman?

Tyler looked guilty. "I know." He swallowed hard making his Adam's apple bob up and down. "I've ridden with you and trusted you with my life. But I never thought you'd look the way you do in a dress."

"She sure don't look like one of us." Rafe giggled. "One Shadow has a few more curves." Rafe moved his hands over his own chest showing how hers rounded out.

Both Tyler and Wolf's fists swung toward the boy. In dodging, he stumbled backward, almost landing in the fire. The warmth sobered him.

Nick reached for her Colt, but the weapon wasn't at her hip. She wanted to shoot all three of them. Rafe thought she was a freak in a sideshow, Tyler couldn't stop staring at her like she was fresh-made apple pie, and Wolf was so overprotective he would smother her completely at any moment.

Grabbing the carpetbag Wolf had bought, Nick shoved her normal clothes inside, then lifted her Colt from the branch where she'd hung it. If this was anything like the reaction of the rest of the world, she'd rather stay here and be shot. Since Wolf wouldn't allow that, she figured she'd need the fine new Colt he'd bought her last year. She didn't know if she could stomach every man from here to Texas acting like his brains had been drained.

Much to her frustration, her anger brought tears to her eyes. Not because of the way the men were acting, but from a memory she'd been trying to bury for months. Adam. He'd never treated her like a freak, gawking and staring. Adam had always acted as though her clothes were normal. He'd even told her he liked her hair short. When he looked at her, he didn't just see a man or woman, he saw her.

"I'm sorry about Rafe." Tyler reached for the bag. "He's just having a little trouble seeing that you're still our Nick, no matter how you're dressed."

Nichole switched the bag in her hands, moving it away from his grip. "And you, Tyler? Are you still my friend?" She could tell he was as shocked as Rafe, only for some reason Tyler was trying to please her with his words, something she could never remember him trying to do. She'd always seen him as a good fighter who had little to say.

"Of course," he answered. "It'll just take a little getting used to. You've always been able to count on me, Nick."

He couldn't hide the smile that spread across his face, and she knew things would never be the same between them. He seemed to have developed a twitch that kept lowering his eyes to her bosom.

"Wolf says I'm to take you into town." Tyler tried to focus on her face.

"All right," Nichole mumbled as she gave Wolf a quick hug good-bye. It was one of the few times they'd touched, and though both tried, the hug was awkward. They moved only close enough to pat one another on the back a few times and then stepped away.

"Don't give the McLains any trouble," Wolf ordered. "They're good folks."

She nodded and climbed into the buckboard. Tyler rounded to the other side and climbed in beside her. Nichole stared hard at her mountain of a brother. She knew he'd find her when this trouble was over, there was no need for him to repeat himself. He loved her, though she doubted he'd ever say the words.

When she and Tyler were out of sight of the others the darkness closed in around them and Nichole relaxed. She was at home in the early spring night. Now her clothing didn't matter, she and Tyler were only voices.

"Tyler?" She finally broke the silence. "Could you be honest with me?"

"Sure," Tyler volunteered.

"Completely?"

"Completely."

"How do I look? I mean as a woman."

He pulled the reins and stopped the horses. She fought down nervousness as he turned toward her. He was her friend. She had nothing to fear from him.

"You look great, Nick," he answered. His voice was lower than normal. "You are prettier than just about any woman I ever seen."

"You haven't seen all that many."

"I've been around a few," he said defensively.

"Then why did you and Rafe act like such fools? Wolf told you I was his sister days ago. You knew I was a girl."

"I guess it didn't soak in until we saw you in that dress. Nick, a man treats a woman different and that's a fact. I may try not to say anything, or look at you, but that don't keep me from thinking things. And after seeing you in that dress, things will always come to mind when I'm with you."

"What things?"

"Things it wouldn't be proper for a man to tell a woman he's thinking even if they're on his mind." Tyler said the words slowly as if they made sense.

"But we've been friends for three years. I've heard you talk about everything. I heard all about that night you left the camp and went into Cortland last year."

Tyler slapped the horses into action. "That wasn't something you should have heard. A woman shouldn't oughta hear about another woman."

"I don't need another brother telling me what to do!" Nichole snapped. "Give me the reins. Suddenly, I'm in a hurry to be rid of the lot of you."

Tyler resisted for a second, then gave her the reins. In truth, they both knew she could drive a team better than him, but she sensed her action hurt his pride. He was right about one thing. It would never be the same between them now that he'd seen her in a dress.

When they arrived at the station, the train was already loading. Several groups stood saying good-bye as soldiers stood at attention near the center of the platform.

"Now, act like a lady, damn it!" he whispered as he forced her to allow him to help her down. "All you got to do is get on this train, and you'll be safe in two hours."

Nichole's fingers dug into his arm as he walked her down the platform. She shortened her steps, making moving in the dress easier.

She thought briefly of breaking away and running back to Wolf. If she raised enough ruckus, he'd allow her to stay. She knew he would. The only thing that kept her going along with this plan was the possibility that he might just be right. Wolf had a quick sense about danger, and if she was captured with the others, it could go badly for her. They might hang the men, but Wolf said they'd send her to one of those women's prisons. She'd die if she were locked up.

Tyler handed her the ticket. ''Wolf said you'll catch a stage tomorrow night. He wired a Doc Wilson in Corydon and received word that the McLains are in Fort Worth, or at least they were a month ago.'' Tyler looked worried. ''You sure about these Yanks, Nick? I wish there were somewhere else to send you. I don't like the idea of sending you to folks we don't know.''

Nick thought of hitting him hard on the side of his head. He'd caught Wolf's illness of being overprotective. Only the knowledge that one of the soldiers was watching kept her hand lowered.

''They're good men,'' Nichole reassured Tyler, who was now back into the big-brother role again.

''Nick . . . Nichole.'' Tyler moved his hand slowly down her arm. Something he'd never done. ''When this trouble is over, I plan to come with Wolf to fetch you. If these McLains mistreat you, they'll answer to me.''

''You do whatever you like.'' Nichole pulled away. ''But if any man mistreats me, he'll answer to *me*.''

She looked up into Tyler's gaze and knew he was about to kiss her. Without hesitation, she turned and stepped onto the train as it shifted and moved. She offered him her hand. ''Take care, Tyler.''

''Take care,'' he answered as her hand slipped from his grip.

Nichole took the last seat in the car and watched Tyler disappear into the night. He'd been a good man and a good friend. He'd never hurt for the sake of hurting, or killed for the fun of it. Tyler had never been unfair or dishonest. He wasn't more than five years older than her and she had always thought of him as handsome.

So why hadn't she let him kiss her good-bye? She thought about it until she fell asleep and still couldn't come up with an answer. She had no one. The only man she'd allowed close to her was married by now. But even if he were single, they were worlds apart.

At Memphis, she switched to the Butterfield Stage Line and grew more exhausted by the hour. The trip was dusty and hard during the day, and by night she was housed with the women and crying babies. Nichole wanted to ask to sleep outside with the men, but didn't dare.

The only thing she found enjoyable about the trip was the surprisingly warm friendships she made with the women. People thrown together for hours looked for anything to help pass the time, and there was something about a stranger you'd never meet again that made conversation easy.

The women talked of their lives during the war, making Nichole realize for the first time the men weren't the only ones who had paid a price. Their natural mothering instinct seemed to want to take her under their wing. Wives told Nichole of their future and the widows talked of the past.

One night, near Fort Smith, Nichole told a small circle of women that her mother had died and there were so many questions she wished she'd asked her about being a woman. The group seemed to take up the cause of telling her all kinds of bits of wisdom mothers pass on to daughters.

When she changed stages in Dallas leaving the other passengers heading south while she headed west, Nichole was sad to part. She felt she'd grown from the chance encounters and that somehow she was a little more of a lady.

The last leg of her trip was silent. She sat back alone in the coach and watched the scenery rolling by. The only other passenger had asked to ride up top and was probably swapping stories with the driver and man riding shotgun. She'd heard him say he was only going a few miles to his farm.

The land wasn't as pretty as Kentucky. There was a wildness about the very air here. She'd felt it since Fort Smith. There were streams laced across the land near Dallas, but not an overabundance of trees.

Just as she found a comfortable position and was almost asleep, the stage rocked violently, throwing her against the windows, then forward into the empty seats.

Nichole swore and tried to straighten her clothing as the driver pulled to a stop.

"Sorry, miss. You all right in there?" he yelled.

"Yes." Nichole balanced herself enough to open the door. "What happened?"

"Nothing much. Just a problem with the wheel. Me and Amos will have it fixed in a blink."

Nichole looked at the man riding shotgun and guessed that unless he was far stronger than he looked, the driver had his work cut out for him. If she'd been in her normal clothes she would have offered to help, but one thing she'd learned in these days of travel was that men didn't appreciate help from a woman no matter how much they needed it. The man who'd been riding up top was gone and Nichole guessed he must have climbed off when they stopped a while back.

Looking around, she noticed the road followed a creek. Along the water's curves were clusters of elm and cottonwood and spruce. The grass was tall near the water and littered with branches from times past when the creek thought itself a mighty river for a few hours. The shelter of aging cottonwoods a hundred yards away lured her.

"I'll be by the stream," she said as she lifted her carpetbag and headed down the incline. "Just call when you're ready to leave, or if you need any help."

"You just rest yourself, miss. We can handle this!" the driver yelled from the boot of the coach.

Nichole lifted her skirts several inches off the ground and disappeared into the trees. She was careful to walk on the balls of her feet, leaving little trail to follow even though there was no reason for her to do so now.

After days of being around people, she needed to be alone. Leaving the natural path to the stream, she walked as Wolf had taught her to, without disturbing nature. After several feet she crawled beneath low branches and found what she'd hoped to find, a cool, shadowy cave made from brush and branches. The floor of her find was covered in dried winter leaves. Once she was settled, even a squirrel entering her cave would make a racket.

Spreading her jacket as a pallet, Nichole used her carpetbag as a pillow and her warm wool man's jacket as her blanket. Within minutes she was soundly asleep for the first time in days. For the first time since she'd left Tennessee she felt at home.

The wind blew, ruffling the branches above her, and the stream rippled over a thousand tiny rocks only a few feet away. Birds, excited with early spring, returned to the tree above.

Nature muffled the screams of Amos and the driver as they battled and died. In her mind, the cries were only a faraway nightmare no longer strong enough to wake her. In her mind, she was alone and safe.

ELEVEN

Adam waited for the stage over an hour, but none came. The wind tried to push him off the street and inside the stage office. Moisture in the air darkened his hair to black, but he waited, wanting to be there when the stage arrived. He turned his collar up and paced the dirt in front of the office so many times the clods became powder. Wolf wouldn't have asked a favor if it hadn't been important. And today was the first day something traveling by stage could have reached him from Tennessee.

What if Wolf asked him to keep something that was important to the South? Could he do such a thing, even as a favor? Would he? He owed Wolf for helping the night the twins were born. He'd heard men talk about how the South wasn't licked yet and how rebs were planning to rise and fight again. Maybe Wolf had something he needed to keep safe until the uprising. What if it were hidden gold to buy guns for another fight?

No, Adam told himself, Wolf wouldn't ask him to do such a thing. The man knew what side the McLains had fought on.

Adam continued his pacing, trying to imagine what would be so important to Wolf that he'd ship it to Texas for safekeeping.

"Doc!" Harry yelled from the Butterfield office. The young man was always moving, dodging invisible bullets with his nervous youth. "Come around to the barn quick! The stage has been attacked, and a rider's tellin' all about it."

Adam joined a crowd suddenly surrounding the large livery at the edge of town.

Harry jogged by his side. "Rider came in a few minutes ago. Said it looked like the coach busted a wheel and made itself a sitting duck about three hours east. Comanche or maybe even Comancheros burned what they could, then killed old Randy, the driver, and Amos who was riding shotgun.''

The young man fought down emotion by staying in constant motion. ''I knew them both, I did.''

Rocking back on his heels, Harry added, ''I figured since you were waiting for the stage, you'd want to know.''

''Were there any passengers?'' A nagging feeling began to throb in the back of Adam's head. He could think of only one thing Wolf valued and protected like a mother hen . . . Nichole.

''Telegram said there was a gentleman and a lady. I don't know if they was traveling together.'' Harry looked suddenly sad for the doctor who'd been waiting so long. ''The rider didn't find any other bodies near the broken-down stage. Maybe the passengers got away or the Indians took her as a captive. If the robbers were Comancheros, she'll be in Mexico before you can catch up to them and it's anybody's guess what happened to the gentleman.''

''Or maybe the rider just didn't find the bodies,'' someone in the crowd volunteered. ''I know I wouldn't stay around to search the place too closely, and they could have drug a woman off to the side for a while before they killed her.''

Adam rubbed his brow. If it were Nick, she could have been traveling as a woman, or a man. He couldn't very well ask about a passenger when he couldn't name the gender.

''If the Comanche have her, they'll trade her, but if those thieving Comancheros have her, you might as well count her dead,'' another man offered. ''As for any man, he'd be killed outright.''

''Fine time for the sheriff to be gone,'' someone mumbled.

''The deputy's organizing a group to go take a look!'' a man at the far side of the crowd yelled. ''He don't want to, but some of us reminded him that, until the sheriff gets back from Austin, Deputy Russell has his job to do.''

As if on command, Russell stood at the front of the crowd and announced he'd be going out to survey the crime scene and he expected every able-bodied man to go with him. The crowd moved away. A few mumbled about Russell being worse than any outlaw they might find. Some went to collect horses and weapons, others to spread the news.

Within an hour a dozen volunteers waited to leave. Adam was among them. He wasn't sure if the shipment would be Nichole, but he had to know. If she'd been on the stage, she wouldn't have died without a fight. There would be signs. If she'd been there, even dressed as a woman, she would have been armed. If she'd been dressed as a man, she might be the "gentleman" who disappeared.

Three hours later the posse saw the smoke from the still-smoldering stagecoach. The horses were gone and the cargo scattered. Two bodies lay facedown atop the overturned stage. Since there was no evidence they'd been tied, they must have already been dead before they burned. There was no telling which had been the driver, nor did it matter.

Icy rain popped and sizzled against the dying fire. Deputy Russell yelled, "Let's take care of these men and look around as quickly as possible! With dark coming on and the rain freezing, we'll all be grave stuffing if we don't get back to town."

Adam watched Russell closely. He seemed mismatched for his job. Though he wore a gun strapped to his leg, he didn't seem the type who would fight for anything except his own life. Maybe. Harry said he'd won the job during the war when every able man was fighting. The sheriff hadn't had any others apply for the job so Russell stayed on, mostly as a caretaker to the office. His red eyes and the shake in his hands told Adam that the deputy had a drinking problem. In this country drinking wasn't all that unusual, for most men forty or older had a lot they needed to forget.

While four men stood guard, others dug graves and the deputy made a great show of investigating the area. From the tracks that had already been muddied in the rain, he determined that there was no woman passenger. He saw no signs, no woman's clothing among the cargo, no blood, no body. If there had been a woman, the tracks of the horses ended abruptly half a mile downstream, so there was no way to follow her or the raiders.

Adam didn't accept the deputy's quick answers. He made his own circuit of the scene. Nothing. He examined the bodies as best he could before they were buried. Both men's throats had been cut deep, but their bodies were curled up in final sleep, making it hard to see any bullet holes. These two men had been alive and active only hours before, but now their arms and hands were withered and black, as though they'd finished a lifetime of aging in death's final moments.

He turned away to join Russell. "Find anything?"

"No," the deputy answered, then yelled, "Mount up!" before Adam could ask more.

The ride back was almost silent. Adam guessed, like himself, the others had seen far more death and killing than they'd have liked and none had enough drink in him to talk about the adventure of today.

When he reached home, it was full dark, but the nun had left a supper for him. Adam tried to eat, but couldn't. He had no way of contacting Wolf. He wasn't sure the "shipment" was on the stage today. There could have been delays anywhere along the line. But one thing he knew, if the "shipment" was Nichole, she would still be alive and he'd find her. She hadn't survived the war as a Shadow to be killed by robbers.

By dawn, he'd decided to see if he could round up a few men and go out to the scene again. He must have missed something, he told himself. If she, or word from Wolf, wasn't on the next stage, he'd be searching until he found her.

He'd planned to go over to the stage office without opening his practice, but folks were knocking on the door before he had time to get dressed. It seemed that several of the deputy's posse finished the night drowning the memory of what they'd seen. Then, when the bartender tried to send them home, they busted up the place and themselves in the process. By dawn their senses, and newfound pains, hit them fully.

Adam added the line of men needing stitches to the usual number of children with colds and old folks with aches. Before he'd had breakfast, the foyer in the middle of the house was lined with people.

The sun was low, almost touching the silver stovepipe chimneys by the time he saw his last patient. He'd sent Nance Edward over to see if anything came in on the stage. The boy reported that they were holding up the line in Dallas for another day so that a few of the troops from Fort Griffin could ride along. He also said Harry told him to let the doctor know that there was no word on the woman and man who were passengers.

Adam tried to read, but couldn't concentrate. He could find no clues in the dark so he'd have to wait another day to return to the burned stage. Another day would cost him dearly in his chances of finding anything.

After listening to a few of his patients, he wasn't sure he could find anyone to go with him. These folks weren't overly friendly, barely said howdy on the street, but when danger came, they were like ants on a rainy day. No one wanted to leave their home.

Giving up reading, Adam stepped out on the front porch. He liked this time of night when respectable folks were all home having supper and the not-so-respectable hadn't started their play. This part of the night belonged to no group. It seemed the twilight between both worlds.

Tonight, the air was cold, the kind of still cold that soaked into your bones before you noticed it. In another month they'd be in full spring, but tonight winter seemed reluctant to leave.

The front of the house faced an empty street. Most of the homes were little more than shacks. Adam had asked around and found that these buildings were built during the time the cavalry called this place home. Most had been constructed in a hurry and were now falling in. The saloon next door had had some repairs but the boardinghouse on the other side of Adam's office would soon join the crumbling buildings if someone didn't use a hammer.

Maybe someone would buy it. People were coming to town every day and construction was going on so fast the town was spreading like weeds. There was talk of turning the old parade ground into a town square. Right now the spot was mostly used as a campsite for those passing through. Fort Worth was turning from an abandoned frontier fort to a town before his eyes.

Adam walked to the end of the porch and wished he were somewhere else. But where? He had an itch to pack but nowhere that he wanted to go. He'd left Corydon, realizing there was nothing for him there, but wasn't sure there was anything for him here either. All he knew for certain was that he was through with fighting, and that he loved doctoring. The past few months had taught him that.

I'm lonely, he thought. *God, I'm so alone.* He was in the world, but no one shared his world. It seemed an impossible dream to want what Daniel and May had if only for a short while. During the war he'd thought his loneliness would end with peace, but it hadn't. He traveled halfway across the country and was no closer than before. The hollowness inside him was still present.

He enjoyed the folks around him, even the nun who never hesitated to tell him his business. But somewhere there had to be more.

"Evening." A man walked in front of the porch, startling Adam.

"Evening, Russell." Adam took a step forward. He didn't particularly like the man, but he might have information. "Any word on the stage robbery?"

Russell made a great show of pulling up his gun belt. "Seems there was a rather heavy strongbox on that load. The line was worried about leaving it in Dallas and that's why they left with only two passengers. The Comancheros would be after the gold, but not the Comanche. I've been around these parts a long time and if it's Comancheros, there's nothing we can do but count our losses."

"Any news of her?" Adam held his breath waiting for the answer.

"On the woman?" Russell shook his head. "If she's not dead, she will be soon. Whoever robbed the stage went to great lengths to leave no clues to tell the story. If she got away, the weather or the varmints will have her by now. Official word from the stage line is that there was no woman on board. They figure she and the gentleman probably got off somewhere along the way at one of the ranches outside of Dallas. The only two men who know are dead and buried by that hull of a stage.''

Adam didn't want to think of any woman being alone in this country, especially not Nichole. If she were the woman, she wouldn't have gotten off. But where was she?

''I'd better turn in.'' Adam nodded his farewell at the deputy.

The man returned his nod and walked on down the street. Adam noticed Russell always made his rounds at sunset, never after dark.

Just as Adam reached the door, something moved amid the boxes and scattered chairs. ''Terry?'' Adam called the dog. ''That you, boy?''

A shadow moved slightly, growing before his eyes. A shadow of a man.

''Who's there?'' Adam's muscles tightened.

The stranger moved again, closer.

''Adam!'' someone whispered. ''Help me.''

In one blink Adam was by her side. ''Nichole?'' He shoved the hat from her head and pulled her into the light. ''Nichole, how—''

Before he could ask, she raised her hands. ''Help me,'' she whispered again.

Adam looked down and saw her hands wrapped in olive green strips of cloth. From the way she held them away from her body, he could tell she was in pain.

''Come in here.'' He led her through the door and into his office.

Without wasting time asking questions, he lifted her up on the table and began unwrapping her hands. The smell of burned flesh assaulted his senses.

''Nance!'' he yelled without slowing. ''Nance!''

The boy appeared in the doorway. ''Yes, Doc?''

''Get me fresh water from the well. Cold water. And tell Sister to make a pot of coffee.'' He glanced up into Nichole's face. ''And bring food, warm and hearty.''

Nance disappeared without questioning. He'd learned over the weeks that the doctor never asked for something unless he needed it fast, and he never requested help unless someone was in pain.

''Relax,'' Adam whispered as he pulled the strips of bandage away from burned flesh. ''Burns hurt a lot more than most injuries, but they heal.'' Blisters on her palms had seeped and dried against the cloth. Flesh pulled away with the cotton strips.

He started with the water in the pitcher though it wasn't cold enough. Tenderly, he patted at the red, swollen flesh, examining each open wound for infection.

Nichole looked into his face. The pain was already starting to subside, and the chill was leaving her bones one degree at a time. ''I found you,'' she whispered.

''Thank God.'' He didn't look up at her. ''I was about to go crazy with worry. I wasn't sure, but I had a feeling you were the shipment Wolf would be sending.''

''I'm fine,'' she answered. ''I only burned my hands trying to pull the drivers from the blazing stage. Then I realized they were dead and it didn't matter.''

''The robbery? What happened?'' He lowered her fingers slowly into cool water.

''I'm not sure. I was by the stream sleeping. There were no gunshots, but the sound of horses woke me. I guess I've spent too long on the run to walk into anything without taking a good look first. I climbed up in the branches and watched as men watered their horses before riding off.''

''Did you get a good look at them?''

''Not really, just body types mostly, but I'd know a few of their horses. I think there were only three, which seems odd that the driver and the man riding shotgun didn't at least get off a shot. The man watering the horses had a belt with conchos the size of silver dollars all around it.'' She bit back the pain. ''They made a few swings at finding me, but were in too big a hurry to really look. If they had, I'd have been somewhere else.''

''I figured that you'd get away.'' He smiled at her. ''But you're not much help on descriptions.'' Adam worked as he answered, ''A lot of vaqueros come up from Mexico to help with the herds. The belts are common. Are you sure they didn't see you?''

''I waited until they were out of sight, then I ran to the stage and tried to help the men, but it was too late.'' She looked at him directly. ''They didn't see me, but from the way they looked, they knew I was on the stage.''

''What about the other passenger?''

Nichole shook her head. ''A young man, about Rafe's build. He didn't say two words to me. I don't remember seeing him with the driver when I left, and I couldn't find his body.''

She fought back any cry of pain as Adam dried her hands. ''I changed into my pants and used my dress for bandages. I walked all night, but with the wind and rain, I couldn't be sure I wasn't walking in circles. After sunup, I headed west and by luck passed over stage tracks. About midafternoon I wandered into town. I asked about a doc and found you, but I wanted to make sure you were alone before I came in, so I curled up on the porch.''

"Why? No one knows about the trouble you and Wolf are in. No one is looking for you here.'' Adam couldn't believe she'd waited for hours outside and in pain.

"No one knows about me,'' she whispered. "But I saw the men riding away from the stage robbery. They were a dirty lot, men raw with meanness. I know their types. They'll try their hardest to slit my throat if they find out I saw them.''

Her statement was obvious. Adam's forehead wrinkled in worry as she continued.

"I've been thinking it over. The attack was too clean not to have been planned by professionals. Maybe the kid on the stage was one of them. Maybe the driver knew whoever stopped to offer help. Otherwise, why would there have been no shots?''

Nichole's voice died suddenly as she looked toward the doorway.

Adam glanced over his shoulder, moving closer to her in protection. "Sister.'' He relaxed. "Thank you for bringing the coffee.''

The nun moved to his side. She took one look at Nichole's hands and wrapped a coffee cup with a thick towel so none of the heat would pass to Nichole as she drank.

"Nick, I'd like you to meet Sister. Sister, this is the shipment I've been expecting for days. She was on the stage that was attacked.''

Both women nodded a greeting, but the nun didn't waste time with small talk. "You're in great danger, child.''

"I know,'' Nichole agreed.

Before Adam could ask any questions, the nun spoke again. "I'll put a bed in the storage room upstairs with boxes all around. No one must know you're here.''

"Including the deputy,'' Adam added. "We must keep her safe and I don't trust the man not to talk.''

"Thank you.'' Nichole let the exhaustion reflect in her voice for the first time. "I knew I'd be all right if I could just find you.''

The nun smiled, turning her face into tiny ripples of skin. "When Dr. McLain gets you bandaged, move upstairs and I'll bring food. Men mean enough to kill and burn the two stagecoach hands won't hesitate to kill you.''

Adam gently wrapped Nichole's fingers as he studied both

women's faces. "I don't know how, but the two of you seem to share a secret. Want to let me in on it?"

She bit back the pain the thin cotton caused. "I'm not sure I understand, but Sister is right. If anyone finds out I'm here, we may all be in great danger. I can't explain. I just sense it. I think she does, also."

Curling his arm beneath her knees, he lifted her off the table. "Then we'd better get you upstairs. I promised your brother I'd guard you with my life, and that is exactly what I plan to do."

An hour later, he helped Nichole eat both her supper and his. She'd told him every detail that she saw of the robbery. If there was a loaded strongbox traveling with her, the men who killed for it wouldn't hesitate to kill again. Something didn't make sense. If they were only after the money, they could have just robbed and taken it at gunpoint, not killed and burned the two men.

Adam took the tray of empty plates downstairs. A low lamp still burned in the kitchen, though it was long past time all were usually in bed. Mrs. Jamison liked a late dinner. She said it reminded her of her youth in Georgia when her family would have huge dinner parties served after nine. But most nights they ate at seven or Nance would fall asleep at the table.

Tonight, the nun sat alone by the window, her rosary circling her hands. When he entered, she looked at him with tear-wet cheeks.

"How is the girl?" she asked in a whisper.

"Better," Adam answered. "I gave her something to help the pain so she can sleep. She was sent here because her brother thought she'd be safe." He laughed, without humor.

"She's in great danger. The men who took the stage would have her dead along with the others. I've heard of these men. They kill for fun and think to become legends."

Adam watched the nun closely. She knew more than she was saying, but he'd learned it was a waste of time to inquire. "You've told Nance to be quiet about our guest?"

The nun nodded.

Adam waited a minute for her to add more. When she didn't, he moved to the stairway. "I'll check on Nichole, then call it a night." He knew that once he turned on his study light, the night people would tap on his door if they needed him. Maybe one of them would have news of the robbers.

"I'll help your friend all I can." The nun went back to her prayers. "And another will watch over her, too."

Adam wondered what more she could do as he climbed the stairs.

When he opened Nichole's door, he found her sitting on the edge of her bed still fully dressed.

"I thought you'd be asleep by now." He stepped inside her room and closed the door.

"I couldn't work the buttons with these bandages." She looked up to him once more for help.

Adam knelt on one knee in front of her and began unbuttoning her shirt in what he hoped was a professional manner. "I'm sorry," he said without looking at her face. If he looked in those green eyes, he'd have trouble remembering how buttons worked.

"I didn't want to come," Nichole whispered. "I wanted to stay with Wolf and fight for our land."

"I understand." He guessed she was trying to tell him that she hadn't traveled all this way to see him.

"Wolf said to find any of the McLains. If you want, I could go to Daniel or Wes."

He pulled her sleeves gently over her bandages as he removed her shirt. "Wes is somewhere on the range rounding up cattle. Daniel is in a settlement near Dallas. You'd probably be safest with him, if we could get you there in one piece."

Standing, she held her arms away from her sides as he worked the buttons on her trousers. "You want me to go?"

Adam stopped with both hands on her waist ready to push her pants down. "No," he answered, feeling her nearness as he always did. "I just want you safe."

Nichole laughed. "I've never been safe."

Pushing the trousers to the floor, he helped her out of them. She wore plain cotton leggings and a cotton chemise with lace at the shoulder. The undergarments were store-bought and plain but far more feminine than anything he'd seen on her.

As he stared, she smiled and touched her leg, pulling the material with a bandaged hand. "They're called pantalettes. Funny name. Wolf bought them for me. I never had any woman clothes, but I like the feel of them next to me, even underneath my trousers."

If he'd expected her to be embarrassed or modest, he was greatly disappointed. She turned around as if showing him a new outfit and not her undergarments. The line of her tall, lean body showed clearly. Her breasts were full, her waist small, her legs long and slender.

"I wasn't sure I was wearing them right until one night at the stage station when I saw other women with them. We all took off our dresses and slept in these. It was almost like a party where everyone came in their underwear."

Adam tried not to notice the way the cotton molded around her breasts or how the lace showed one shoulder almost bare through the fine material.

"You ever see such clothes?"

"No," he lied. "They look quite serviceable to sleep in."

Sweat dripped off his forehead, but he wasn't about to tell her that he'd seen women dressed in chemises made of all lace and no cotton. They'd had big breasts and painted cheeks and offered their services by the hour . . . but they hadn't been half as alluring as Nichole.

"You'd better get to bed. With the salve, your hands will feel much better in the morning." He tried to sound like a stern father, or a worried doctor, anyone except a lover, which is exactly what he'd like to be.

"All right." She climbed into the tiny cot of a bed and let him pull up the covers.

"Good night." He leaned and planted a brotherly kiss on her forehead.

"Good night, Doc," she answered, already half-asleep.

TWELVE

Adam spent half the night thinking of reasons not to go up to Nichole's room. She'd told him she hadn't wanted to come to Texas. The burns on her hands must be hurting. She needed sleep. Wolf had sent her to him for protection.

So he paced his study, then went across to the two rooms he used as his doctor's office. After cleaning and restocking everything he could think of, he wandered into the little room by the kitchen that he'd made his bedroom.

His room was stark, plain, and colorless, but it had two advantages. The one curtainless window faced the east and caught the morning sun and the room was always warm from the kitchen fire. But tonight the very walls were closing in around him.

He'd spent six months having conversations with an absent Nichole and now she was only a floor away. They had nothing in common, she wasn't the kind of woman he should be attracted to, yet the need to see her was an ache in his gut the size of a cannonball.

He wanted to tell her what he'd done and how he helped people, all kinds of people. He wanted to remind her of that morning when he'd almost given up being a doctor. She'd verbally slapped him hard with her cutting words and lack of sympathy. She'd woken him up to the fact that he had to be satisfied with the best he could do sometimes. The effort counted, not just the outcome.

Adam finally convinced himself he would only check on her, and stepped into the darkened foyer in the center of the house. In the corner of his vision, where the last touch of moonlight lit the back of the stairs, he saw something move.

A chill slid down his spine like a crawling glacier. His first thought

was that somehow Nichole had been followed and someone was trying to kill her.

But the figure moved past the stairs and into the kitchen at a slow,
almost painful pace.

Adam pulled down his rifle he kept hidden over the foyer cabinet
and followed. The people of the night knew he would help them
without asking questions. They always came to the side door off his
office. This was no patient creeping through his house. Even in
shadow, this unknown guest was crippled and twisted with age, or
pain.

The kitchen was dark with only a low glow from the banked fire
to dust any light across the room. Before Adam's eyes could adjust
to the blackness, the back door opened slightly with a low creek, then
closed just as quietly.

In long strides, Adam reached the door and stepped onto the porch.
Nothing. The porch and the alley beyond was silent, deserted except
for old Terry who raised his head in greeting.

Adam knelt and patted the dog. Terry was a good watchdog. He
always barked when strangers stepped on the porch. Whoever passed
through the house tonight was no stranger to the animal. Somehow
the knowledge disturbed Adam far more than the possibility that
someone might have tried to break in.

Silently, he moved inside and up the back stairs. When he opened
the door to a storage room where they'd hidden Nichole, he was
surprised to see the nun sitting by her bed. The room was cluttered
with boxes and old furniture, but he noticed she had covered the
boxes beside Nichole with a cotton tablecloth.

Adam straightened to his most professional manner. "How is
she?"

"She's restless." The nun closed her prayer book. "I'm afraid
she'll wake herself by hitting her hands against something. She keeps
moving, fighting in her sleep."

He leaned over the bed. Nichole was sleeping, her hair tossed
wildly, her face slightly sunburned. She'd never looked more beautiful. What was it about this woman that made him feel like a thun-
derstorm was going on inside him? She was as far from a lady as
she could get with her short hair and men's clothing. Yet she touched
him in a way no one ever had, and he found the idea disturbing.
Seeing her was like coming down with the croup and waking up to
Christmas morning at the same time.

"The young woman is almost starved." Sister broke into his

thoughts. "I plan on making it my calling to get at least three meals a day into her."

He looked more closely. She did seem thinner and her hair was a few inches longer than he remembered. The months since they'd seen one another must have been hard on her. She was a free spirit who would have to learn to settle down now that the war was over.

"Do you think we can protect her here?" he wondered aloud to himself.

"We can try. I'll do what I can. You give her the medicine that helps her sleep without the pain and I'll keep watch."

"Her brother sent her here to safety. Now that she's witnessed a murder and robbery she could be in great danger if anyone found out she was on the stage. I wouldn't want to depend on the deputy for help."

"She's safer here with us." The nun nodded in agreement. "The only one we have to be careful about is Mrs. Jamison, and she only comes out of her room in the afternoon. The rest of the time she likes to sit by the window and pretend she's in better times."

Nichole moved in her sleep, reaching across the covers for something that wasn't there. The movement made her cry out softly in pain.

Kneeling to her coat Adam pulled out the handgun she'd wrapped so carefully out of sight. Gently, he emptied the shells and placed the weapon at her side. A bandaged hand passed over the metal, and she relaxed in sleep.

He looked up expecting the nun to be frowning, but she showed no judgment in her face.

The nun finally whispered a statement that awaited no answer as she pulled the covers over Nichole. "Our poor Nichole, she lives by the gun, doesn't she? I'll keep watch on her tonight, Doctor."

Adam nodded, realizing the foolish notion he'd had of kissing Nichole good night was just that, foolish. He'd better get a handle on this unreasonable attraction for Wolf's sister before he made an idiot of himself. They had nothing in common. *Nothing.* Except that every time he saw her he had to fight himself to keep from holding her, and he knew deep down she felt the same.

Walking slowly back to his room, he thought that just as Nichole needed the comfort of her weapon, Adam knew he needed her at his side. It didn't matter that they'd only slept in one another's arms twice. His need to hold her was basic, primal. He needed to feel her heart beat next to his once in a while. But she respected only strength and would think him weak for ever saying such a thing.

His job was to guard her until Wolf came, nothing more. All he had to do was keep her out of harm's way. Then they both could get on with their lives and never cross paths again. Nichole loved adventure, excitement. She needed to be free. All he wanted was to settle down and live a quiet life as a doctor. Bergette had taught him that to dream for more was only that, a dream.

But by midmorning the next day, it seemed dreams turned quickly into nightmares. Trouble arrived wrapped in lace and any hope of a quiet life seemed shattered.

Troops from Fort Griffin rode in with the stage. Half the town turned out to see them and Adam joined the crowd, watching from across the street. Adam was relieved there had been no trouble and turned to go back home when a tiny woman stepped from the stage.

She was dressed in a wine red traveling suit and wore a hat to match with long enough feathers to have bothered everyone who rode the stagecoach. Her blond curls were tied with ribbons and decorated one side of the front of her jacket from shoulder to waist. She was stunning.

Everyone in the street stopped to watch her. But only Adam's face turned pale.

Bergette looked slowly around until her gaze met his.

From across the street he could see she'd lost none of her beauty.

She walked directly toward him, smiling as if she hadn't threatened to have him sliced to bits the last time she'd spoken to him.

"You must be Dr. McLain," a cavalry officer voiced from just behind Adam as Bergette crossed the street toward them.

"Yes," Adam answered without smiling. He wouldn't have been surprised if the officer pulled his gun and arrested him. There was no telling what Bergette had said about him. Maybe she hadn't been happy ruining his name in Indiana, maybe she planned to spread his mistreatment of her through the West.

"You're a lucky man. The little lady hasn't stopped talking about you since Dallas." The lieutenant slapped Adam on the shoulder as Bergette grew closer. " 'Morn-ing, Miss Dupont. I was just telling your fiancé how lucky he is to have you willing to come all this way to be his little wife."

Bergette's smile could have melted a Gatling gun from a hundred yards. "Thank you, Lieutenant." She placed a gloved hand on the officer's sleeve. "But I'm afraid I have given my dear Adam quite a shock. You see, he wasn't expecting me."

Adam knew the small crowd around him was listening. Harry was bobbing up and down to see over the heads of those in front of him.

In a town where most women considered dressing up putting on a starched apron, Bergette was quite a sight.

"Welcome to Texas, Bergette," Adam managed to say with a forced smile.

"Thank you," she answered sweetly as she leaned and almost touched his cheek with a kiss. "I just couldn't stay away from you any longer, darling."

"I see she's here! That's her, ain't it, Doc!" Harry yelled. "I'm mighty glad she wasn't the woman on the stage two days ago." Harry's normally twitchy body seemed to have been wound to double-time with the excitement of seeing such a pretty lady.

The young station operator broke the spell on the crowd and everyone moved about their business. The young officer excused himself to return to his duties, and the stage driver pointed toward two huge trunks left behind as though he expected Adam to do something about them. Bergette simply turned away, as always, expecting someone else to take care of the details.

"You surely didn't come alone, Miss Dupont?" Adam looked around at the other passengers across the street claiming luggage.

"Of course not." Bergette giggled. "Charles and Lily are with me, but I'll know true hardship without my cook and personal maid."

Adam offered her his arm, and they moved into the shade. He'd recovered from the shock, but still found his muscles tense as if waiting for a blow he knew would come. "Why are you here?" he whispered between clenched teeth as they strolled.

Bergette pouted a moment, as if hating to answer. Her temperament made him almost laugh aloud. Could it be possible that she thought he'd run to her when he saw her step off the stage? Surely she wasn't that short of memory, or that vain?

"When Papa returned from Indianapolis, he wasn't happy about our broken engagement." She played with one of her perfect curls as she spoke. "You're a returning hero, a doctor, a McLain."

Adam stopped walking. "What does my name have to do with our engagement being canceled? Or anything else for that matter."

Bergette looked around, as if hoping to be distracted from this conversation. "Your father was one of the immigrant bosses on the work crews that built the canals."

"That was years ago!" Adam snapped.

"But if my papa runs for state office, people have long memories. The older men will remember your father, the younger may remember you or your brothers. Papa had no son in the war, and you know he didn't have the health to fight." She began to pout again. "He said I let him down. I hurt his chances of election. Oh, Adam, you wouldn't believe how he talked to me!''

"I'm sorry," Adam tried to sound sympathetic. To be honest, he doubted his family name would help much in getting the old man elected. Dupont had been a selfish, self-centered, money-hungry fool for far too long. His only talent in life had been to father a beautiful daughter.

"So." He tried to follow her reasoning. "You ran away?"

"No," she answered as she dabbed at dry eyes. "I ran to see you once more. I just had to talk to you."

Adam didn't want to talk to her. He'd said all he planned to say the morning he'd left her house. "Have you already arranged for a place to stay?" Adam asked, knowing she probably hadn't and hoping to change the subject.

"I thought you'd recommend a hotel or boardinghouse. But the officer who rode in with the stage said he thought the doc in Fort Worth *lived* in a boardinghouse." She tilted her head and smiled, as if for a portrait. "Isn't that wonderful?"

"I do," Adam could feel the hinges of the trapdoor beneath his feet starting to creak, "but there are only three rooms vacant, and they need a great deal of work before they can be rented. The owner is recovering from a long illness. And I'm making noise all day and night with patients coming. And—"

"I'll survive." Bergette lifted her chin. "Show me the way. Papa made sure I had enough money to be comfortable in this primitive state."

Adam planted his feet square apart and folded his arms. "Hold on. First, I don't know if Mrs. Jamison is willing or able to take on three new boarders, and second, we need to get something straight right now, Bergette. We are not engaged to be married." He wanted to add a third that he had all he could handle hiding a woman from Mrs. Jamison, much less bringing another home.

Bergette pulled at one of her curls so hard it needed reironing. "All right, Adam. We're engaged to be engaged. And we will be no problem to this Mrs. Jamison. Charles and Lily will take care of me. I'll offer whatever's necessary to talk her into letting me stay. But I've decided to give you another chance and I'll hear no argument."

She lowered her voice. "And before you get all upset you might as well know I'm only staying a month. Papa says I can come home then, alone, or with you if you come to your senses."

Adam forced himself to breathe. He could endure one month of anything, even Bergette. Maybe he could figure a way to only look at her and not have to talk to her. The nun would help him keep Nichole out of sight. *One month.*

"I'll go check with Mrs. Jamison about you renting her extra rooms." He hated giving in. If he could have thought of another way for her to turn he'd have sent her packing, or left her on the streets. But this town was no place for a lady alone.

Knowing she'd won the first battle, Bergette smiled and motioned for Charles and Lily to follow.

An hour later the smile faded as she climbed the steps to her new home. What had been a serviceable alternative for Adam was enough to make her cry out in horror. Only Adam's description of the hotel kept her from running for other lodging. She'd shown no interest in meeting the nun or Nance Edward and barely glanced around at Adam's office. But Mrs. Jamison was different, she received the full measure of Bergette's charm.

After the short tour, she rested in his office while Adam helped Charles move furniture upstairs. Lily, the maid, cleaned. In less time than Adam thought possible, they'd transformed the three extra rooms into living quarters for Bergette. A bedroom, a sitting area, and a dining room. With all new furniture, lace and linens from the stores, Bergette thought the space livable. Carpenters arrived by mid-afternoon to enlarge the two windows facing the front and to build a second-floor balcony for Bergette.

Adam dropped in on Mrs. Jamison, fearing the noise would not allow her to rest. Surprisingly, he found her happy. She assured him that Bergette had offered to pay for all repairs and planned to leave the furnishings when her stay ended. On top of everything, she insisted on paying full rent not only for her three rooms but for her employees. The tiny little blonde had won Mrs. Jamison over by treating the widow as if her position as proprietor were of great importance. Bergette acted as though she valued the widow's advice and thanked her for being so kind in allowing her to stay. For the first time in years, Mrs. Jamison forgot she was an outlaw's widow and felt important.

Lily made a cot in the laundry room off the kitchen with the agreement that she'd do all the house's laundry, and Charles rigged himself a tent on half the back porch. Suddenly, the boardinghouse was full.

By late afternoon Bergette hired a buggy to take the Jamisons and her employees shopping. As soon as they were out of sight, Adam went in search of the nun.

He found her cuddled between boxes in the storage room with Nichole asleep beside her.

"Heaven help us, Doctor," the nun cried, "the devil has blond curls."

Adam laughed. "You'll get no argument from me." He helped the nun to her feet.

"What are we to do with our poor child?" She touched Nichole's head. "I'd let her stay with me, but my room is little more than a closet. There's not enough room for another cot in it. And here isn't safe, I've spent the day hiding her from people bringing in items to store. This close to the fancy little lady would never be wise."

"She could stay in my study," Adam suggested. "I could move my books to the medical office across the hall. Anyone would have to cross through my bedroom to get to Nichole and trust me, Bergette will never be in my bedroom."

The nun showed no surprise at his announcement. She was a woman who looked deeper than ruffles and lace. "I could easily bring her food and tell the others you hate having your things disturbed so they are never, never to go in your quarters. Nance hears everything said in this house, he could let us know if they suspect something, and he loves a secret. He'd be a fine ally."

"It might work," Adam agreed.

"You bring her, Doctor, while I carry the cot down. We have to move fast before they come back."

Adam lifted a sleeping Nichole. He knew the medicine he'd given her and the days she'd probably gone without sleep had caught up to her, but when he put his arm around her she snuggled into his chest making his heart jump a beat. They moved her downstairs as silently as they could even though there was no one else in the house.

"Do you really believe, Doctor, that you can keep your fiancée from finding out about this one you call Nick?" The nun frowned as she made space for the cot in Adam's book-lined study.

"I don't know," he answered in frustration. Bergette introduced herself to everyone as his fiancée, and he would have looked like a fool following behind calling her a liar. "All I know is I have to protect Nichole."

Nichole stirred in his arms and mumbled, "You don't have to protect me. I can take care of myself."

He could see anger banking in her sleepy eyes. Anger and hurt mixed as she came awake.

"And I agree with Sister Celestine, this study is no place for me," she argued. "I'd be safer outside, hiding on the land. Just get me out of town. There's a grove of trees not an hour from here that would suit me fine. I can fend for myself."

Adam's head snapped up so hard he felt it pop. "Sister Celestine?" He looked from the woman in his arms to the nun. "She told you her name?"

"No," Nichole said. "I read it in her prayer book. There wasn't much to do upstairs."

"Is Nick right?" He lowered Nichole's feet gently to the floor as he stared at the nun.

No emotion marked the old woman's face. "The other sisters called me Sister Cel. I wish no one else in the house to know my name. Having them call me Sister suits me fine but you and Nick can call me Sister Cel."

"Thanks." Adam knew she'd given him a gift by allowing him to call her by name. "Sister Cel, will you help me hide Nichole here even if it's not the best place?"

"I will," she answered proudly. "When I saw others moving in, I thought I should be leaving. Now I see I'm needed. The very wind whispers trouble."

"You're not superstitious, too?" Adam raised an eyebrow.

"No," she answered. "It's not superstitious to listen for trouble's footsteps."

"Well, however you know, I think you're right and you are also greatly needed," he added, guessing that he'd touched on her one reason for living.

The nun nodded as she went about making the small bed they had moved from upstairs.

"Stop acting like I'm invisible and defenseless!" Nichole snapped.

She was only a few inches shorter than he and now faced him squarely. "I do what I want to do and answer to no one, no matter what you believe or Sister hears in the wind. It that clear, Doc?"

He couldn't help but wonder if she always woke up with such fire. Then he made the mistake of smiling. She attacked.

"If I decide to stay here in your study, we might as well clear the air. First, don't take the bullets out of my Colt again, ever. Second, you're not the only one in this house who is engaged. Tyler will come with my brother to get me as soon as the smoke clears at home."

Adam was so busy trying to hide his surprise that he didn't bother explaining to her that the engagement to Bergette was a farce. "Tyler?" he questioned. "Tyler? The man who was in command that night you were dying?"

"He took me to the train," she answered with a lift of her eyebrows that seemed to say more.

"Wonderful." Adam felt as if it had been raining on him all day. Why should he be surprised now when lightning struck him? "I'm happy for you both. Now you can marry and run around the country raising little Shadows."

"Fine," Nichole answered. "I feel the same way about you and little Miss Silk."

"Fine!" Adam snapped as he faced Nichole.

Sister Cel stepped between them as she passed. "Now that everyone is fine here, can we get back to work? There are people waiting to see a doctor."

"Where?" Adam hadn't seen anyone all day.

"She said she'd wait till dark, but if you got time now, she needs care. You can have her doctored long before the others return." The nun nodded toward the house on the left where several women from the saloons stayed. "Her name is Dancing, and I'm not sure she can walk over here. Her friend came over to check if you were seeing anyone and if you'd let them bring her over before dark."

"I'll go get her myself before the others get back." Adam had never asked her opinion, but he imagined Mrs. Jamison would not be pleased by the people who sought his help during the nights. Her husband might have died an outlaw, but she considered herself a respectable widow.

The nun on the other hand made no judgment. People were people. Several times, when he'd needed another set of hands, she'd appeared in the hallway and helped.

He glanced at Nichole. "Stay here, and stay quiet."

She didn't argue.

Ten minutes later, she watched through a crack in the paneling as he carried a woman into his office. She was badly bruised and bleeding.

"Sister!" Adam yelled. "Sister!"

He laid the woman down on the table and began pulling bandages from the cabinet.

"She said she had to leave for a while." Nichole rolled her sleeves up with clumsy bandaged fingers. "What can I do?"

Adam hesitated. "You shouldn't be here. I told you—"

"Stop giving orders. This woman looks too near death to say anything. I may not be able to help much, but I appear to be all you have. When we hear the others, I'll disappear. You seem to forget I can melt into nothing and vanish like smoke."

"But your hands?"

"They're better. I can stand a little discomfort if help's needed." Nichole looked down at the woman. "What happened to her?"

"The owner of the saloon accused her of stealing whiskey and slapped her around last night. When he found out she was planning to come to me, I guess he thought it would look bad for his reputation. So he beat her into silence." Adam moved a scarf away from her face. "You wouldn't know it now, but she's a pretty girl, probably not out of her teens."

Nichole touched the woman's bleeding hand with her bandaged one. "Tell me what to do."

Adam pulled off his coat. "Talk to her, keep her calm. If you have to, hold her down. Her left leg's broken in two places, maybe more, and there are several cuts that need stitching. I don't know if there are any injuries inside her or not. Her name's Dancing."

As Adam began examining the cuts and mentally ranking them in order of need, Nichole leaned beside Dancing and, in a soft, Southern voice, began to speak. "You're going to be fine, Dancing. This here is the best doc in Texas. He'll have that leg set and you back twirling across the dance floor in two shakes of a possum's tail."

Adam listened as Nichole whispered. He felt Dancing jerk when he set the leg, but she held on to Nichole's arm without crying out. The nun returned and took up the job of keeping anyone, mainly Bergette, from bothering the doctor while he was working.

By the time they finished, it was long past dinner and the new arrivals to their household had turned in for the night. Adam and Nichole ate dinner in the examining room while watching Dancing sleep.

"Thanks for your help," he finally broke the silence. "I seem to be saying that every time I see you."

"I did it for her. No one should be beaten like that. She's like a wounded animal, too frightened to let out a cry."

He didn't miss the fire in her eyes as she added, "Someone should do something about that man."

"Agreed. But with men getting shot in gunfights and the stage being attacked, I doubt the deputy will take time for a barmaid. Some folks consider beatings as an occupational hazard of such women."

"You mean no one will do anything?"

"He could have killed Dancing and no one would do anything, Nick." He moved his chair closer and shoved his plate away. "You've put me off twice this afternoon. It's time to take a look at those hands now."

Nichole started to pull away, but decided to give in. In truth, her hands were throbbing.

Adam doctored them with the same care he always showed. "You've opened a few of the blisters, but you're healing nicely." He wrapped each finger slowly. "Tomorrow I don't want you doing anything. We'll unwrap them and let them heal. As for tonight, I'll give you something to help you sleep without pain."

"They don't hurt anymore," she lied. "Compared to Dancing, I've only a scratch. I don't matter."

Adam turned her newly bandaged hands over in his own. "You matter to me," he whispered. His knees were so close to hers they lightly brushed her trouser leg. "Despite everything, I'm glad I have the chance to see you again. I've thought of you often."

"Why?" She leaned forward watching his warm brown eyes study her.

"I feel—" He stopped suddenly, unable to look anywhere but at her. "You're so beautiful," he whispered his thoughts. "So beautiful in so many ways."

Nichole knew if she spoke she'd break the spell and they'd return to reality. She also knew with her ugly men's clothing and short hair she was anything but beautiful. But if he wanted to believe it, if only for a minute, she wasn't going to stop him.

Without a word, she leaned forward and pressed her lips against his. For a moment, he didn't move, then without breaking the kiss, he slowly stood, pulling her into his arms.

No! his mind shouted. *You can't be doing this!*

But his body wouldn't listen. If it were only just this once, he wanted to hold her and feel her against him.

When she raised her arms around his neck and leaned her body into his, his mind stopped yelling and all he heard was the pounding of their hearts.

THIRTEEN

NICHOLE FOLLOWED NANCE EDWARD THROUGH A TINY CRAWL space and into the attic. The musty air danced in the light from dirty windows. Spiderwebs hung as thick as drapes between rafters. Voices drifted from below in muffled rumblings of conversation.

During the week Nichole had been hiding in the study, Nance decided she was his playmate. He sneaked into her room every afternoon when his chores were done and told her of all the happenings in the house. He seemed to hear every conversation, though many he was too little to understand. Nichole had nicknamed him General Ears.

With his help as lookout, Nichole had found ways to move around the house, otherwise she would have gone crazy in the little study. Most of her time was spent taking care of Dancing. No one came for the young prostitute, so Dancing took up residence in Adam's examining room. Fever kept her in its grip. Each day she seemed weaker, not better, though Adam did all he could.

"You sure you can make it, miss?" Nance pulled Nichole from her worries as he slowed his climb into the attic and looked over his shoulder.

"I can make it," Nichole answered. "Lead the way, General Ears."

The little boy moved into a dusty space between the rafters. "It ain't really an attic." He straddled one of the beams. "There's not enough room to store much up here. Mom says it wouldn't be worth the trouble to try to shove it through the opening, so she just uses the room below for storage."

Nichole found a level spot that looked sturdy enough to hold her weight. She sat, crossing her legs underneath her. This wasn't much of an adventure, but at least it was a change. Plus Nance was showing her one of his secrets, and that was important to him. He was a boy who loved secrets as other boys love fishing.

"My dad told me," Ears whispered, "that if I was ever real afraid I was to come up here and hide. He said not even the devil could find me here. When my dad and his partner rebuilt the house, they put these and other spaces in the walls like they weren't there at all. My dad used to say you can never have too many places to tuck things away for safekeeping."

"It would make a good hiding place." Nichole looked around. The area was the width between two windows with only a little square tall enough for an adult to stand between the beams.

"But I've checked all the openings and passages except the cellar and my dad didn't leave nothing for me to find."

"But you found something to hide away yourself," she whispered. "That's much more special than something left behind by someone else."

Nance agreed and leaned closer, loving having someone who would talk to him. "I never showed this to anyone because nobody has the time to listen. Mighta been a waste of time for me to learn to talk." He smiled. "But you listen, Nick. So I want to show you something."

He pulled a box from between the boards. "When my dad died, my mother threw his things in the trash to burn. I dug 'em out and brought 'em up here." He handed the box to her. "I figured I'd hide 'em just in case anyone ever wanted to look."

Nichole opened the box slowly. A black silk shirt with pearl buttons lay on top, the kind a gambler or dandy would wear. "These were your father's?"

"Yeah." Nance smiled. "I don't know what to do with 'em. My mama says they're trouble clothes. She said once that my dad thought he was bulletproof in 'em."

Black trousers unfolded across Nichole's legs. A belt with a thin silver buckle was laced between the folds.

"Do you think these clothes are magic?" His eyes danced as he rocked on the beam. "Maybe my dad couldn't be seen in the dark in them. Maybe that's why he never got caught until the day he didn't have time to change into them. Maybe they *are* magic."

"I don't know." Nichole didn't want to destroy the boy's daydreams.

"I heard some men talking one night outside the bar, and they said my dad wasn't no bum of an outlaw. He had class, they said. Dad and his partner never killed nobody.''

He fought back the tears. ''When they went to prison, the sheriff came by and told Mama my dad got sick and died. But the men in front of the bar said someone tried to beat where my dad hid his money outa him. He wouldn't tell and they finally beat him all the way to death. When his partner heard the jailers killed my dad, he went crazy and started fightin' like a wild man. He broke out of that jail killing maybe six, maybe twenty, men on his way out.''

''Nance, are you sure?''

''Heard 'em talking, I swear. They had no reason to lie. They didn't know I was listenin'. My dad didn't die of any fever in a prison . . . he was killed.''

Nichole wanted to pat his hand, but she knew he didn't want sympathy. Not this little boy. He needed to believe in his father even if no one else in the world did.

''I think this is a fine outfit.'' She moved her hand over the silk. ''I bet I could put this on and move through the night like a whisper.''

Nance picked up the idea. ''Sure you could. I got a black hat and gloves too. You could go anywhere and no one would see you.''

Nichole laughed at the fun it would be to move about the town. She had all the skill she needed and with these clothes it would be easy. ''But where would I go? It wouldn't be any fun unless I had a mission.''

''We'll wait for a mission,'' Nance whispered. ''Maybe we'll find out who killed my dad and you can go round them all up.'' He laughed. ''Or maybe you could just walk around making sure nobody's doing nothing wrong.''

''And we'll never tell anyone,'' Nichole could see the excitement in his eyes. She laughed just thinking of how Adam would react if he knew of such a plan. ''We'll keep it a secret, acting all surprised when we hear about it the next morning.''

Somewhere, far below, they heard Nance's mother calling his name.

''I got to go,'' he whispered. ''You wait by the opening and when the coast is clear I'll signal. I'll help you make it all the way back to the study.''

''I'll wait.'' Nichole watched him slide through the opening as she folded the clothes and put them back in the box. For years she'd been free, always on the move, living on the land. Now the confines of the house were like bars. Logic told her to stay with Adam and be safe, but she was restless. She liked Adam, he felt right beside her, but she could never live his way of life. Maybe marrying Tyler wasn't such a bad idea. At least with Tyler she'd be free as a bird.

She waited almost an hour before Nance reappeared. "Everyone's eating lunch." He made a swipe across his chest as their secret signal. "All clear."

Nichole climbed out of the space and moved silently, first down the hall and then the stairs to the first floor. She could hear Bergette in Mrs. Jamison's room sharing lunch and gossip. The doctor had told her that Mrs. Jamison seemed to thrive on Bergette's small talk, growing healthier every day since she arrived. Nichole couldn't understand why. The times she'd eavesdropped, she found Bergette's conversation reminded her of a colorful bird constantly chirping the same boring tune.

She might not be able to see herself in Adam's world, but he didn't belong in Bergette's.

Turning the corner, she slipped into the back entrance to Adam's examining room. Dancing was sleeping on a bed by the windows, and Adam stood next to her.

"How is she?" Nichole knew this was a safe room for her because no one except Adam and Sister Cel came in. The only danger lay in crossing the open hallway to his bedroom and study. She'd discovered that with patients in the hall, if she lowered her gaze and walked straight across, no one paid any notice. "Any improvement in her condition?"

Adam shook his head. "Yesterday I thought she was better. But today, I don't know. The leg is healing and the cuts are all clear of infection, but she's not fighting. Twice this morning I thought I saw her open her eyes and close them again as if life was too much bother."

"You want me to sit with her?" Nichole asked.

Adam nodded. He, the nun, and Nichole had been taking shifts for days waiting for Dancing to improve enough to answer them. Adam believed she'd be frightened and would need someone with her. He'd seen men in war wake up screaming, still believing they were in battle. Dancing might react the same.

"You might try talking to her. It couldn't hurt." He shrugged.

Nichole touched Adam's arm as she passed him. The touch was light, but she felt him tense.

Since the night they'd kissed, he had avoided touching her again, but she could see the longing in his glances. She wasn't sure if the lie about her being engaged to Tyler, or his engagement to Bergette, was stopping him.

"How are your hands?" He lifted her fingers from his arm.

She looked down at the strip of cotton around each of her palms. "Much better."

He cupped his other hand beneath hers. For a long moment, he held them protectively in his grasp. Since childhood, she'd always thought of herself as big. There were few men she had to look up at, and Wolf said once she was as strong as a man. Yet her hands felt small in Adam's grasp.

"Do you think you could manage with Dancing this afternoon?" He slowly stepped away from Nichole, looking slightly embarrassed that he'd caressed her hands for so long. "I've got a woman just outside of town who is due any time. I need to check on her."

"Of course," Nichole answered, knowing that watching Dancing would be no problem. Every few hours they forced a couple of swallows down her. The rest of the time, they mostly just observed.

"Thank you," he said almost formally as though they were no more than strangers.

"You're welcome," she answered, wishing she could talk to him . . . really talk. Why couldn't she tell him how she watched him sleep, the few hours he allowed himself to rest each day? How did she ask this polite, kind man to hold her? Why did all her bravery vanish when she thought of making the first move?

He slipped on his jacket and moved through the door leading to his office. Since Dancing had nowhere else to go, Adam's office now also served as his examining room.

Nichole heard Bergette calling him just before Adam closed the door between the two rooms. Instinctively, she pressed against the wall, out of sight. Moving closer to the door, Nichole listened.

Bergette's whine was growing very familiar. Like a fire wagon rushing through the night, they usually heard her clanging before they saw her coming into view.

"Adam, aren't you coming up to lunch? How can it be possible you never have time to sit down to a meal?"

Nichole covered her mouth to keep from giggling. Adam had developed a habit of avoiding Bergette. A few times Nichole had shared her supper with him in the study, because he would rather miss dinner than have to eat with his fiancée. Sister Cel must have anticipated his actions, because Nichole's tray became fuller.

"I have to go," Adam answered. "I have a patient to see just out of town."

"Can't you let them wait for a few minutes?" Bergette's song of sorrow drifted through the office door. "Honestly, Adam, don't I count? Maybe I'm getting sick of your excuses and this town that civilization hasn't seemed to touch yet. All day you have your work, and at night you have to read. It's like living upstairs from a ghost.''

''We'll talk of it later,'' Adam said.

Nichole fought down a full laugh. This appeared to be the only conversation Bergette and he ever had. For a man planning to marry, he acted like he feared the pox every time he got near his beloved. She hated his town, his work, and didn't seem all that fond of him either. And Bergette would probably die of shock if she knew just how many ''ghosts'' lived below her.

Nichole heard Bergette storm up the stairs in a most unladylike stomp. The front door closed, telling her Adam had gone. Dancing mumbled in her sleep. Nichole turned her attention to helping.

It was twilight when Sister Cel relieved Nichole and still no word from Adam. Both women talked of all the reasons he could be delayed, as they worried.

Dancing drank most of the glass of milk Sister brought her but still didn't speak to them. She curled up and went back to sleep, crying softly with pain each time she moved.

Sister Cel picked up her mending. Nichole tried to get interested in a book as they waited for Adam's return. A half hour later, a tapping on the side door made them both jump with alarm.

''Don't answer it,'' Nichole whispered.

''It might be someone needing help,'' the nun suggested.

''It might be someone bringing trouble.'' Nichole moved into the shadows. ''Let them come back when the doc is home. We can't help them.''

''No.'' Sister Cel hurried to the door. ''I won't turn away someone in need.'' As she turned the handle, a tiny woman resembling a red ball of yarn almost fell into the room.

''Help me,'' she whispered with hands reaching toward the nun as though she were drowning. ''All I said was I was going to see Dancing, and he started hitting me.''

The visitor kicked the door closed with her foot and hurried to Sister Cel.

''I'm bleeding, but it ain't nothing.'' She patted her face with a square of lace. ''Please, can I see Dancing?''

Nichole moved from the dark corner and pointed toward their patient as the nun collected supplies to bandage the cut at the woman's forehead.

The visitor had wild, long red hair, a color nature never produced. Her clothes were layers of undergarments and frills tied together with faded silk ribbons. Wide red lips spread into a smile as she saw Dancing sleeping. She hurried to her side and closed her hand over the sleeping woman's as she looked back at Nichole.

"I had to see Dancing, no matter what he tried to do to stop me. We came out here together four years ago from Arkansas. We figured to find ourselves real western men."

She laughed as the nun tried to doctor the cuts and bruises on her face. "And we did. We found plenty of them, but most was as wild as the land. If they wanted a wife, it was to slave out on some farm all alone. Dancing and me like town life, so we kept working our way west hoping to find a town wild enough to let us stay. Finally, we stumbled on Fort Worth and Mole. He's the bottom of a barrel full of scum, so rotten the rats won't nibble his body when he's dead."

She smiled, her red lips spreading from ear to ear. "By the way, my name's Rose. You got any whiskey, dear? For medicinal purposes, mind you."

"No," Nichole answered. "I don't think so."

"Oh, well, hard times all around. Like I was saying, Mole ain't worth nothing, but he pays better than most. He treats us worse than my pa used to treat his lame hunting dogs. He expects his girls to do everything he says, like he's our master and we're mindless slaves. But it's about time somebody told him slavery's over."

Before anyone could say more, the door opened with a pop as loud as gunfire.

"Where is she?" a man in his mid forties yelled as he stormed in the room at full charge. He wasn't tall, not much over five foot, but he was made of hate from his dirty straight hair that hung halfway down his back to his scarred hands that opened and closed in a hunger to hurt someone. "I'll kill Dancing for sure this time and that no good bedbug she calls a friend."

The woman with the bruises across her cheek screamed and ran behind the nun. Nichole moved in front of the table where Dancing lay mumbling.

Glancing at Sister Cel, Nichole watched the nun fold her arms and widen her stance like she was the wall of Jericho and it would take a thousand trumpets to blow her down.

"Get out of my way!" the man shouted as he headed straight to Nichole. "Both these girls have been nothing but trouble since the day I took them in. First Dancing tried to drink all my whiskey. Now she's got the others thinking they need to leave work and come visit.

Well, they can visit her at the funeral. It's no crime to stomp out trash, and I aim to finish the job this time.''

Nichole glanced around for a weapon. This madman wasn't going to touch Dancing without a fight. She grabbed a pitcher and hurled it at him. As he dodged, her hand slid down her leg and pulled the knife from her boot. Seven inches of thin, shiny steel reflected the lamplight.

He growled like an animal and jerked a thick-bladed hunting knife from a sheath at his side. "I'll cut you deep for interfering with my business."

She knew she could take him in a fair fight, but he didn't look like the kind of man who fought fair. She took a step backward.

His growl fouled the air as he moved toward her. His free hand caught Dancing's arm as he passed her. He jerked her from the bed, sending her tumbling to the floor between Nichole and him. Dancing screamed with pain and fright.

In the second Nichole glanced down at her, the madman slashed forward.

The first swing missed by an inch, the second lunge brushed across her shirt.

"Run!" Nichole yelled to the others. "Get out!"

Sister Cel lifted the screaming redhead and moved toward the door as Mole kicked Dancing out of his way and closed in on Nichole.

She swung once, twice, missing him by a hair.

He was huffing now, snorting like a bull. "I'm going to slice you up good," he growled. "No one interferes with me."

Nichole dodged another lunge and countered with a cut across Mole's forearm. He swore and swung wildly, slinging blood through the air. Nichole ducked and darted a few steps away, but the windows pinned her.

He took a great breath and began closing in, leaning his entire body from side to side as he walked. Teasing her to try and get past him.

Suddenly a shot blasted through the room, shattering a window above Mole's head. "Hold it right there!" Adam's clear voice shouted.

Mole and Nichole both turned toward the door as Adam took a step closer. "What's going on?" he demanded without lowering the rifle from his shoulder. "Nick, are you all right?"

"This ain't none of your business, Doc. Stay out of it." Mole lowered his knife an inch. "I got a right to deal with my girls the way I see fit, and I don't like the idea of Dancing coming over here whining to you about her sorry life.''

''She's very ill. You almost beat her to death.'' Adam moved closer, the rifle still pointed at Mole's chest.

''I didn't give her any more than she deserved,'' Mole reasoned. ''And I don't take kindly to your butting in where you ain't wanted. You don't know how these women are in my place. I got to keep them in line or they'd steal me blind. They're all lazy, or they wouldn't be making a living on their backs.''

Adam didn't lower his gun. ''Get out,'' he said. ''Get out and don't come back.''

Mole glanced around the room. ''I ain't no fool,'' he said as he took a step toward the side door. ''But no man treats me wrong and gets away with it, not even a doc. You'll get yours sometime when you ain't got a gun pointed at me. And you can tell Dancing, she's as good as dead. I'm through with her and that mouthy friend of hers. They can starve, for all I care. When I toss them out there ain't a person in town who'll give them a bread crumb.'' He turned and was gone as quickly as he'd appeared.

''He means it.'' Nichole moved to Adam's side.

''So did I.'' Adam put the rifle down. ''Are you all right?'' He glanced first at Nichole, then at Sister Cel.

''We're fine, but Dancing—''

Before she could finish, Adam knelt beside Dancing. The patient looked like a rag doll someone had kicked into a corner and forgotten. She wasn't even crying anymore.

Adam's hands moved carefully down her body, feeling for more breaks in her bones. After a moment, he ordered, ''I'll need more bandages, hot water, and all the light we can set up about the table.''

Nichole hurried to the cabinet just as she heard footsteps rushing down the stairs. In a blink, she had vanished into the corner by the cabinet.

''What is going on, Adam?'' Bergette screamed as she rounded the corner and rushed past the nun and into the office. ''Did I hear a shot?''

Adam carefully lifted Dancing to the table. Blood was spilling onto her bandages in several places and his shirt-front was stained with crimson rain. ''We have an injured woman,'' he said calmly. ''Would you like to help?''

Bergette looked first at Dancing, then at the redhead standing next to the nun. ''Does Mrs. Jamison know about the kind of people you see?'' Her voice held a hint of a threat.

"She knows I'm a doctor." Adam was far more interested in Dancing than in Bergette. "I see people who need help. I suggest you either help or get out."

"You can't talk to me like that!"

"I don't have time to talk to you any other way."

Bergette opened her mouth then snapped it closed. She ran from the room yelling for Charles to bring her pills. Everyone knew the argument wasn't over, she'd just run out of ammunition. She was the kind of woman who would make him pay dearly for his harshness.

"Sister, lock the door," he ordered. "And you," he looked at the redhead.

"Ro-Rose," the frightened woman hiccuped her name. "Just Rose."

"Do you think you can hold your friend? Cradle her in your arms and try to keep her still. We've got to reset her leg, and she's got a bad gash on her head from the fall. We'll have to work fast, she's losing a great deal of blood."

The prostitute joined him. "I can do whatever I have to do. My ma was a midwife back in the hills. Blood don't frighten me none." She seemed happy to be asked to help and she hugged Dancing. "And Doc, no matter what happens, thank you."

When Nichole heard Sister Cel lock the door, she joined Adam. They worked for hours trying to repair the leg and cool Dancing's raging fever. While Nichole and Sister Cel followed Adam's orders, Rose seemed to know what to do. She'd been honest about having no fear of blood for by the time Dancing's head was stitched Rose's top was wet with her friend's blood.

She pushed away the nun's efforts to clean her up and continued to cradle Dancing.

Finally, long after midnight, Dancing slipped away. They'd all tried but couldn't hold her to this earth. She died without a whimper, without a fight.

Adam pulled away in defeat, Rose cried softly as she held her friend's cooling hand to her cheek. Sister Cel prayed in a soft voice that was almost a song. The smell of blood and death hung in the air, weighing on everyone.

Adam heard Nichole follow him as he walked into the darkness of the porch. Without a word, he opened his arms and they held one another tightly. He could feel his heart pounding against hers, her breath brushing the side of his throat, the warmth of her body pressing against him.

This was part of it, he wanted to scream. Part of the magic she thought he had. Part of being the doctor she wanted him to be. Not the wonder of saving a life, anyone could handle that, but the ability to keep going when death wins.

He didn't kiss her. He only held her. There were no words for him to tell her why, or how dearly, he needed her close. There were no words needed for her to understand.

When the nun called him, Adam slowly pulled away. He touched her hair, silently saying thank you as he returned to the house.

Without a word, Nichole slipped into the foyer. Moving up the stairs, she climbed into the attic. She retrieved a box of clothes that would make her invisible and maybe even bulletproof. She now had a mission.

FOURTEEN

Standing in the shadows of a quarter moon, Nichole stripped off her warm wool trousers and heavy cotton shirt. Slowly, she removed her undergarments, knowing that where she was going she might get hurt. She couldn't stand the thought of ruining them.

The musty air was cool against her bare flesh as a spiderweb brushed her shoulder. She pulled a roll of bandages she'd taken off Adam's supplies from her trouser pocket. The wide cotton strip was tied with a piece of midnight blue yarn. Laying the yarn on a beam, she wrapped the bandage around her rib cage and across her breasts, pressing the soft tissue as flat as she could.

The familiar wrapping gave her a sense of coming home. The tight bandage made her straighten, as though placing on an invisible cloak of the warrior inside her. Her muscles tightened, her stance widened, her senses became more alert.

A smile touched her lips as she thought that this was Adam's bandage that now bound her. The memory of the morning so many months ago at his farm came drifting back to her. She could almost taste him as she recalled the way he'd kissed her and how his hands had spread over her breasts forever branding his touch on her skin.

What if they'd had longer that morning? What if he'd made love to her?

High in the dusty attic, his memory kept her warm as she dressed in bandit's black. The silk shirt slid across her skin like a caress. The pants were a little baggy, but the tarnished silver-buckled belt held them tight. She used the yarn to tie her hair back knowing that if she continued this disguise, she'd have to cut it a few inches shorter. Nance's father's hat fit low but securely. She used her own soft leather footwear that laced high, a cross between a moccasin and a boot. Wolf had them specially made not to make a sound or leave a heel print, even in sand.

Last, she wrapped her gun belt around her waist, high and secure. A gunman might think of wearing it low so that his draw would be a second faster, but not a Shadow. A tiny circle of leather hooked the Colt in place so that it wouldn't accidentally fall from the holster. If she did her job correctly, she'd never need her gun, Wolf used to lecture. She slipped the knife into its casing at her calf and straightened.

More than her clothes had changed. Her entire carriage, the very air around her had been rearranged. Any softness was gone, any hint that she was a woman. A tall thin man seemed to have been born in full armor. She pulled black gloves over her bandaged hands and the transformation was complete.

She moved silently to the opening and dropped down to the storage room. For an instant, she thought she saw something move among the boxes.

"Nance? Sister?"

No one answered.

Nick pulled her Colt and moved between the boxes. Nothing. She crossed the room twice. No one. If there had been someone in the room, they were as good at disappearing as she was.

She slipped into the hallway and down the stairs. Adam's voice drifted from the examining room. He was talking with the undertaker, offering to help so that Dancing could be buried soon after dawn.

As she passed the office, she saw Rose sleeping in a chair behind Adam's desk with an empty bottle of whiskey next to her. She once again reminded Nick of a ball of red yarn, for her hair was a flaming blanket covering her. Sister Cel must have retired and Nick guessed Adam would think she had also.

Tiptoeing across the room, Nick kept an eye on Rose. Silently, she opened a window and slipped out. She'd learned years ago that doors caused too much noise and draft. Windows were a far easier porthole. The darkened porch on the moonless side of the house would be the perfect place to penetrate the world outside.

She crossed to the house next door and entered the same way she'd left the boardinghouse. It was only an hour before dawn and everyone was asleep in this establishment that housed most of Mole's employees.

Nick passed from room to room, looking, listening. The rooms were cluttered and smelled of old whiskey bottles and bodies in need of washing. Most of the rooms had two or more women sleeping together, their customers having left for the night. A few men had paid to stay till dawn, but they didn't stir as Nick walked past.

She entered each door, checking first the location of weapons, and then studying each man.

In the last room on the second floor, she found what she searched for. A stout, barrel-chested man spread across the bed on his belly. His right forearm had been bandaged with what looked like a bar towel. The smell of blood and filth assaulted her nostrils as she moved closer and forced herself to stare at the nude man. His body was hairless and rounded, reminding her of his name, Mole.

He snored unaware as she circled the bed. The cut she'd slashed into his arm had bled through the towel, but the injury didn't seem to be bothering his sleep. The back of his body was scarred and ugly like a sand sculpture that had been pitted by rain and distorted by wind.

Nick fought down the bile that climbed in her throat. Without looking away, she moved to the chair where he'd draped his clothes. Slowly, she slid her hand into his pants' pocket, thankful for the gloves.

Nothing.

She moved to the other side of the chair and felt inside the other pocket. Mole grunted in his sleep and rolled to his side as her fingers touched a key.

Clutching it, she almost ran from the room. She should have moved slowly but realized she couldn't endure seeing more of his body than she already had.

Once she was in the hall, Nick leaned against the wall and listened, afraid to breathe. Mole's snoring continued.

Slowly, an inch at a time, she relaxed.

Within minutes, she was back outside and once more in the fresh night air. She slipped into the total blackness behind a building and took a deep breath, enjoying the rush of excitement through her body.

Something rattled in the alley behind her. Nick froze. Someone had followed her from the Mole's house. Her first thought was that Mole, still nude, was stalking her, but he couldn't be. She'd left him snoring and his stocky body could have never moved down the stairs without waking half the house.

She waited several minutes then relaxed. Probably only a cat, she thought as she started down the street staying well into the shadows. In the wild, animals were like allies, warning her of danger. In towns, they could confuse even the best Shadow.

The rules turned over in her mind like a lesson long ago memorized. Stay behind the light, never between it and something that might show your outline. Move slowly as if melting, for fast actions cause attention. Pick your next hiding place before you leave where you are. Listen. Listen.

Glancing at the sky, she calculated. Thirty minutes maybe before the first hint of dawn. Thirty minutes to complete her mission.

Slipping into the doorway of the first saloon, she tried the key. Nothing. It would have been a great help if she knew which saloon Mole owned. But she could hardly ask Adam. If he had any idea of what she planned tonight, he would do everything in his power to stop her.

The second saloon. The third. The key didn't work. She moved on into a part of town less well kept, more lawless.

Finally, half a mile from the boardinghouse, the key worked on one of the most run-down saloons. The door swung open, and Nick slipped in. A moment later, she almost cried out in repulsion. The floor gave with her foot. Slime, tobacco spit, and filth covered the floor thick as a greasy chicken skin.

Nick forced herself to progress across the open area to the bar outlined by moonlight. There were no tables or chairs, only a long horseshoe-shaped bar and a pair of stairs leading to a second-floor landing, with doors off it every four feet. Men who patronized this place came to drink and to womanize, nothing more.

Behind the bar was cleaner. Sawdust coated the floor. She felt her way in the blackness for a door that must lead to storage. She found one beneath the stairs. The lock was a simple one she'd practiced with as a child. Within a minute the lock was opened, not broken, so it could be refastened. She opened the door and found stairs leading down. A lantern and matches were on the first step. Nick took two steps into the blackness, closed the door and lit the lantern.

"Thanks, Mole," she whispered as if he'd left the light there for her.

Barrels of beer lined one side, whiskey the other. She sat the lantern on the third step and went to work.

With the sharp point of her knife, she chipped a hole in the back of each barrel. Guessing no one would be in the saloon before noon, most of the barrels would be empty before anyone checked and the basement floor would be a foot deep in whiskey-smelling mud.

Her act wouldn't pay Mole back for the life he'd tossed away, but it was a start. Maybe without any liquor, he'd have to close and let the girls go somewhere else.

Something stirred near the steps, and Nick turned to stone. What if someone had followed her? What if someone had been sleeping beneath the steps? No, she told herself. The door had been locked. Mole would never imprison anyone inside his supply of liquor.

She moved slightly and saw a rat dart between two steps. "Rats," she whispered. "I hate rats."

Turning out the lamp, she retraced her steps, stopping to relock the door. When she made it back outside, the first touch of dawn brushed the sky. She hurried down the alley to where Mole slept and slipped the key back into his pocket, without even glancing at him snoring on the bed. She'd done what she came to do. If he caught her now, she'd simply fight her way out.

A woman on the first floor rose a few inches as Nichole passed, but a man leaving the house at dawn was not an unusual enough sight to fully awaken her. She rolled over and let Nichole pass without saying a word.

No one confronted her as she crossed between the houses and slipped back into the open window. Rose still slept in the chair, and Nick heard Adam and the undertaker working in the examining room. The smell of coffee came from the kitchen.

She climbed the stairs and entered the storage room, taking her first deep breath. But as she pulled herself into the attic entrance, she had the feeling that someone was watching her. Someone who wouldn't be there if she looked back.

FIFTEEN

Nichole slept through dancing's funeral. Only Adam, Rose, and Sister Cel attended. Bergette refused to even discuss the possibility of going, and Mrs. Jamison wouldn't let Nance out of the house. Nichole knew she couldn't attend, so after they left, she curled into the little bed in Adam's old study and fell into a deep sleep. The night's adventure had eased her sorrow and made her feel alive again.

When the sun was high, she came awake with a jerk at the sound of Bergette's voice close by, too close.

"What do you mean I shouldn't be in here?" Bergette shouted loud enough for the entire house to hear.

Adam's low voice reached Nichole as she slipped from the covers and moved behind the open door. Through the crack, she could see Bergette standing over Adam who lay atop his covers fully dressed.

"I'm trying to take a nap, Bergette," he said in a voice that left considerable doubt that he'd been asleep when she barged into his room. "I didn't go to bed last night and I'd like to sleep an hour before I start seeing patients."

"Oh, forgive me." She pouted. "I forgot you were up all hours, first with the whores and then the undertaker. It seems you have time to talk to everyone in this town but your fiancée. Well, I've had enough. I don't care how tired you are, it's time we had a few words."

"You talk," he mumbled. "You seem a lot better at talking than listening. But can't we move somewhere else besides my bedroom? Bergette, it isn't proper."

She laughed. "Are you suggesting that I wouldn't be safe in here alone with you? What a joke. You haven't made any effort to so much as touch my hand since I've been here. I find it very unlikely you'd attack me in passion's fever now.''

''I played that game when I returned from the war. Remember, you pushed me away.'' He leaned on one elbow and resigned himself to having to talk to her. ''I'd wasted years thinking of coming home to you and all you thought about was that my clothes were dusty.''

''Well, a girl should never make it easy. I'm not some old maid who would jump in your arms despite what people would say. That doesn't mean I planned for you to stop trying.''

''What people? We were alone in your house when you ran down the stairs and stopped just short of my arms.''

''There were the servants,'' Bergette defended. ''I hoped you'd try again when we were alone and in more proper surroundings.''

''Did you?'' he asked. ''Do you want me to keep trying, now? A bedroom seems the right surroundings.'' He made no move toward her. ''Or do you simply enjoy the control as you enjoy controlling everything around you? The day I came home it seemed we were never alone, nor did you make any plans to be. Tell me, Bergette, what is it you wish me to do? Crawl at your feet and beg for a touch, a kiss, any scrap of feeling you have inside?''

''Nothing. I want nothing from you if I have to tell you what to do.'' She paced beside his bed, her silk skirts making a swishing sound as they brushed his quilt. ''I've come to a conclusion about you, dear Adam. I understand that there are some men who are not turned toward wanting women. They might not even know it themselves until they're in the army, or something.''

Adam laughed. ''You think I'm a man who doesn't like women?''

''It wouldn't matter to me if you were,'' she answered quickly. ''We could still be married. You could live your life, and I could live mine. I understand many of the royalty in Europe live apart and are happily married. When my father dies, I'd see that you have a fair allowance. You can go about healing all kinds of trash, and I can go about my pleasures.''

''You're not saying you want a marriage in name only?'' Adam looked as if he couldn't believe what he was hearing. He'd always thought her cold, but not that cold. ''Surely there are hundreds of men standing in line to love and marry you, Bergette?''

''I've looked!'' she snapped before she realized what she said. Then her pride wouldn't allow her to back down. ''Do you honestly think I would have waited for you if there had been a man worth having? I don't want to be passed from my father to a husband to be regarded as only something pretty to decorate a house. If we married with an understanding, I could be respectable and still travel and shop and go to parties with an escort." She smiled and lowered her voice. "You're a doctor. You could make sure there were no children born."

Adam couldn't hide his laughter. "But you see, dear Bergette, I want a wife in my bedroom as well as in my life, and I want children, dozens of them."

She stopped and stared at him a moment. "I would agree to share your bed occasionally, and we could talk about children later, after we've been married a while."

"But I wouldn't share a bed with you." He crossed his arms and leaned back on the pillows.

"Now, are you saying you wouldn't sleep with me?" Her eyes opened in shock.

"That is exactly what I'm saying. Not even at gunpoint. Not even if it were my last night on earth."

Bergette stomped her foot. "Then something is wrong with you. You're not a man. Something is missing inside you, Adam McLain. All you think of is your work and your studies. That isn't normal."

Adam looked at her with anger in his eyes for the first time. "Nothing's missing in me just because I think I can live without you in my life." There was something missing, he thought, only Bergette couldn't fill the void.

She saw doubt blink in his gaze and jumped on it with hope. "Yes, it is, Adam. You try as hard as you want to help others, you study without sleep, but you'll never find what you're looking for." She smiled, hoping she was hurting him. "There's no fire inside you. No man beneath the blood and bone. You look whole, but the war crippled you as surely as if you'd returned on crutches."

"That's a lie!"

"Then prove it," she challenged. "Take me in your arms and kiss me. Take me to your bed, and we'll seal our marriage right now. You'll never find anyone more beautiful or more generous once we're married. Take me in your arms and prove you're a man. Prove you're a man with an ounce of passion running in your blood."

She held her arms open as if she were a saint sacrificing herself to save one poor soul.

"Stop it!" Adam turned away in disgust.

Bergette pulled the laces of her bodice open, revealing most of her well-powdered breasts as she moved before him once more. "Go ahead, prove you're a man, Adam. Take me."

"Get out, Bergette."

His whisper was so low Nichole barely heard him but she could feel the anger in him from a room away.

"What's the matter?" Bergette leaned forward, knowing the front of her dress would pull open slightly. "Haven't you ever had a woman? Don't worry, I'll teach you what to do. I didn't spend all the war locked away waiting for you."

"Get out," he said again in controlled fury.

"Or are you afraid you can't satisfy me? You're not man enough to even kiss me. Wait until everyone hears about you back home. One of the McLains isn't a man at all but only a shell."

Adam stood and opened the door with forced slowness. "Good day, Bergette."

Bergette laughed. "You can't even bring yourself to kiss me. I feel so sorry for you, Adam."

"Good-bye." His knuckles whitened on the doorknob.

"It's not good-bye. I plan to stay another three weeks and have lots of talks with you." She moved out the door. "We'll discuss every detail of this problem."

Adam closed the door behind her and turned the lock, then closed his eyes and leaned against the wood. His dream, his perfect woman, had turned to a monster even fairy tales couldn't describe.

Nichole moved from the study. She didn't know what to say. Bergette had hurt him, but he'd allowed her to without striking back. She would have cut the woman in half if she'd been Adam. But he'd stood the insults. In some strange way, he seemed the stronger for it. It would have been easy to kiss her and end her protest, or slap her and send her screaming from the room, but he hadn't. And he hadn't yelled or threatened to strike her. What Bergette saw as weakness Nichole suddenly realized was strength. A kind of strength proven only to himself.

"I forgot you were there," he whispered when he opened his eyes and saw her at the doorway.

"I didn't mean to eavesdrop. She woke me up."

They looked at one another, not knowing what to say. His brown eyes seemed full of pain and she had no idea what medicine could help him.

Slowly, Adam walked to her and circled his fingers around the back of her neck.

"Your hair is all a mess of curls." He brushed the back of her head with his hand.

She looked down for a moment. "I didn't comb—" When her gaze met his once more she forgot what she'd been saying.

With a sudden move, he pulled her to him and kissed her fully on the mouth.

Nichole pulled away. "Don't," she said. "I don't know how to play games."

"I'm not playing any game." His hand still rested on the back of her neck.

There was loss in his eyes, and pain, and anger. He was searching.

"Then don't try to prove something to yourself, Adam. You're not really kissing me, you're simply not kissing Bergette." Nichole wanted her own kisses, not those denied his first love.

Adam slammed his fist into the wall behind her head. "I—" He couldn't put his feeling into words. He grabbed her by the shoulders and pressed his lips against hers with bruising force.

Nichole shoved with all her strength and broke the hold, then slapped him hard across the face. She felt herself boiling over inside. She wanted Adam to hold her, but not this way. Not to prove something to himself.

Without a word, she ran back into the study and closed the door. There was no lock, but she knew he wouldn't come in. She crawled into her covers feeling cheap and used. He'd kissed her because she'd been there and because he was angry and hurt. Somehow the kiss that had been so perfect before had soured and turned ugly.

Half an hour later someone tapped lightly on her door. When she didn't answer, Sister Cel opened the door and placed a tray of food by her bed.

Nichole was awake, but she didn't want to face anyone, not even the nun. By midafternoon, she gave up sleeping. There was no reason to cross over to the examining room. Dancing wasn't there. So she began to pace, feeling very much like a caged animal.

"Nick?" Nance whispered from the doorway to the bedroom. "Nick, are you in here?"

She stepped from the shadows. "What is it, General Ears. You got news?"

"I got news like you wouldn't believe. Lots of talk going round today. Some of the things Miss Bergette is saying I wouldn't repeat to my own mother, 'course I don't have to since that's who Miss Bergette is telling them to. But first, Doc needs to see you if you can cross the hall safely, but he said don't take any chances." Nance added, "He said, 'Please come.' "

She pulled on her coat and shoved her hair behind her ears. "I'll come. Give me the sign."

Nance stepped into the hallway where she could see him. After a few minutes, he rubbed his hand, with fingers spread wide, across his chest.

Nichole moved into the hallway. A moment later, she disappeared into the back room of Adam's office.

Rose, Dancing's friend, sat alone, fiddling with her dress as though the extra layer of clothing was uncomfortable. She looked up when Nichole entered and smiled her wide smile. "There you are, honey." She cocked her head sideways, sending hair flying around her shoulders. "I was wondering where you disappeared to. When you weren't at the funeral, I figured you had your reasons."

"Is something wrong?" Nichole noticed a bruise covered with powder. "Mole hasn't hit you again."

"No, I'm fine. I went over to my bedroom and collected my things after the funeral. I knew Mole would be down opening the bar." She smiled. "I ain't working for him no more. In fact, I'm getting out of the business for good. When Dancing and I left home, I was a pretty fair cook, so I thought I'd come here and ask the doc for a job. Mole will kill me too if I stay with him, and I ain't ready to meet my Maker yet. Have to do a few hundred good deeds to balance out the scale, you know."

"What did Adam say?" Nichole wanted to hear about Mole and what he found in his saloon, but she couldn't come right out and ask.

"He said he had a few people to talk to at the sheriff's office, then he'd talk to me. He told Nance to go fetch you and Sister and to tell you both that he'd be back in a few minutes." She tried to straighten her hair. "I know I don't look respectable, but I'll work on it."

"You look fine," Nichole lied. She didn't even want to think about how Bergette would yell if the doc hired Rose for a cook. Bergette's favorite hobby, besides picking on Adam, was complaining about Lily's cooking.

"While I was packing up my things, I got to thinking about you. You were in this room with Dancing and you fought for her, but you didn't come to the funeral. When the doc talked to the sheriff, he left out you even being in the room when Mole came in. Mole was so drunk, he couldn't remember what happened." She raised one painted eyebrow. "You do a good job of dressing like a man, but one good look told me you were a woman. So I figure you got your share of reasons and secrets."

"I do." Nichole moved closer, wondering if the woman would attempt blackmail.

The redhead watched her closely. "I also figure it's none of my business."

"You're right," Adam answered from the doorway. "I ask you never to mention that you saw Nick. She's our guest here, our secret guest."

"I never saw her." Rose winked at Nichole. "I got books full of things I never saw. Fact is, in my life I don't see more than I do see, if you know what I mean."

Adam moved to the washstand and scrubbed his hands. "What can I do for you, Rose?"

She straightened. "I come to ask for a job. I'm a fine cook. My ma was a cook for a big house, and she taught me."

Adam lifted a towel and dried his hands. "I don't do the hiring around here." He looked up as the nun entered the room and closed the door behind her. "What do you think, Sister, do we need a cook?"

Rose lowered her head, her hopes disappearing before the aging nun.

Sister Cel shook her head. "After the fit Miss Bergette threw about your treating the ladies of the evening, she wouldn't have a chance. Which is a shame, because Charles and Lily argue over every bean that goes in a pot. Seems both think they're above cooking and have too many duties already. My cooking is far too plain to satisfy the lady upstairs."

Rose looked up with hope in her eyes. "I ain't a . . . you know . . . I ain't one of those no more, Sister. But I got to have work, or I'll be on the streets starving. You folks were the only ones I have to turn to. You're the only ones who have ever helped women like Dancing and me. All the girls talk about how the doc treats them like they was a lady, and how Sister gives them sweets when they leave, like they was Sunday company come to visit. And this here invisible woman fought for us. No one's ever fought for—"

"Hush," Sister Cel ordered in a gruff tone that didn't reflect in her face.

Adam smiled. "You give them sweets, Sister?" He couldn't hold his laughter when the nun blushed.

"I might have. Don't concern yourself with the workings of others, Doctor."

The old woman never gave him an inch. She might toss her undying loyalty to Nick at first glance, but she would challenge him at every turn. He couldn't decide if she liked him and was trying to hide it, or only tolerated him.

"Of course," he answered. "This house is bulging at the seams with secrets. Why should we not add another?"

Sister Cel faced him directly. "I agree. There is always room for one more." She looked at Rose. "Can you wash that color out of your hair?"

"Yes," Rose whispered. "I worked real hard getting it in, but half a bar of lye should chase it away."

"Even if we could get her looking like a cook, where's she going to sleep?" Adam couldn't believe they were adding another to their number.

"I'll sleep on a cot in the kitchen." Rose looked excited. "And I'll work for room and board. I wouldn't expect no pay."

"This is insane." Adam glanced at Nichole for her opinion.

"I heard Bergette say she'd be gone in three weeks and I'll be leaving as soon as Wolf comes. Then you'll have plenty of room." Nichole shrugged. "If you had a cook, Sister could help more with the patients."

"But I'll only stay while I'm needed," Sister Cel added. "I didn't sign on for a full tour of duty."

"All right," Adam gave in. "Get her looking respectable. I'll talk to Mrs. Jamison." He pointed at Rose. "But remember, nothing about Nick being here. As far as you're concerned she's a ghost in this house . . . and no drinking."

"I don't even see her now. But I do tend to cook more than folks will eat." Rose lifted her chin proudly. She not only would have a respectable job, she'd be entrusted with a secret and that was a great honor. "As for drinking, I promise not more than one after sundown. My ma always said not to go too far with redemption, or salting."

"Fair enough." Adam offered his hand. "Welcome."

The nun led Rose upstairs to clean off the paint and powder and dig through boxes of old dresses Mrs. Jamison kept in the storage room. Adam and Nichole were left alone.

He moved to the window and looked out, as if there were something to watch. "I don't know what to say about what happened between us this morning." He hesitated with each word.

"It isn't necessary to say anything," she answered, feeling his hurt as she'd felt it earlier in the bedroom when Bergette had tormented him.

He folded his arms and leaned against the wall. "I'd say I'm sorry, but it would be a lie. I've wanted to kiss you again since that first night."

"Why didn't you?"

How could he explain how different they were, how they didn't belong in the same world? She was just visiting his, no more. And he no longer believed in love, or living a life with another. Bergette had taught him that all too clearly. If he pulled Nichole as close as he wanted to, he wasn't sure he'd have enough heart left to pump blood when she walked out of his life.

"I'll make you a promise," he whispered. "I'll not touch you again no matter how much I want to. You'll have no fear of me."

"I have no fear of you now," she answered, shoving her hands into her pockets.

"I'm glad I didn't destroy that between us." He looked at her, wanting to clear the air. Too much of their lives had crossed for them to part as strangers. "Any questions? Or any more you want me to promise for the remainder of your stay?"

Nichole smiled and moved to stand beside him. "Only one. How about me touching you? Is my behavior part of your promise?"

Adam relaxed a little. "No. It doesn't figure in. Any time you like, I'm available. And unlike Bergette, you'll never have to ask, just make a move. Being close enough to touch you would be a pleasure."

Nichole wasn't joking. But she'd take him up on his offer some other time. First things first. "Mind telling me what the deputy needed? Any word on the stagecoach attack?"

"No. But I thought I saw a paint horse tied around back of his office. After we talked I went to look, but it was gone. Probably not the one you saw that was with the raiders. There are lots of paints."

"So what was so important that Russell had to see you right away?"

"He only wanted to know where I'd been early this morning after Dancing died. The undertaker said I'd been with him so that ended my being questioned. It seems someone broke into Mole's saloon and did quite a bit of damage." He looked at her closely. "You wouldn't know anything about that, would you?"

"Sure. I crawled out the window of your office, snuck into Mole's bedroom across the way, stole the keys and broke into his place just before dawn. Then, of course, I retraced my steps and put the keys back while he slept nude only inches away, snoring like a pig."

Adam laughed. "Sure you did, Nick. Sure you did. And I've no doubt Sister went along as your sidekick."

He walked out of the room still laughing. Nichole shrugged her shoulders. "So much for honesty."

An hour later, Nichole hid behind the door and watched Mrs. Jamison meet Rose, a silent little woman who looked like she'd been raised in a girls' boarding school. Her hair was brown, her face scrubbed, her dress only slightly reminiscent of a gown Mrs. Jamison had worn years ago.

Within minutes Mrs. Jamison welcomed her and turned the duties of the kitchen over to her. By noon, Rose had prepared a simple but hearty meal, and by dinner the smell of fresh-baked bread filled the house. Even Bergette approved of Rose's cooking, but complained that now she'd gain weight.

When the house settled down for the night, Nichole slipped up to the tiny attic room and dressed in black. As soon as the doctor's light went out, she had another mission.

SIXTEEN

Adam leaned back from his desk and tried to relax. His office and examining room looked like there had been a savage raid on the place, leaving no survivors. He'd had little time to put away the books he pulled from the study to allow space for Nichole's bed. All the volumes lined one wall like a narrow unstable bench. Remains of the carpentry work for Dancing's casket littered the floor of his once spotless examining room along with soiled sheets and discarded bandages.

The day had been endless. After Bergette said he wasn't a man because he didn't want to make love to her, she refused to speak to him. Mrs. Jamison informed him he'd have to pay for Rose, though she was cooking for everyone. She also hinted he look for another place if he planned to continue treating whores or allowing them to die beneath her roof. She didn't come right out with an open threat, but her words sounded more like Bergette's than the ailing landlady's.

Charles and Lily thought themselves above Rose and offered little help in the kitchen, only ample advice. To Adam's surprise, Rose held her own with them, taking on her share of the work and no more. She might be yes-ma'aming Mrs. Jamison, but she was a scrapper in the ranks.

To make the atmosphere more hectic, the deputy had been by three times trying to wrangle a confession out of everyone including Sister Cel. He seemed convinced that since Dancing died there before dawn, someone in the house was responsible for Mole's worries at the saloon. The deputy proclaimed himself a close friend of Mole's and swore to catch the culprit. But Mole had his share of enemies. The doctor was far down on his list to "make pay."

Deputy Russell also reported the stage robbery was officially blamed on a small band of outlaws in the area. Since there were no living witnesses, the deputy planned to let the stage line worry about the crime. He had all he could handle investigating Mole's break-in . . . and of course, Dancing's death, though he didn't see how Mole could be involved in the crime since he wasn't even present when the woman died.

Looking into the blackness beyond the window, Adam tried to put the pieces together. One thing he couldn't figure out was that the nun *did* show signs of being guilty when Russell questioned her. She ran and hid every time the deputy knocked and refused to answer his questions. If the idea hadn't been so outrageous that an old nun would commit the crime, the deputy might have taken her in for a night in jail.

And Nichole. Adam rubbed his forehead, trying to push away the headache. Since she slapped him that morning after he'd kissed her, she hadn't said more than a few words to him. Not that he blamed her. She probably thought him both a fool and a coward. How could he explain to her that fighting just wasn't in his blood any longer? Maybe it never had been. All he'd ever wanted to do since he could remember was to be a doctor and help people.

He guessed that she wanted him to challenge Mole, maybe even kill him for what he'd done to Dancing. He knew she would have enjoyed hearing him yell back at Bergette this morning. Or maybe she wanted him to prove he was a man and accept Bergette's offer to go to bed?

Adam wasn't sure. All he knew was that Nichole had believed him to be the perfect man and he'd let her down. Her dream of what he was like was just as unreal as his old dream of marrying Bergette and being happy. He wished he could convince Nichole that the perfect man didn't exist any more than the perfect life did. They were both dreamers caught in mourning a loss made of vapor.

Moving to the porch, he leaned against the railing and closed his eyes, listening to the sounds of the night . . . the faraway tinkle of a piano, voices drifting on the air too thin to be words, and horses. He'd grown up with the sound of horses always in the background. His father had been magic with the animals. People said he had a gift.

Adam chuckled. What Nichole longed for was not one man, but several rolled together in one form. She wanted his brother Daniel's goodness, and Wes's hardness, and his . . . his what? What was it Nichole saw in him?

Voices from the balcony above interrupted his thoughts.

"I don't care if we are hundreds of miles from home, Lily, if you disappear on me again, you'll be looking for your own fare back to Indiana." Bergette's voice was high with anger.

"But I only went to the telegraph office."

"Don't bother with excuses. Now that they've hired a cook, I expect you to be more timely with your duties." Bergette's voice seemed to pop through the air like dry lightning. "Go get my bath ready while I have a few words with Charles."

Adam looked up, as if he could see through the wood and onto her balcony. Footsteps, probably Lily's, moved away.

Bergette's voice was little more than a whisper and the words were unclear as she addressed Charles. Adam thought he heard her say, "see that it's done."

"Tonight?" Charles' voice was hard with anger.

"Tonight," she whispered. "I expect you—"

Adam turned back into his office suddenly not wanting to eavesdrop. He didn't care what she had to say, nothing about her interested him.

"Doc?" Nance Edward walked in eating a hush puppy the size of his fist. "You busy?"

"Nope," Adam answered.

"Good, 'cause I got a question." He finished off the cornbread roll and wiped his hands on his overalls. "Do you believe in ghosts?"

Adam did his best to look thoughtful. "What makes you ask?"

"Oh, I'm asking everybody. Sister says there's no such thing as ghosts except for 'the Holy,' of course. Mom says she has to live with one every day of her life. Rose told me she slept with a ghost once, but when I tried to ask a few questions, she give me a hush puppy and told me to get along."

"And now it's my turn," Adam said. "But first, what got you to thinking of such a question?"

Nance leaned on the desk. "I hear things, you know, better than most. Some nights I hear walking late in the night and I know it ain't Nick, 'cause she don't make no sound when she crosses the house. I sleep right by the door in Mom's room so nothing passes that doesn't usually wake me. Whoever it is walks up and down the stairs sometimes with slow steps, sometimes fast like he's in a hurry."

"Well, I don't know about ghosts, Nance, but next time you hear someone walking, get up and see who it is. Maybe we have a sleep-walker, or an unwanted guest.''

''Or a ghost,'' the boy added.

''Or a ghost,'' Adam agreed. ''When you find out, if you think it's trouble, yell real loud and I promise I'll come running. I'll leave my door open a few inches so I can listen.''

Nance grinned. ''I'll do that. Maybe we'll catch us a ghost from the fort. I heard Mom tell Miss Bergette that this house was a bar-racks once. She said, 'If these walls could talk,' whatever that means.''

''Should you be eavesdropping on others?'' Adam asked, feeling a little like a father.

''I got nothing else to do.'' Nance shrugged. ''I have to listen to a bushelful to find a pea that's interesting.'' He grinned and disap-peared around the corner before Adam could ask more.

Adam laughed. The boy did seem to be everywhere in the house.

Looking back, Adam remembered the outline of someone he'd seen moving through the house one night. Could that have been Nance's ''ghost of the old fort?'' Now there were so many people living under one roof, he'd be surprised if there was ever a time day or night that everyone was asleep. The house he'd once thought so big was fast becoming claustrophobic.

Lifting a book, Adam stretched back in his chair and opened to the first chapter. By chapter four, his headache had grown worse. He twisted out the lamp and propped up his feet, thinking he'd rest his eyes for a while before trying to finish the volume.

All in the house seemed asleep, and the breeze blew in cool from his open window. Adam wasn't sure how long he slept, but as a cramp in his leg woke him, something moved across the moonlight at the window.

Alarm jolted him full awake. The thin outline of a man reached the inside door leading to the hallway. Adam realized his rifle was several feet away and the intruder would be deep into the house before he could fetch it. Bolting from his chair, Adam slammed into the figure, thinking he had to save those sleeping.

The intruder and Adam rolled across the floor, the figure not taking as much force to topple as Adam suspected.

''I've got you!'' Adam rolled on top of the man he suspected must be their unwelcome guest or someone Mole sent to cause havoc. ''I've caught Nance's ghost.''

''Get off me.'' Nick fought to free herself, slugging at him more with anger than any need to defend herself. "I'm not a ghost any more than you are."

"Nick?"

She gave up her struggle. "Of course it's me. Let me go, you idiot."

"But . . . I thought you were asleep hours ago." He rolled off her. "I had no idea it was you. Nance said something about someone coming into the house late at night, and I thought . . ."

Nick raised to one elbow. "Are you sure you weren't just attacking me for the second time in twenty-four hours? Tell me, Doctor, is this going to be a frequent habit like some kind of twitch you're developing?"

"I wasn't attacking you." He felt the fool, for he had attacked her. "Are you hurt?" If he'd knocked Bergette off her feet, she'd have probably shattered like a china doll.

"You're lucky I saw you in the chair. My mistake was in thinking you were still asleep." Nick rubbed at her knee. "And it'd take more than the likes of one, Yank, to hurt me."

"Why am I lucky?" he asked.

"Because when I stepped through the window and noticed you, I slipped my knife in its case. Otherwise a second after you touched me, a blade would have been tickling your backbone through your belly button."

Adam tried to see her face to decide if she was kidding. He slid his hand along her leg and felt the holster. "You're armed?"

"I usually am when I walk the night. There's always the possibility that some fool out there might attack even a whisper."

Standing, Adam reached for the box of matches. Nichole appeared before him as the match lit. She was dressed in black shirt and trousers. But he saw her for only a moment before she blew the light out.

"No," she whispered. "This time we talk in my world." She no longer felt like Nichole, Wolf's little sister. She was a Shadow now, an equal. Adam was on her ground now.

Adam dropped the matchbox. "All right, we're in your world. Only I'm guessing your vision is better than mine in this midnight." He leaned back against his desk to steady himself in the floating blackness. "How about answering a few questions? Like where you were tonight and how long you've been doing this?"

"Doing what?" she almost sounded innocent.

"You know what. Leaving the house after dark and . . . and . . . I'm not sure I know what, or want to."

Her outline moved from the floor and stood in front of him. He could see little, but he could feel the warmth of her body so near and hear the light intake of her breath. The smell of leather drifted past him as she raised her hand and touched his hair.

He ignored the touch. "Where have you been, Nick? Don't you realize how dangerous it is in this town after dark? This isn't the woods of Tennessee."

She pressed closer, her height equal to his as he leaned against the desk. He felt the length of her body only a fraction away from his.

"What if someone saw you?" He tried to keep his words angry. "Maybe even one of the raiders from the stage? Your life would be worthless if they knew you could identify them. You've got to stay hidden at least until the sheriff gets back."

Nichole didn't answer but moved her gloved hands to his shoulders. Her fingers lightly brushed from his neck to his arm and back.

"What do you think you're doing, Nick?" She was driving him mad with her nearness and her silence.

"I'm touching you," she finally whispered. "I seem to remember you telling me I could this morning. Are you backing down on your word?"

Adam raised his head and folded his arms across his chest. But the action only brought him in contact with her, and she refused to step away. "No," he answered. "I'm not backing down, but we've a great deal to talk about. You have to look at what you're doing logically. The war is over now. There is no . . ."

Her hand stroking his jaw made him forget his point. He felt starved for her touch.

She pressed close to his forearms and brushed her lips against his ear with her words. "Talk. I won't stop you, Doc."

Adam closed his eyes, trying to think of what it was he'd had to say. All he could think about was the movement of silk at his arms as she touched her lips and cheek against the side of his face. Her journey didn't reach his mouth, but moved over his skin, exploring the feel of him with her lips.

Didn't she know that a woman didn't advance so? Only right now he couldn't understand why women didn't, for the feel of her was intoxicating. Maybe she was just punishing him for the way he'd acted this morning. If he reached for her, she'd probably pull away and remind him that he said he'd never touch her again.

He tightened his grip on his elbows and found the muscles in his arms became more sensitive to the brushing of her shirt.

Her warm breath tickled beneath his ear as she slid her cheek along his jawline.

His head leaned back as her hands moved across his shoulders and began unbuttoning his collar. "Nick." His voice was so low he hardly recognized it. "We can't do this. You can't do this." He knew they were both attracted to one another, but they had to fight it. There were other considerations. Though logic told him this was insane, he seemed to be the only one fighting any urges at the moment.

"We aren't doing this," she whispered as she removed his collar and unbuttoned the top few buttons of his shirt. "I'm doing this. You'll stand still and keep to your word. After all, you made a promise to welcome my nearness."

Her fingers clutched the material and pulled his shirt open. "Are you telling me to stop, Adam? Are you pushing me away?"

"No," he answered. "Never."

She moved her hands beneath the cotton.

Adam closed his eyes once more and swore beneath his breath. She was torturing him, paying him back for the cold kiss this morning. Now he was positive if he reached for her, she'd be gone.

She tugged at his arms and he unfolded them, gripping the sides of the desk. Let her play this game, he thought. She was too much of an innocent to take it very far.

Without moving away an inch, she pulled off her gloves and dropped them on the desk. Then to his surprise she went back to unbuttoning the remainder of his shirt. With each button, her fingers spread the starched cotton apart so that she could feel his warm skin. The tips of her fingers moved along his chest, painfully slow.

He felt her light touch a hundred times stronger than if it had been a blow. The fresh, wild smell of her surrounded him, making him feel like he was taking her very being inside him with each breath.

"I want to feel your skin," she whispered. "Do you mind? After all, you've touched mine. Even that first night when my body was filled with pain, I remember how you touched me as you washed the blood away. And in your bedroom just before dawn months ago. I'll never forget the way your hands moved over me."

"I said I wouldn't touch you again," he answered. "And I won't."

How could he tell her that the pleasure of her fingers against his skin was shattering any calmness? She didn't need to remind him of the times he'd touched her. Each moment was vivid in his mind.

She spread the shirt wide and leaned into his bare chest as her lips brushed his so briefly he wasn't sure if it was reality or dream. Then she lowered her face to his chest and rolled her head from side to side, taking in the feel, the smell, the touch of him like a wild animal choosing a mate.

"We have to talk," he mustered his last ounce of sanity. "Nick." His mouth touched hers and his words only traveled a breath away.

Without a word, she pressed her lips against his and ended all conversation. He didn't react to her kiss but let her kiss him.

At first he thought, let her take what she wants, let her torture him. But she wasn't being fair. She wasn't taking, she was giving.

She moved her fingers into his hair and pulled him closer, molding the length of her body against him. His resolution shattered. Without thought of how she might reject him, he moved his arms around her waist and matched her kiss.

For a moment, she felt a jolt of surprise and pleasure, then she settled into his arms as if she'd been there a hundred times.

All the reasons they should stay apart crumbled as he kissed her. He felt a wonderful sense of coming home with her in his arms. Even if they could never get along in the real world, here in the night, they were a perfect match.

He plowed one hand into her short curly hair. The thick, midnight silk of it drove him mad. While he was listing reasons for his insanity, he'd have to add the way her lips tasted and the way she pressed against him without holding back and . . .

Her mouth opened and all other thought vanished as the kiss turned to liquid passion.

He had no idea if minutes or hours passed, nor did he care. She pulled away suddenly, leaving his body a cavern from the loss.

"Listen!" she whispered in sudden panic. A moment later she vanished into the blackness of the room.

SEVENTEEN

Nick slipped her knife from her boot and crept into the hallway. A thin beam of light from the kitchen cast a glow along the narrow space turning the center of the house into a wood-lined cave.

The sound she'd heard came again. She felt her way along the wall until she reached the front door. The thin windows on either side of the door were black with the darkness of predawn.

"Let me!" Adam whispered from just behind her as he reached for the knob.

"Don't open it," she answered. "It could be the deputy, or even Mole."

"Step back and cover me." He placed his hand on her shoulder as he moved past her. "I can deal with the deputy . . . or Mole"

Before Adam could finish the order, she'd vanished with only the sound of her Colt clearing leather hanging in the still air. He blinked twice, fascinated by how she could evaporate.

He straightened and slowly turned the lock on the door. Hinges creaked as he pulled the door toward him. The thin light spread onto the porch.

"Mornin', Adam," a deep voice mumbled. "I didn't mean to wake you."

"Wes?"

The tall man in leather and chaps pulled off his wide-brimmed hat. "I know I'm sunbaked and it's still dark, but I thought you'd know me. It may be a little early, but I wanted to make sure I was in time for breakfast. I haven't had nothing but campfire cooking for weeks."

Adam pulled his brother in with a slap on the shoulder. "Of course you're in time." He looked back into the hallway. "Nick, it's Wes."

To both men's surprise, Nick unfolded from the shadows and jumped into Wes's waiting arms.

"Well," Wes laughed with his arm still around her. "I wasn't expecting to see you, kid." They moved into the study as Adam found the lantern. "Is Wolf here, also?"

"He will be as soon as he takes care of a few claim jumpers on our land." Nick slapped at the cowboy's hat. "And I'm no kid. Name the time and I'll outride, outshoot and outfight you. I've seen the way you Northern boys ride. They must not have anything but milk cows across the Mason-Dixon line."

His smile reached the scar on his cheek. "I've no doubt you could outride me. For four years I felt like I lived in the saddle, but since I've been to Texas I'm sleeping in it as well." He winked at her. "To top it all, kid, you're getting prettier every time I see you. Isn't she, Adam?"

Nichole felt her face warm.

"Beautiful's the word, brother." Adam didn't look at her for fear he'd give too much away to Wes. The brother just a year older had always been able to read him.

Wes studied her seemingly unaware of how warm the room had become for everyone else. "That she is. Of course, I thought so the first time I saw her. I remember thinking that if she could look that good in baggy men's clothes, there wasn't any telling how many heads she'd turn in a dress."

Nick paced to the window, not knowing how to handle the sudden praise. "Well, you'll never know, because I cut up the only dress I owned for bandages when my stage was attacked on the way out."

"You were on that stage, darlin'?" Wes looked concerned. "I heard the Comancheros killed everyone and burned the bodies."

"It wasn't Comancheros, just three outlaws, maybe more. I got a quick look at two of them and their horses. At the time I didn't know they'd already killed the men on the stage so I stayed in hiding and let them pass. Lucky for them. It would take more than three men to kill a Shadow."

Wes laughed. "I would have thought you'd given up that line of work since the war."

The quick glance she gave him told Wes she hadn't.

Adam changed the subject. "What brings you here?" He didn't miss the way Wes nodded toward Nick. She nodded back, silently agreeing to continue the discussion later. The pair was leaving him out of any future discussion and Adam didn't like it.

Wes didn't take his gaze from Nichole as he answered Adam.

"I've got a herd a day's ride from here. I thought I'd ride ahead and pick up supplies while they move closer. I wouldn't want to let my men stay too long in a town. They're great on the trail, but as ornery as longhorns around civilization. Plus, I've heard talk that Fort Worth has more meanness then oughta be allowed in a town and only a deputy on guard."

"You're starting to sound like a Texan." Adam motioned for him to take a chair.

"I'm becoming one. I went down below Austin looking around, and this state is something to see. You can ride for miles and never see any sign that man touched this land. The war seems a long way away from here, but the wildness of this state keeps your heart pounding and makes you know every minute you're alive."

Nichole folded into a chair and draped one long leg over the stuffed arm. "You both are becoming Texans." She watched the brothers. They belonged in this land with its wide-open spaces and self-law.

"Wait till you meet my partner, Vincent," Wes answered. "He was born here. You wouldn't believe the stories he can tell, but he swears they're all true. I'll be camped just north of town until he catches up with me. I made good time, but heard he hit bad weather and may be as much as a week behind with the rest of the herd."

Footsteps sounded in the hall, and Nichole moved off the chair and vanished into the drapes without stirring the air. Wes glanced at Adam, then nodded his understanding to remain silent. There was no need to explain.

"Mornin'." Rose popped her head in the office door. When she saw Wes, she squealed. "Oh, I'm sorry, Doc. I didn't know you had a patient." She looked Wes over as only a woman of the night can examine with a glance. "You don't look all that sick, mister. Couldn't you wait till full dawn before you came waking the doc?"

Adam tried to hide his smile. "Rose, this is my brother. He never could tell time. He's not ill, only hungry."

Rose moved her head slightly from side to side, making her newly made bun wobble. She gave Wes another onceover. Her lips might no longer be bright red, but they were still full and expressive when she smiled. "Well, hungry's something I can cure. I got coffee boiling and apple turnovers about ready to come out of the oven. I didn't know what time folks got up around this place, so I started early."

"Apple turnovers?" Wes stood slowly. "Take me to the cure."

As Wes followed Rose out of the room, Adam pulled Nick from the folds of the curtain. "I wish you could join us," he whispered as he pressed his cheek against her hair. He was hungry too, but only for another taste of her.

"Me too," she said honestly. "But I can't take the chance. None of those upstairs will be down for another hour, but Charles or Lily might wander through the kitchen. Tell Wes I'll talk to him later."

Adam wrapped his arm about her waist. "We've a lot to talk about, you and I." He pulled at her gun belt.

"I answer to no man," she whispered in almost a challenge.

"Then maybe you'll listen to one." He kissed her lightly. "Get some sleep. We'll have time to talk later."

He couldn't resist tasting her lips once more. He felt he could stand there all day and kiss her. She had a way of giving so much with a kiss. The world seemed a long way away when she was in his arms.

"Go," she whispered, and shoved him gently.

She watched him move away knowing she couldn't tell him where she had been during the night. He wouldn't understand what she had to do. He'd shown that when he allowed Mole to live after Dancing died. How could she tell Adam that she found one of the raiders from the stagecoach killings just before she crawled into the office window? She'd followed the bandit for an hour, then lost him to a whorehouse that never quieted enough for her to enter.

Adam would never understand that this time justice wouldn't depend on the sheriff's office. She'd lived too long as a Shadow not to know what had to be done.

As Nichole moved to Adam's room, she could hear Wes teasing Rose. Nichole wondered if she'd ever be able to step into the light and live like a normal person. She could hardly remember life when she hadn't had to watch her back and judge every sound for danger. As she crossed into her tiny bedroom, she heard Rose whack someone with what sounded like a wooden spoon. Wes yelled, giving himself away as the victim.

"Now, I draw the line at your eating four dumplings!" Rose shouted. "You may be the doc's brother, but you can starve a few minutes while I scramble up a dozen eggs for breakfast. We'll have to roll you out of here if that dough rises again after all you've eaten."

Wes rubbed his hand as though she'd hurt him greatly. "Oh, Rose, darling, those are the best things I ever put in my mouth."

"Don't you Rose-darling me. I know you're just after my dumplings. Besides, maybe they ain't all I can cook. Wait till you taste my biscuits layered in butter and honey."

Wes winked at Adam. "Rose, darling, I think I'm in love. Will you marry me?"

"No, sir." Rose huffed and moved over to the stove. "I got me a respectable job now, I do, and I aim to keep it." She smiled over her shoulder. "But you're welcome to come by anytime for a taste of whatever's cooking." Her dancing eyebrows indicated there might be quite a selection on the menu.

Both men laughed. Adam wasn't sure just what the cook meant, but Wes was smiling like it didn't matter one way or the other.

As Wes lifted his second forkful of eggs, Charles walked through the kitchen acting as if he didn't see anyone in the room. He took a handful of fresh towels from the counter and vanished into the hallway.

Lowering the fork, Wes stared at his brother. "Bergette's here?"

Adam nodded without stopping eating.

"Hell," Wes shrugged. "I thought this place was too good to be true. What's she doing here?"

"It seems Papa Dupont wanted her to marry a McLain. Thought it might help him win a state office," Adam mumbled. "I've made it plain that I'm not interested, but I could put in a word for you if you're interested in the job. To the old man one McLain is as good as another and Bergette's always been so fond of you."

Wes shoved a forkful of eggs in his mouth. "You do that, little brother," he challenged. "I'd love to talk it over with the sweet little thing."

Adam leaned back and enjoyed his coffee. "She's come to tell me she forgives me and I can go back to Indiana with her. She doesn't seem to care that I'm no longer interested in marrying her." He grinned. "But you'll hear all about it from Bergette. She should be down soon and my shortcomings are her favorite topics."

"Rose!" Wes finished his eggs and grabbed his hat. "You think you could wrap up a few of those biscuits for me? Miss Bergette may love my brother here, but she hates the sight of me. If I'm lucky, I can get out before Charles wakes up the witch and she flies down the stairs to stomp on me."

"You ain't afraid of her, are you?" Rose laughed.

Wes looked surprised she'd ask such a question. "Any man would be a fool not to be."

Rose handed him a tea towel wrapped around hot biscuits. "You come back anytime. I'll protect you, honey."

Wes laughed. "I just might do that, darling."

Adam followed his brother to the front door. "Send word when you camp tonight and I'll join you for supper."

"I'll do that if you bring Nick. I'd like to hear what old Wolf's been up to these past months."

"Nick doesn't follow orders, but I'll tell her about the invitation."

They moved onto the porch as dawn lightened the sky above the run-down houses across the street. "You're crazy about the girl, Adam," Wes said.

"She's not right for me. We're too different, but she's in my blood. Half the time I'm so mad at her I can't get words out, and the other half I have to fight from crushing her against me."

The balcony creaked above them and both men silently saluted a good-bye. Wes walked to the side of the porch where he'd left his horse tied. Adam leaned against the wall and listened. Someone was above him, he could feel a presence even though he guessed whoever it was wouldn't move until he went back inside.

After waiting a few minutes, he decided he didn't care who heard him talking with Wes. Unless it was Nichole, no one else would understand what they were talking about.

Walking slowly back in the house, Adam turned down the hallway to his bedroom. If he was lucky, he could get a few hours sleep before the day started.

Sister Cel stepped from his room as he reached for the door.

"Morning, Sister," he whispered. "You're up early." In truth he'd decided the nun never slept. He'd seen her moving about the house after midnight and always before dawn.

"Morning, Doctor," she answered formally. "I brought Nichole a tray, but she's sound asleep. I guess she hasn't recovered from the loss of sleep while taking care of Dancing."

Adam yawned. "I think I'll try to catch a few hours of shut-eye myself. I spent the night in my office chair after I fell asleep reading." He stepped past the nun. "Will you wake me if any patients come in this morning? I don't have any scheduled, but that doesn't mean much in this town."

"If I have time, Doctor. If I have time. I have much of the Lord's work to do this morning. I'll pass the message along to Rose if I leave the house."

He didn't pry. The nun usually left with a basket of food each morning. No one questioned her or objected. Several of the farm families paid in trade and she saw that none of the food went to waste.

"Thanks," he mumbled.

"If the Lord meant us to sleep the day away, He wouldn't have the sun come up every morning." She crossed her arms, as if judging him. She reminded him of a bully who only picked on one person, and somehow he was the unfortunate one.

But Adam knew her better than to fall for her badgering by now. "Is that in the Bible, Sister?"

"Well, if it's not, it should be," she said as she moved away, already in a hurry to be about her work. "And if you read the Good Book more often, you wouldn't have to ask."

Adam stepped inside his room and chuckled as he locked the door. He stretched out on his bed and closed his eyes, thinking today had to be calmer than yesterday.

Just before he fell asleep, he felt Nichole slide in beside him and put a blanket over them both. She must have been tired, for she'd only removed her Colt and boots.

She didn't say a word, or make a move to wake him. She only curled next to him as she had twice before and placed her hand on his chest.

"Good night," he whispered without opening his eyes.

"Good morning," she answered sleepily.

She felt so right against his side, he couldn't help the long sigh that escaped his lips. Adam curled his arm about her and spread his fingers out across her back. Then, he felt it. The bindings. She wasn't just walking the night. Whatever she was up to, she'd been a Shadow.

The thought brought a chill no blanket could warm.

EIGHTEEN

A FEW HOURS LATER, ADAM SLIPPED FROM NICHOLE'S SIDE AND BE-
gan his day. Two men, badly beaten, were brought in by the deputy.
Russell claimed they got in a fight when left locked in the same cell,
but Adam found it strange that the pair seemed to bear no hatred
toward one another or fear when left side by side to wait.

As he treated each, he found bruises only a fist would make on
both bodies, but neither man bore any marks on his hands. They were
silent about the fight and no one could remember how it started.

By midafternoon the sky seemed to boil with clouds. Adam finally
took a break. While the nun jotted down information on his next
patient, he slipped through the back of the examining room and into
the kitchen.

"Got any coffee?" he whispered to Rose as Charles polished a
sterling silver tea set at the table. Bergette's butler had the habit of
ignoring everyone unless he needed something. His very stance told
Adam how much he hated being in such primitive surroundings. Even
the tea set he worked on was small and common compared with what
he was accustomed to. His every stroke silently spoke of his distaste.

"I keep it on the back of the stove warming for you, Doc." Rose
smiled proudly. "Whenever you want it just yell. There ain't no need
of you having to leave work. I'll bring it to you."

"You don't have to wait on me, Rose. I work here just like you."
He pointed with his head. "And Charles."

"No, sir," Rose objected. "Not like the rest of us. You've got the
gift as my ma used to say. You got healing hands. And that's some-
thin' rare." She glared at Charles. "We all ought to respect that."

Adam poured his coffee. "They used to say my dad had a gift

with horses. But my talent comes from books I read. I had a professor in medical school who used to say, 'Be kind, help as much with the suffering as you can, and try not to bury too many who come to you.' I do no magic, just the best I can to help.''

"Say whatever you like, but I know the truth.'' Rose raised her head with pride. "I was in the general store this morning picking up a few things, and I heard one of the women say you are ten times the doctor Doc Tillie was. 'Course he still used his barber chair to do most of his surgery.

"I told them I was your new cook and they all treated me like I was somebody special. So don't go telling me you ain't got a gift. You would have saved Dancing too if Mole hadn't come over and rekilled her.''

Adam laughed. "All right, I'll keep it as our secret if you'll set another cup of coffee in my bedroom in a few minutes. I usually drink two cups.''

Rose cut her gaze to Charles for she knew who the doctor planned to give the other coffee to. "I'll do that. And I'll remember you like one there with a few cookies on the saucer.''

He left the kitchen and by the time he reached his bedroom door, Rose was behind him with the other cup. "Thanks,'' he whispered as he took the cup from her and moved inside his room.

Rose winked. "Anytime.''

Nichole still lay sleeping in his bed. She looked so soft and sweet curled up in a quilt with her hair half covering her eyes. He remembered how passionately he'd kissed her in the shadows before Wes arrived. Adam never thought he'd feel that for any woman. Passion just wasn't a feeling he saw himself losing control over. Or any other feeling for that matter.

But she brought a side of him to the surface he didn't know existed. She made him want to forget everything else in the world and just hold her. When he did, he felt powerful and lost all at the same time.

"Nick,'' he whispered as he sat the cups down. "Nick, wake up.'' He couldn't resist touching her hair. Curls circled around his fingers in welcome. Midnight curls just as she was somehow his midnight woman.

Beautiful green eyes opened, then closed again. "Go away,'' she mumbled, and turned to her side. "I just got to sleep.''

"No, you didn't.'' He pulled her back to face him. "You've been sleeping all day, which makes me wonder what you're doing besides sleeping at night.''

"Nothing," she answered as she lifted her head following the smell of coffee.

Adam handed her the cup with the cookies on the saucer. "We've got to talk, Nick, but I only have a minute now. I've two more patients to see, then I'll saddle a couple of horses. Do you think you can be dressed and ready to ride out to Wes's herd by dark?"

"Sure." She took a sip and smiled as the coffee warmed her. "I'd love to go for a long ride."

"On the way out, we'll have a *long* discussion as to where you were last night before you climbed in my window. And just out of curiosity, I'd like to know where these black clothes came from. They seemed to have just appeared like you did last night."

The memory of how they'd kissed in his office filled his thoughts once more, but he pushed it away. "Lock the door when I leave."

He stepped away from her. "And stay out of sight until I bring the horses around to the side of the house."

Nichole looked at him as if he'd just told her to remember to breathe.

As his hand touched the knob, he added, "And sleep in your own bed." If someone had walked in early this morning, they'd never believe she'd just lie beside him to cuddle. He knew his words were harsh, but he had to protect her even against himself. He'd lost control so easily, he no longer trusted his own actions. If Wes hadn't shown up, Adam wasn't sure what might have happened.

All day his mind had drifted to the possibilities and none of them were what he should be doing with Wolf's little sister who'd been put in his care. *In his care.* Adam almost laughed aloud at the words. She was no more in his care than she was in control. The problem was that her lack of control seemed to be spreading to him.

"Any other orders?" Her words were cold.

"No." He opened the door and stepped into the hallway. A moment later, he heard the lock snap. Good, he thought, at least she'd followed one order.

"You pestering that child?" Sister Cel whispered from a few steps up the stairs. She was leaning over the railing looking down at him as though he were a boy. "Because if you are, sir, you'll answer to me. She's not like other women. She knows no fear and leads with her heart. A rare combination."

"I wasn't pestering her," he defended. "She's the one driving me crazy. And as for the 'like other women,' I've yet to find two alike enough to be able to mold a standard of comparison."

The nun relaxed slightly. "Well, if she's bothering you, that's another matter. That, sir, is none of my concern. I came to tell you the patients are ready.''

Adam followed the nun down the hall, wondering why Nick bothering him was no crime, when him pestering her seemed to be a capital offense. Most of the time he felt like Sister Cel extended all her charity to others and never allowed him a drop. Maybe the Lord sent her here, all gift wrapped in her habit, as some punishment for a sin long forgotten. No, Adam thought. He already had Bergette. Surely there could be no added punishment?

An hour later, the sun was a golden red on the western horizon as Adam and Nichole rode out of town. Clouds fenced the northern sky, promising a cool evening. But at sunset, nature was cloaked in green.

Suddenly, this land he'd thought was so barren and gray only months ago was bright and alive. Wildflowers dotted the rolling land, and oak and cypress trees followed the river like children frozen in play as they ran alongside the water. This location had been a wise place to station a fort with plenty of water and high ground. Adam felt like he could see miles in all directions.

Nichole kicked her horse into a faster gait and laughed. ''I'm glad to get away from the smell of people.''

''I wasn't aware I smelled,'' Adam said as he caught up with her.

''Not you, the entire town. Anywhere folks collect there's the same smell that follows them. Cookstoves and lye wash and bodies and blood and breathing through tobacco-tinged air. Sometimes I think of civilization as one huge deformed, splintered creature that settles in a place just long enough to smell it up. At night, when I pass by each home, I can tell if the laundry was done that day, or if they killed a chicken for supper, or if there's sickness, just by the smell.''

''You're right,'' Adam agreed though he'd never thought of it before. ''I remember during the war, I could find the hospital tent or the mess tent just by the smell. Some mornings before dawn, I would swear that I didn't open my eyes until I was putting on my white coat at work.''

For the first time since they'd met, they talked, just talked. Each told of where they had been and what they'd done. Adam was surprised how many times during the war their paths had almost crossed. He wondered if he might have gone into some town for supplies and not noticed her passing him. Or if she'd walked silently past his tent at night when crossing the line.

Adam wondered where the time had gone when they reached the herd almost an hour later. He'd meant to question her about where she'd been the night before, but somehow they'd started talking. And they talked of everything, not just subjects she might be interested in. Except for May, he could never remember talking with a woman so.

Wes waved them into the camp with a wide smile, but Adam didn't miss the guards posted around the herd. Double the men that would be needed to watch sleeping cattle. He slowly looked around, searching the land beyond the herd for trouble as he neared Wes.

"I know," Nick whispered. "I feel it, too."

He glanced at her, realizing she'd read his thoughts, but the night hid her face. As their horses walked toward Wes, he heard the leather of Nick's gun belt sliding into place about her waist.

"I was about to tell the cook to throw out the stew!" Wes shouted as he stepped forward and held their mounts. "You city folks may dine late, but on the trail we eat at sundown."

Adam stepped around his horse to Nichole's left side as she swung from the saddle. Her long, limber body needed no assistance, but he let his hand slide along her side as she stepped to the ground.

"Stew sounds great," Adam said as he touched Nichole a moment longer than needed even in his pretense of steadying her. "Sorry we're late. Seems every wife in Fort Worth is pregnant these days. Lucky all the menfolk didn't make it back home on the same day or I'd have a landslide nine months to the day after the war."

Adam kept his voice casual as his hands circled Nichole's waist in a gesture that told her he wanted her closer to him.

Wes was busy tying the horses and didn't hear Nichole whisper, "You're in my world now, Doc. The night."

Her words haunted him through the meal, for he knew she was right. He'd never liked the night, not even when he was a child. But she was a creature of the darkness, more comfortable there than in day. Another reason they didn't fit together, he thought. Another reason to stay a proper distance away.

But what bothered him was that in the darkness, she seemed to set the rules, not him. He might tell her in the light to sleep in her own bed, but he knew if she came to him in the shadows, he wouldn't push her away.

"I figure I'll lose ten percent of the herd along the trail, maybe more." Wes pulled Adam back to the present. "But for every cow that gets to rail, I'll make five times what I paid per head." Wes sounded excited. "Some of these cattle I didn't pay a dime for, but found on the open range.

"I've hired the best cow men I can find and an extra dozen to ride along as protection. I've heard tell that some herds make it as far as Kansas just to be lost to bandits.''

Nichole looked at the herd. ''Not much to lose. Longhorns, the ugliest cattle I've ever seen.''

''Kid, don't talk about my fortune that way,'' Wes complained. ''These are the kings of cattle. They can survive any weather, and they've been roaming wild since Coronado dropped them off in Texas some three hundred years ago. I heard a man down South call them rainbow cattle because they come in so many different colors.''

Nichole studied the herd. In truth she saw black, white, blue, bays, reds, and some spotted with every combination of color. Many had horns spreading four to five feet.

Following her gaze, Wes added, ''We found several mature long-horns with the horns twisted down. Some of them had about starved to death trying to graze on winter grass. It wasn't an easy job, but we caught them and cut the horns down so they could reach the short grass, then turned them loose to graze and fatten for another year.''

Wes continued to tell his brother of his plans while Nichole stood and returned her plate to the wagon. She'd been one of a group for so long it never occurred to her to leave her plate for someone else to wash.

''Thanks.'' A cowhand with a towel for an apron startled her. ''That's one plate I won't have to wash tonight.'' A light flavoring of an Irish accent blended in his words.

Nichole looked at the stack of dirty plates next to the tub of soapy water. ''Want some help?'' Without waiting for an answer, she lifted half the stack and lowered them into the wash.

''Sure. Most the men around here are nothing but coffee coolers.''

'' 'Coffee coolers?' ''

The cook chuckled. ''Ye know, men who stand around all day waiting for their cup to cool enough to drink before they go back to work.''

The cook winked at Nichole and smiled with his few remaining teeth showing. ''Me name is Lloyd, miss.''

She looked at the short, graying man carefully. ''I guess I didn't do a very good job of acting like a man tonight.'' In truth it was hard to remember all the rules with Adam around treating her like a woman.

''From a distance, I thought there was two men riding in, ye being so tall and all. But when I saw the way the boss and his brother stared at ye and how they both waited until ye sat down, I knew ye were a woman. I got four daughters meself.'' He pulled a tintype from his shirt pocket showing a chubby little woman with four chubby daughters around her. "A lady's a lady no matter how she's dressed. But ye're smart to travel like ye're dressed in this country. I told my Gina Kay not to come out here until I tame the place down a bit."

Nichole handed him a plate to dry. "You expecting any trouble?" She fought to keep her voice calm, conversational.

"We've heard talk. Boss hired three more men yesterday. There's lots of men wandering these days, and they don't feel any guilt taking another man's land or property. It's like the whole country's got fighting in their blood and can't wiggle it out."

The cook looked sideways at her to make sure he hadn't lost his audience before continuing. "Mr. McLain's partner, Vincent, said there's a gang of outlaws operating near Fort Worth, so we're taking our time and being real careful."

"So Wes takes extra precautions?" She kept her eyes focused on the dishes so he wouldn't think her interest too great.

"Ye bet yer spurs he does. Between the guards and the hands there's a circle around this camp no man could get through. One thing about McLain's partner, he may be young but he's an honest man and everyone in the state knows it."

Nichole looked around her. In truth the camp was very well protected. Each guard could see the post of the next so if one man on the outside circle was taken out at least two of the others would know it. Without an opening of at least three men, no one could enter.

She handed Lloyd the last plate and picked up the pan of dishwater. "I'll toss this," she said as she walked toward the horses and away from the stream.

As she poured the water onto rocky ground, she glanced at the row of horses tethered for the night. A paint caught her attention. A paint marked exactly like the one she'd seen at the stagecoach fire.

NINETEEN

"Where's Adam?" Nichole tried to keep her voice calm as she approached the cook fire where Wes stood talking with Lloyd. "I have to see him."

Wes pointed to a place beneath the trees where several bedrolls were spread. On a warm night like this, there was no need for the men to sleep by the fire. A single lantern blinked like a firefly amid the trees. "He's checking on one of my men who has an infected cut on his leg."

Giving his full attention to Nick, Wes studied her as he continued. "Franky claims it's nothing, but I'd rather Adam took a look at it since he's already out here. He'll be right back." Wes moved closer and motioned with his head for Lloyd to finish banking the fire. "What's wrong, Nick?"

"Nothing," she lied, instinctively gliding her fingers over her gun belt. "I just need to talk to Adam."

"Don't try and fool me, kid. Something's bothering you." Wes rolled a cigarette and knelt to touch a stick to the fire.

Nichole didn't want to alarm Wes without reason, but he had a right to know. "Adam told you how I was on the stage that got attacked?"

"He told me and I wasn't at all surprised you survived." He brought the tip of the burning stick to his cigarette, then stepped away from the fire with her at his side. "Nick, I know you're a beautiful woman. Adam can't seem to keep his eyes off you, but I never forget you were a Shadow. To have stayed alive, you must have senses most people don't. During the war, if you went through half what those men did—"

"I went through all that the men did," she countered. "And while I'm correcting you, Adam doesn't care about me in the way you think. He looks at me as only someone he should protect until Wolf comes. I'm only part of a promise he made to my brother."

"Like hell he does," Wes mumbled. "But before we argue that, tell me what you see in the darkness that I've missed. You walked over to the horses to toss the water, but you returned with the movements of a seasoned fighter on enemy ground."

Nick explained about how she'd hid near the stage and saw men watering horses after they'd robbed the stage. "One of the raiders rode a paint marked just like the one over there," she ended, pointing toward the horses.

"There are lots of paints," Wes added.

"Does the rider have a belt with silver conchos on it?"

"Maybe." Wes nodded. "But most of the good herders come from Mexico and several of them wear the belts."

She grew frustrated with his denial. "Your circle of guards will do no good if the enemy infiltrates the ring. They can kill your men one at a time if they are already among them."

"Without anyone hearing?" Wes shook his head.

Nick moved her finger across her throat. "Somehow they were able to slit the throats of both the men driving the stage without me hearing a word."

"But how—"

"The stage line reported one male passenger. I remember him as young, about average size. He could have gotten as close as your men would let the bandits, since they're working for you. They'd each die before they could make a sound."

The grim facts finally settled over Wes's face. "The men are already on post for the night. What do you suggest?"

"They won't make their move until the camp's settled down. It's to their advantage to have as many men sleeping as possible. When are you moving out?"

"A few days, maybe a week. I pulled in early. My partner, Vincent, is picking up a few hundred head southeast of here. He's due in by the end of the week."

Nick shook her head. "Then my guess is they'll attack tonight or tomorrow night. These men don't want to put in too many days of honest work, and once you're on the trail there could be other complications.

"Once your partner is here, that's more men to worry about, so they have to strike before he arrives. Here they know exactly where their backup is. The way this land rolls, raiders could be waiting unseen within a mile or two to help with the stolen herd. By dawn you and your men could be dead, and they'd have the herd moved out before your partner arrived. No one would be the wiser. We'd just never hear from you again, and we'd have no idea if you were killed in Texas or Kansas.''

"I see your point about tonight or tomorrow," Wes answered. "And I let ten of the men who've been with me for a month go into town for the night. That's ten men I can trust that are gone." He tossed his smoke into the fire. "The latest to be hired are the ones with me tonight."

"And, I'm guessing, three you can't trust are here with you," she hesitated, "maybe more."

"Maybe," Wes said. "But most of the others have been with me for a while." He walked a few steps toward the sleeping men.

Nick followed, allowing him time to think things out for himself.

"If they've got any sense, they'll go after me first," he mumbled. "Take out the leader if you can get to him. Then the men would have no one to follow. A few of my hands might try to fight, but most will run if given the chance. They hired on for a cattle drive, not a war."

Wes paused. "I'm trapped in the darkness with no law close by or backup in sight. I'm not even sure who's on my side."

"You've got one ace in the hole." Nick patted him on the shoulder.

"I do?" he asked.

"Sure," she answered. "Me."

Wes stood beside her and watched Adam walking toward them. "I don't want Adam here. This could get ugly, and it's not his fight. I used to worry during the war that if he were ever forced to fight, he'd hesitate a moment, deciding what was right. And that moment would get him killed."

"If it's your fight, it's his. He's your brother," she answered. "But I know what you mean. Men like him weren't born to listen for danger and smell trouble on the wind. He's worth too much to this world to die with a bullet in his back."

Wes pushed her gently with his shoulder. "And I *am* worth so little?" he teased.

"Definitely, and a waste of lead at that," she answered, and nudged him back with double the force he'd used.

Wes laughed. "Better watch it, kid, or I'll take you down a notch off that high horse you're riding on."

Nick shoved again. "You and what cavalry, old man?"

Both laughed, releasing tension the way soldiers do waiting for the dawn of battle.

Adam watched them as he walked toward the campfire. The realization of how well they fit together struck him like a blow. He'd never seen Wes laugh like he did around Nichole, and even in the firelight shadows he could tell they were teasing one another about something. They were alike in so many ways. A matched set.

This could be the answer, Adam thought. If they married, Wes would settle down and finally lose the coat of hardness he'd molded during the war. And Nichole would have a man who understood her. She loved the free life, the wild life, and she'd have that with Wes in Texas. His big brother needed a wife who could keep up with him, who didn't mind the hardness of the land or the wildness of the country. They were perfect for one another.

Adam took a deep breath. If they were so right for each other, why did he feel like he'd had rocks for supper?

"How's Franky?" Wes asked when Adam was within ten feet.

"He needs the cut cleaned properly and stitched," Adam answered. "Otherwise there could be a bad infection."

"I hate to leave him behind," Wes grumbled. "He's so excited about going. Plans to use his wages to start a farm down by Austin. Got a girl waiting for him. If he doesn't make the trip, it'll be another year before he can start his dream."

Adam sat the lantern down. "If we unloaded the supply wagon, I could drive him into my office and fix him up right, then bring him back by dawn. It might mean a few days riding in the wagon for him, but by a week the leg should be fine. If left as it is, it'll take weeks to heal, and the chance of infection is great."

"Sounds like a good plan, Adam. Take him in and do what you can." Wes glanced at Nick. "Want to stay here, kid, and watch cattle all night?"

To Adam's surprise, she nodded.

Within minutes, the wagon had been unloaded and the cowhand placed on blankets in the back. Adam checked the reins as Wes talked to Franky, assuring the boy that the doctor would bring him back in time.

Nichole moved behind Adam without saying a word. She was so close he could feel the warmth of her body. She had no idea of the effect she had on him, Adam decided. Just standing close made him fight the urge to reach for her.

"I wish you were going back with me," he grumbled as though not wanting to say the words, but having to.

"I'll be safe here," she said. "At least you'll know where I am tonight, and I won't be bothering you by sleeping in your bed."

He wanted to tell her that she didn't bother him. This morning had been heaven with her curled into his side and he'd been a fool for suggesting she return to her own bed. But now wasn't the place or the time. And if she spent the night talking with Wes, there might never be a time or place for him.

Adam closed his eyes and remembered the feel of her against him. He wouldn't stand between Wes and Nichole if it was meant to be, no matter how much he might ache inside.

He pulled himself onto the wagon seat. "Take care," he whispered to Nichole, wishing he could kiss her good-bye. The night, with her here and him back in town, would seem endless.

"Take care." Nichole's fingers brushed his knee. "I'll see you at dawn."

She watched Adam drive the wagon toward town, knowing she might never see him again. He was the one man she'd kissed, or ever wanted to. The only time she slept soundly was in his arms. This man who hated war and violence had somehow crept into her heart. He didn't want her, he'd proved that this morning when he reminded her to stay in her own bed, but that didn't stop her from wanting him.

She couldn't be the kind of woman he needed, but maybe she could save Adam's brother tonight. That would be one thing she could do for him. Wes was just the kind of honorable, straightforward fool who'd get himself killed by outlaws. He was what the Shadows used to refer to as a "predictable." They knew by the way he'd been trained how he'd react.

"Well, he was easier to get rid of than I thought," Wes interrupted her silence as he moved up behind her and they both watched Adam driving the wagon into the darkness. "Give him someone to doctor and he's on his way. He didn't seem all that upset that you were staying, kid."

Nick wasn't listening as she turned and watched the guards changing shifts. She didn't want to think about how easily Adam had left. She now had a job to do. "How often do the guards rotate?"

"Every two hours a third of the men change. That way each man gets at least four hours sleep at a time. This is the ten o'clock switch."

"It won't be this shift," Nichole studied the camp layout. "The moon's still too high, and a few men haven't settled down for the night. My guess is it'll be midnight or two before something happens. Four would be too close to dawn and they'd have to deal with the chance the men might ride in from town.''

"What do we do in the meantime?" Wes adjusted his gun belt.

"We walk the perimeter, casual like, talking. But keep your eyes out for which guards seem to be watching us more closely than the others. If we spot him, that's the point man. The one assigned to start, probably by taking you out of the fight first. He'll be working this shift or the next, so that he can be in camp close to you when the fighting starts.''

Wes took a deep breath and straightened. "Sounds like a good plan. All we have to do is walk, watch, and wait for someone to make a move to kill me.''

Nichole forced her body to relax. She leaned down and picked up a handful of rocks, then casually tried to toss them into the stream.

Wes watched her. "Talk," he said as if giving himself an order. "I feel better knowing Adam's safe.''

Nick reached down for another handful of rocks. "He'll be madder than hell if he finds out we let him go back to town when we thought there was going to be trouble. He's a worse mother hen than Wolf.''

"I'll never tell him we suspected anything," Wes promised. "It will be our secret, just like your loving him.''

"I don't love him!" Nick snapped, and dusted the dirt from her hands. "Love's a weakness for fools. Something no one needs.''

"I agree." Wes fell back into step with her. "But that doesn't stop us all from playing the fool now and again. I fell in love once just before the war, when Adam was still in medical school.'' He rubbed his scar with the tip of his thumb. "I got this in the first battle. Months later, when I made it back home, there was a big party for my return and Adam's graduation. After one dance, the young lady I'd given my heart to told me she couldn't live every day of her life staring at this scar.'' He took a deep breath. "By the last waltz, she was engaged to Adam.''

"Bergette!" Nick let the word rush out before she could stop it. "You were in love with her? Does Adam know?''

Wes shook his head. "I figured he'd see for himself what kind of woman she was after he was around her a while, and he did.''

"Would you have stopped him if the wedding had been set?"

Wes wrapped his arm around her shoulder as they passed through low branches. "Not stopped him, but helped him see the light. When you and Wolf showed up that first night we were home, I saw my opportunity. You see, Bergette's a schemer who always gets her way. I had no idea what you wanted of my brother, but I figured you'd help him see Bergette for what she was.''

Nick laughed. "I guess we did ruin Bergette's plans. We were the uninvited guests.''

"When I got to the house, the minute I saw the way Adam looked at you, I knew my worries were over. Bergette would never sleep in our family plot. She can tell everyone they're still engaged, but that doesn't make it so.''

"He may have broken off with her. They don't seem too friendly. But it doesn't mean he loves me.'' She wished she could believe Wes's words. "Adam made it clear this morning and other mornings that there could be nothing between us. He's only paying back a debt by taking me in.''

"And what about at night, kid? How does he act when you're both in the shadows?''

Nick watched the outline of the riders on guard, not wanting Wes to see her tears. "Sometimes,'' she whispered, "he holds me tight, like he never wants to let go. And when he kisses me, I can feel the heat all through my body.''

"He's got it worse than I thought,'' Wes admitted with a laugh. "I know my brother. He'll fight his feelings with logic and rules, but he'll lose this time.''

"But I'm not the kind of woman he needs. I'm not pretty with hair piled on my head and a dress that floats around me. I don't even own a dress. Compared to Bergette, I must look like a toad.''

"Never. He sees what I see,'' Wes assured her. "Dressed any way, even bald, you're one hell of a woman. A man would be proud to have you at his side in war, or peace.''

"Well, I'm here with you tonight.'' Nick lowered her voice. "And I just spotted our man.''

Wes slowly turned his head, looking at the three men on horseback that he could see. Their faces were in darkness and they weren't close enough to recognize, but after a few minutes, he felt it more than saw it. One was watching him.

"What next?'' he asked.

"Simple.'' Nick turned back toward the camp. "You go to sleep and wait.''

"I can't go to sleep. What do you think I am, crazy?''

"No.'' She laughed. "You're not crazy. You're bait.''

"Oh.'' Wes shrugged. "That's comforting.''

TWENTY

Wes unstrapped his gun belt as they walked toward camp. "You've been a marvel at guessing what will happen tonight, kid, but I've got something to add."

Nichole waited as he strutted with pride at having thought of something she hadn't.

"We've no use for our guns. These men know as well as I do that one shot could send the herd into stampede. They want the beef, but not bad enough to chase them two hundred miles to claim them."

"So every man must be killed silently?" Nick followed his thoughts. "Not an easy job."

Wes nodded. "And another thing, once the snakes show themselves, we don't kill them."

"We don't?"

"No, we take them alive. Otherwise, we might kill two or three but the gang waiting out there somewhere would get away. Our only hope of catching the whole kit and caboodle of raiders is to take the ones in our midst alive and hope they'll talk once they're behind bars. These men may be the very gang that's been pestering travelers around Fort Worth for months."

Nick started to unbuckle her gun belt, hesitated, then stopped. "I won't shoot, but I'd feel undressed without my Colt. Besides, if a stampede happens, and I'm caught in the middle, I plan to take a few of them ugly longhorns down before they trample me."

She slipped her knife from her boot, showing Wes she was armed with more than the gun. "I have little faith in the deputy in town getting anyone to talk."

Wes tossed her a bedroll from a shoulder-high pile made when they unloaded the supply wagon. "Well, if you won't undress, kid, we might as well go to bed."

They moved over by the trees where several men, finished with a shift, were bedding down. Without a word, she spread her blanket between Wes and the trees. He watched her as best he could in the darkness. She seemed to be settling down, but he noticed a tree branch very close to her feet. Within minutes, her bedroll still looked as though she were sleeping soundly. But Wes knew she wasn't beneath the hat and blankets. He hadn't seen her move in the shadows, but the branch had disappeared. Nick was in the wooded area behind him. He didn't need to see her. He knew she was there.

Leaning back, Wes tried to relax, knowing that Nick was on guard. She was good, he thought, maybe the best he'd ever seen. He admired her talent, but didn't want to think about all that she'd gone through to polish her skills.

The moon passed behind the clouds as midnight approached. The low sounds of the cattle rumbled in the air as the men traded shifts once more. One by one the guards came in, walked among the bedrolls until they found their replacement, and shook him awake. The cook checked the coffeepot from time to time. As the night aged, so did the coffee, filling the air with a rich aroma.

When all the men had settled back to sleep, Nick moved to the tree closest to Wes. She guessed he was still awake, but he was doing a good job of staying still. From this point on, he wouldn't be out of her sight.

She eased down the trunk of an old cottonwood, blending into the gaps where bark became root. Without a sound, her outline became a part of the roots spreading out on the ground. Wes would be safe with her on guard.

Half an hour passed. Nick studied the camp. All were asleep. A lone man moved among the horses, then slowly ventured toward the bedrolls. Something about his movements made her come alert. As he neared Wes, she slipped her knife from her boot.

"Boss," the lone cowhand whispered as he knelt beside Wes. "Boss, I need you to take a look at my mount. I'm afraid he may have gone lame."

One sleeping cowhand rolled away from the conversation. No one else stirred.

Wes rose slowly and grumbled.

Nick was within jumping distance of touching the man. But she had to wait for him to make the first move. He could be just what he pretended, a rider with a lame mount.

The cowhand led the way toward the horses tied on the other side of a dying campfire. "Mine's tied near the other end," he said as he seemed to hurry Wes toward his horse.

"Couldn't this wait till morning?" Wes complained.

"I figured we'd be too busy come daylight." The cowhand pointed toward his horse. "This is him."

Wes patted the animal on the rump so he wouldn't startle the horse as he knelt. Nick watched as Wes ran his hand down the hind leg of the paint.

As Wes tightened his grip and lifted the horses hoof, Nick saw a blade slip from the center back of the cowhand's belt and rise high in the air.

In a heartbeat, she closed the distance. Before he had time to lower his knife toward Wes, hers pressed across his throat hard enough to draw a blood line.

"Move," she whispered, "and air no longer reaches your lungs."

Turning, Wes stood slowly. With the light of the distant fire, he could see the man's eyes were wild with anger and fear. His knife was still held high, flickering in the light like a fractured moonbeam. Another moment and he would have sunk the weapon into Wes.

Wes took the knife from the man's grip, then pulled a leather strap from his back pocket and bound the outlaw's hands. He used the man's own bandanna as a gag.

Silently, Nick and Wes worked together until the man was safely deposited in the trees.

As they moved away from him, Wes grabbed her by the shoulder and kissed her on the cheek. "Thanks, kid, for saving my life. I'd about convinced myself that you were wrong about the raid. I was half-asleep when I looked at that horse."

Nick rubbed her cheek with the back of her hand. "You're not supposed to kiss a Shadow. Show a little respect."

Wes laughed. "Respect isn't enough of a word for you, lady. I owe you my life."

"I'm sure you'll pay me back in time. Right now, we may have two more men to catch. If the others think you're out of the way, they may already be working. We've got to find them before one has time to call in backup."

"But couldn't he have acted alone? Maybe he was going to kill me, then signal the others to move in," Wes whispered as they reached the edge of the trees. "There's no reason to believe there were three."

Without answering, she lowered her body into the shadow of the supplies piled in one place.

Wes stayed close beside her, frustrated that she wouldn't talk to him.

A man stood on a small rise, watching away from the cattle. The silver disks on his belt reflected the firelight. Every few minutes he glanced toward the horses as if waiting for a signal.

Nick pulled a few rocks from her pocket and began tossing them in the water ten feet from the watcher. After a few plops, he moved down off the rise and walked cautiously over to the stream.

They were on him with little more than the sound of air rushing from his body. Nick shoved him to the ground and Wes tied him. Within five minutes, he sat beside his friend in the total blackness of the trees.

"Now what?" Wes asked as Nick circled along the tree line.

"I don't know. I figured there would be an assassin, and a lookout, but your guess is as good as mine where the third man might be."

"If there is a third man," Wes added as he followed her along the tree line toward the campfire.

Nick froze in place with her head high in the air. Listening. Smelling.

Wes took another step, then tried to stop. But he was too slow. He stumbled over something, almost falling face forward.

Nick knelt as he regained his balance and then joined her.

"What is it?" he whispered.

"Blood." Her word floated on the air as her hands moved slowly into the undergrowth without making a single leaf rustle. "I smell blood."

Wes extended his fingers in the direction of what had tripped him. His hand brushed over Nick's as hers rested on something warm.

His fingers spread wider, covering hers and more. The feel of material. The warmth of a body. The wet stickiness of blood.

She slowly raised a towel that had been tucked around the body's waist like an apron.

Suddenly Wes was pulling the injured man into the light.

"Wait," Nick warned, knowing that all he cared about was that a man of his was down. "Don't go into the light!"

Wes wasn't listening. Carrying the body, Wes ran toward the campfire.

She hung back in the shadows as she watched Wes pull the man close to the light.

"Lloyd," he said as he shook the lifeless body. "Lloyd!" Wes's voice was hard as though he could order the cook to breathe once more.

Nick fought all her training not to step into view. Wes needed her comfort as he tried to awaken his friend from a sleep that would never end. But she was a Shadow. She knew both their lives might depend on her ability to keep her head.

She watched as Wes pulled the shirt away from Lloyd's chest and listened for a heartbeat. When he turned the body to the light, Nick saw the two deep cuts on either side of the Irishman's throat. A savage way to kill someone, sliding a sharp blade into one side and out the other in a second before the victim could move. Either side might kill a man, but both cuts would bleed him dry in a matter of heartbeats while it sliced through his voice box so that the victim couldn't even whisper a death cry.

Wes slowly closed Lloyd's eyes and lowered him to the ground. "There's one more," he whispered to himself as he raised his bloody hands toward heaven. "One we haven't found."

A stocky man stepped around the boxes and growled like an animal protecting his fresh kill. Wes had only time to glance in his direction before the man flew at him.

For several seconds they rolled, slugging, fighting wildly.

Nick drew her gun. She couldn't help Wes, but if he lost, she cared nothing for stampeding the herd. If the stranger proved the victor, he'd feel her bullet as he stood.

The men rolled near the fire, kicking and swinging wildly. Several men in bedrolls were awakened and drew near. But like Nick, they didn't know how to stop the fight.

Finally, Wes rolled on top and pinned the man down. "Get some rope!" he yelled at one of the men. "We're taking Lloyd's killer into town to the law."

All at once the camp was alive with movement and voices. Several men looked at Lloyd's body, then suggested justice be carried out "trail-court" style. A few men helped Wes tie and gag the third outlaw.

After watching awhile to make sure it was safe, Nick stepped from the shadows of the trees and listened to the men talk. She blended in among them as easily as she'd blended with the trees . . . a part of the whole, yet unto herself.

When Wes calmed down, he told his men what had happened. No one thought of sleep as they sat around the fire discussing what had taken place and all that might happen farther on down the trail. A few thought it a bad omen that even before the long drive started there should be a killing. Others suggested it might help keep every-one on their toes. Each took a turn saying how grand old Lloyd was and how sad it would be for his family.

Every two hours men came in off guard and the stories were re-visited.

Nichole listened to campfire stories, feeling at home with the men as she had during the war. No one said much to her, a few slaps on the back, a few nods of approval. The group hadn't yet bonded to one another and she seemed no more a stranger than most.

When dawn washed over the land, Wes told everyone to settle in. They'd be camped here for a time while he took the men into town and waited for the rest of the herd. A few decided to make breakfast while several returned to their bedrolls until the next shift change.

Following Wes to the stream, Nichole watched as he tried to wash off Lloyd's blood.

"I'm sorry," she whispered when he looked up at her. "I wish we could have found the third man before he got to Lloyd. I should have guessed. A cook moves around too much checking the fire. He would be a man the outlaws would have wanted out of the way."

"Listen, kid, if it hadn't been for you, we'd all look like Lloyd this morning. They might have moved around in the night and killed us one by one. I owe you a great deal, Nick."

"I'm glad I could help." She sat down beside him as he leaned back against a tree. "I'm glad my skill could be of some use."

He opened his arm in a friendly gesture and she leaned against it, letting all the tension of the night pass away with the sound of the stream dancing over pebbles and the sun warming her face. It felt good to be with Wes. He was the kind of friend who she knew she could always count on. The kind who would save her from any sit-uation or anyone, even herself.

Wes closed his eyes and relaxed at her side. Within moments, they were both sound asleep.

Neither heard the wagon approaching from the direction of town.

TWENTY-ONE

Adam helped the men unload the wounded cowhand named Franky from the back of the wagon as he looked around for Wes and Nick. Stitched properly, Franky's leg would heal nicely, leaving only a thin scar to remind him of his days on the trail.

Several men told Adam what had happened during the night and how Nick had saved the camp. A few of the men confessed they'd been shy in thanking a woman, but that didn't stop them from praising her to Adam. By the time he finished reloading the wagon, some were bragging about her as though they were the proud papa of such an outstanding woman.

A rider had already left to fetch the deputy so he could take the raiders off their hands. Everyone felt sure that the cattle thieves would confess who rode with them after a few days in jail.

Lloyd's body was wrapped in a blanket his wife had quilted and would be buried as soon as the deputy had a look at him. Several of the men thought it would be a good idea to use the extra horses as packhorses so that Franky would have more room to ride in the wagon till his leg healed.

When Adam had heard the stories more than once, he asked about Wes. Someone pointed to the trees and commented that they thought the boss went to wash up an hour or so ago.

Adam moved slowly toward the creek. He felt relief that Wes and Nichole were all right, and a nagging anger that they might have known something was amiss before they sent him off last night. What was he, some child to be pushed from harm's way? Did his brother think him so weak or helpless he didn't want him around during any battle? Did Nichole think him a coward?

The two were alike . . . born to fight. Surely they understood his fights were elsewhere. Logic told him they both understood him, but Adam couldn't help feeling a little left out.

As he turned into the trees, the sight that greeted him shattered any remaining calmness. Wes leaned against a tree trunk, his cheek resting on the top of Nichole's head. Adam saw her curled against Wes's side as easily as she'd curled against his own. Both of them were sound asleep.

Fury and hurt blended with the relief that they were both safe.

"This is what you wanted!" He voiced the words in his mind, slamming them against his brain. But no matter how many times he repeated them, he couldn't stop the pain of seeing Wes and Nichole together.

Adam watched as though made of stone as Wes's fingers touched her hair. The hair Adam loved to touch. She stretched against his brother as she awoke. Adam felt his blood stop moving.

This is right, Adam told himself, but if it was right, how come he felt so wrong inside? He'd thought Wes and Nichole were well matched, would be good for one another . . . but he'd never thought of Wes touching her hair, or of her resting her head against Wes's heart and not his own. He'd never thought of them sleeping side by side.

"We'd better get back, kid," Wes mumbled as he squeezed her shoulder.

Nichole rubbed her eyes with her fists like a child and leaned forward, stretching her body awake.

Wes looked up and met Adam's gaze.

Adam couldn't speak. He couldn't move, and he knew he wasn't hiding any of the anger he felt inside. Wes could always read him. If Wes read him now, he'd better walk softly.

But Wes took Nichole's hand and helped her to her feet, keeping her back to Adam. He bent close to her and whispered something, then kissed her full on the mouth. If he cared that Adam was watching, he showed no sign of it.

Adam stared as she tilted her head slightly, just as she'd done when excepting *his* kiss. Only it wasn't his kiss, it was Wes's. He stayed only long enough to see that Nichole did nothing to shove Wes away, then he turned and walked back to camp feeling like something had died inside him. Somehow in his world of logic the sun was dark at midday, the earth had stopped rotating, the air was liquid and he could no longer breathe.

Within minutes, Wes and Nichole joined him. She seemed happy and excited about all that had happened the night before. Adam didn't miss the way her smile came easy to Wes, or the way his big brother touched her lightly, comfortably, like old friends.

Adam thanked her for saving his brother's life. He knew his words were too formal. Her stare told him as much, but he couldn't help himself. He felt like someone had plowed through his heart. The logic he'd always depended on didn't work now. Why waste time telling himself that this was what he wanted to happen between them? That they were right for one another? That Wes deserved a little happiness? All the reasons in the world couldn't explain the way he felt.

What made matters worse was that Wes kept smiling at him. He was still smiling when he helped Nichole on her horse and told them he'd drop by later to let them know how it went at the sheriff's office. He even laughed about going out on the town now that Nichole had no reason to hide. When she didn't say no right away, he offered to buy her a dress, something that had never crossed Adam's mind.

Touching his hat in farewell, Adam didn't wait for Nichole before kicking his animal into a gallop. As he rode out of camp, he thought he heard Wes laugh.

It took her a half mile to catch him. Adam might claim to be no great horseman, but today he was riding as though racing a twister.

"What is it?" she yelled. "Is something wrong back in town?"

"No." Adam wouldn't look at her. He couldn't look at her and hold to his pride at the same time. "I just want to get back." He urged his horse faster.

Nichole fought to stay even. "What's wrong, Adam?" Her mind filled with all kinds of worries that might have happened. "Is Nance hurt? Sister? What's happened?"

"Nothing! Nothing's wrong!" His words were so angry they boomed like sudden cannon fire.

"Stop!" she shouted. "You'll kill our horses at this pace." The ground was too uneven for such speed. Surely Adam knew this. But he'd gone mad.

"Stop!" Nichole yelled again as Adam turned into the high buffalo grass. "This grass is full of prairie dog holes."

"No!" he yelled back without looking at her.

She couldn't endure another moment of his insanity. Without hesitating, she pulled her feet from the stirrups and jumped toward Adam, hitting him hard and full against his side.

He rolled from his saddle into the tall grass with her knocking the breath from him as she landed on top of him. Shaken, he jumped to his feet and turned on her. "You could have gotten us both killed." Finally, he was too angry to allow the beauty of her to affect him.

He faced her. "Must you always be so wild? We could both be dead with broken necks right now."

She dusted herself off, moving her head from side to side as if testing her neck. "Better killed than crazy." She shrugged. "Which is exactly what you are, Doc. I knew I might kill you by hitting you like that, but I had the horses to consider. They don't deserve to break a leg because you've gone loco."

Adam marched away from her for several feet, then turned and stormed back. "I'm not the one who's crazy. You knew there was trouble in that camp last night before I left. That's why you stayed, but you didn't bother to tell me."

"I felt something, sure. You felt it too when we rode in, remember. But you don't trust your feelings, and I do." Nichole rubbed her elbow. "I wasn't sure anything would happen, but I wanted to stay and find out. I could have been wrong and you needed to doctor Franky."

"You could have also gotten yourself killed. What if there had been four raiders?" Adam questioned. "You could be the one wrapped in that quilt back at camp."

Nichole looked up in surprise. "Is that what you're so all-fired mad about? I could have gotten killed by a few tough riders who think they're mean? I could have taken all three of those drifters on at the same time. Not one of them had a chance of getting within ten feet of me and my not knowing. Surely you weren't worried about me?"

Adam pulled off his hat and rubbed his scalp. "Yes," he started, realizing he'd insulted her pride. "No," he changed. "Oh, shut up. I don't even want to talk to you."

"Well, I don't want to talk to you either!" Nichole snapped. "I save your brother and you go crazy on me. So much for good deeds. And as for dying, I've spent most of my days with Death riding shotgun everywhere I go. Why should last night have been any different?"

"You didn't save Wes to do me any favors. I saw the two of you at the stream. I saw the way he kissed you, and you didn't look like you were fighting." Adam was so angry all the control he'd spent a lifetime accumulating vaporized. "Tell me, was he a gentleman while he held you, or was he more to your wild liking?"

She swung before he had time to block, delivering not a feminine slap, but a full-blown slug knocking Adam off his feet.

Adam, flat on his back, stared at the sun as he felt his jaw.

She moved above him. "Get up!" she shouted. "I want to hit you again."

He rose to one knee before she did what she wanted, sending him rolling across the grass with another punch.

"Stop it!" he yelled as he stood.

"No," she answered. "You want a fight, then fight like a man."

"No." He watched her closely, guessing he'd be counting his teeth in his hand if he didn't stop her. "You're not a man."

Nichole took a step toward him. "I'm not a woman to you either. What am I, Doc? I'm not woman enough for you to bed, or man enough for you to fight. You don't want me. So get out of my life." Her voice lowered slightly. "When I'm around you, I don't know who 'me' is anymore."

He turned his back, unable to look at her any longer. If she thought he was confusing her, it was nothing compared to how greatly he was disturbing himself. She was about as practical for him as indoor rain, but he still wanted her so badly he felt he'd die without her near.

She came closer but continued to shout as if he were having trouble hearing as well as thinking. "I thought I was helping you last night by saving Wes. I thought finally I'd do something right. Wes isn't just your brother, he's my friend. And so what if he kissed me? It's something you'd never do in the broad daylight."

Before she could react, he twisted around and grabbed her, pinning her arms to her sides. The quick action sent them both tumbling to the grass. They rolled for several turns, and he held her closer with each twist.

A low roar seemed to echo through him as all the calmness snapped inside him.

When they stopped rolling, he was on top of her. She struggled, knowing that she could reach her knife easily, but unsure how badly she wanted to win this battle.

"I don't care," he said the words with such anger it frightened her.

She tried to push him away. "You're mad!"

"I don't care if you already love Wes," he whispered into her hair. "I will kiss you in the light." His mouth closed down on hers with bruising force.

The kiss was wild and hungry. She tried to push away, but he held her tightly as his mouth imprisoned all cries. He pressed his body against her, letting her feel the weight of him and his need for her. His hands moved from her arms to her hair, plowing his fingers deep into her curls, knotting her hair around his fists, demanding a kiss that had always been his for the asking.

She felt the world spinning around her, but she didn't move as he continued to kiss her. Her arms were free, resting on the grass like a rag doll. She could push him away, but she didn't as he rolled slightly to his side without breaking the kiss. The warm pressure of his fingers moved along her side, feeling her body with a possessive touch.

His need for her was a storm of passion and haste. He wanted to drink her in so deeply he'd never lose the taste of her. He needed to feel her so completely that his touch would linger a lifetime on her flesh. She should feel his passion and his pain as thoroughly as he felt it.

When his hand reached her Colt, he stopped suddenly and sat up, breaking the kiss so abruptly Nichole felt as though he'd taken her breath away.

"Why don't you shoot me?" He stared away from her feeling the emptiness of the land. "Put me out of my misery. I had no right to kiss you like that, but I'll be damned if I'll say I'm sorry."

She knelt behind him and gently placed her hands on his shoulders. The muscles were iron tight with only the layers of his clothes to soften them. For the first time since she'd met him, she wasn't sure how he would react. Maybe he wasn't a "predictable" like she thought. "I don't love Wes," she whispered. "And I don't want to kill you—though you make it awfully tempting."

His head leaned back slightly, resting on the front of her shirt. "I want to make love to you," he whispered. "I can't get the feel of you out of my mind . . . or the taste of you . . . the smell of you . . . the way you move. No amount of reason seems to matter. I want to make love to you until there is no one in the world but you and me."

Nichole pulled away.

He didn't say more as she slowly walked to the horses and caught the reins.

When she moved back to him, she said, "Follow me," as though he'd asked for water. Without another word she climbed on her horse.

They rode southwest for a mile before she turned into a cluster of cottonwoods. "When I was walking, after the stage robbery, I found this place. I guessed town to be only a few more miles, but I needed to rest. So I stopped here for a while."

She tied her horse in the trees and walked down a slope to a circle of blackberry bushes.

Adam followed. He wasn't sure what she had in mind, but he had no plans of apologizing. The creek was high with spring rains. Water almost covered the huge roots of the trees as they reached down for a drink. The grass was already green, but most of the bushes were still blooming a golden red, making the stream look like it was banked by fire.

She pulled a carpetbag from one of the bushes. "I hid this here, hoping I'd get the chance to come back for it. I knew, dressed as a man, I'd cause talk if I walked into town with this carpetbag. Wolf had to pick out one with flowers on it.''

Adam watched her pat the bag as though it were an old friend she'd missed.

''Wolf bought this for me along with the dress the night I had to leave Tennessee. I cut the dress up for bandages when my hands were burned.'' She opened the bag and pulled out a brush, a comb, and a bouquet of colorful ribbons. ''The ladies I met along the way said I'd need these when my hair grew out.'' Her hands brushed over the ribbons of velvet, silk, and lace. ''In a few more months it'll be long enough to tie back with one of these.''

Adam moved around the tiny clearing guessing that she was talking more to herself than to him. She'd picked a good place to hide. They'd crossed the stage tracks half a mile back, so she knew where she was and the trees offered her plenty of shelter. Suddenly, he realized Nick didn't need him to take care of her. She could take care of herself. She always could. She'd proven it over and over. Did she have to slug him again to get him to see the truth?

He touched his jaw. She was no helpless woman, he admitted. She could have even stopped the kiss he'd given her anytime she'd wanted to. This last fact left him a little more unsettled.

''This is the only piece of my dress I have left.'' She walked past him and dipped the material in the stream. ''I thought it might help your lip.''

Adam stood frozen as she touched the cold rag to the corner of his mouth. A slight sting made him flinch, and she pulled away. Blood spotted her rag.

Touching his lip, he tasted blood for the first time. ''I hadn't noticed,'' he answered as she placed the cool cloth on his mouth once more.

''Be still,'' she ordered. ''How can I treat you if you're jerking all the time?''

Adam smiled. ''I make a poor patient.''

''That you do.'' Nichole leaned closer and lightly kissed the corner of his mouth. ''There, all better.''

''Kiss me again,'' he whispered as he widened his stance so that they were the same height.

She raised her arms to his neck and pressed against him as she repeated the light kiss on the corner of first one side and then the other side of his mouth.

''Again,'' he asked as his hands moved over her b

Her kiss was light, airy, irresistible.

"Take off your weapons, lady," he requested between kisses. "You won't be needing them for a while."

Slowly, she lowered her arms and unbuckled her gun belt. He felt her hands moving against his abdomen as she worked. Without looking, she tossed her valued Colt in the grass a few feet away. Her knife followed.

Adam smiled as he unbuckled her belt and tugged her shirt up over her head. He'd expected to see the undergarments she'd been sleeping in, but instead were the wrappings that bound her chest tightly. Bindings like she'd worn the first night they'd met.

His hand slid along the cotton until he felt the end tucked beneath her ribs. Slowly, he unwrapped her, feeling her breasts swell with each layer removed. When he pulled the cotton away, he let his hand pass over her chest, feeling more of her warmth with each layer.

When the last strap fell away, Nichole took a deep breath and Adam lowered his head to taste what he'd uncovered.

She cried out in surprise as his wet mouth closed over her warm flesh. But his hands around her waist held her steady as he drew her tender breast into his mouth. She arched back giving herself fully to his need.

Gently, he lowered her beside the water and continued to taste her. She relaxed as her surprise turned to pleasure, filling her with a warmth and a need for more.

When he finally returned to her mouth he kissed her lightly, whispering how much he enjoyed the warm taste of her breasts and how he planned to kiss far more than her lips in the sunlight of this day. As his kiss lengthened, his hands moved over her, stroking with long, possessive movements. Each time his fingers reached her pants, he shoved them lower, baring more skin to his touch.

She sighed into his mouth as he pushed the trousers below her hips and covered her bare flesh with his hands. Trying to stop the world from spinning, she closed her eyes and stretched against his touch. The earth was solid beneath her back, the sun warm on her skin and his touch was heaven.

Moving over her slowly, kissing her lightly, caressing every part of her, he convinced her of how dearly he treasured her. She knew nothing of making love, but she knew he was somehow performing a timeless ritual, preparing her for what was to come . . . preparing her body for mating.

She loved each touch as she'd loved every touch he'd given her. Slowly, she grew used to the way his hands dug into her hair pulling it gently, and the way his mouth closed over her breasts with a greater hunger to taste each time, and how he kissed her as if there would never be another time or place for them.

Pulling off his shirt, he pressed his chest against her. As the material moved away, replacing cotton with flesh, she laughed with pure joy.

The feel of his skin touching hers as he removed her clothing brought a new warmth inside her. She moaned in pleasure and arched to meet him, loving the way the soft hair across his body tickled her skin. Loving the feel of him fully over her.

The more he felt her move beneath him, the more he needed her. His kisses were deep and wild one minute and tender the next. She was a need so deep he'd spend a lifetime trying to satisfy and finally die still wanting more.

He fumbled with his trousers, then leaned his face against her hair. For a moment, he seemed to hesitate, unsure.

She reached for him, pulling him close, knowing that this was what had to be from the time they'd met.

Slowly, he lowered his body over her, covering her like a warm blanket, welcoming her to the home of his arms. He moved above her allowing her to grow accustomed to the feel of him. His body was lean and strong and warm as he pressed her against the earth, rocking her world with each slight shift.

His breathing grew rapid and irregular in the hollow of her neck as his hands closed over the top of her legs and he pulled them apart. When she resisted, his mouth covered hers and silently asked again. After several deep kisses, his hand moved once more to her legs and she let him part them without hesitation.

Biting her lips, she felt a sudden pain shoot through her as he entered her, hard and fast. His hands held her shoulders as she cried out but he didn't stop. He pushed again and again.

For a few minutes, she drifted with the pain, then his mouth covered hers once more with a warm kiss that told her all would be right. She didn't move as he continued kissing her, touching her breasts, filling her with passion.

Tears came to her eyes. She knew he was making love to her. And she wanted him to as she had from the first, but no one had told her of the pain. Now she understood what men meant when they said they "took a woman," for he was taking her. He was pressing into her very soul, touching her as no man ever had, or ever would again. This gentle man, with all his kindness and goodness, was taking her with hard, demanding strokes. And she was letting him.

Then, from deep inside she felt it, a stirring rumbling through her body like a landslide rolling slowly at first, only pebbles, then turning to a great avalanche. Suddenly, his kisses were fire and his touch pure pleasure. She shifted with him, feeling the movement inside her like a mighty stampede running wild over her senses, awakening every feeling, every joy. She wrapped her arms around him and fully gave herself over to the pleasure.

Suddenly, she was taking all he offered and begging for more.

The very center of her body exploded, sending out lightning bolts in every direction. She cried out his name and fell back to earth only to find his arms caught her.

For a long while, he held her. Stroking her hair, brushing his fingers gently over her breasts, cupping his hand along her hip. She closed her eyes and let him touch her. There had been so little touching in her life. His hands made her feel beautiful and cherished.

When she moved her leg, he mumbled an oath and rolled away.

Opening her eyes, she watched him pick up the rag she'd used on his lip. His tall lean body reminded her of a wild animal as he knelt by the stream and washed the cloth.

When he returned, she closed her eyes pretending sleep. Gently, his hand touched her knee. He raised her leg slightly and placed the cloth between her legs where the pain had been.

"I didn't mean to hurt you," he whispered as he stretched beside her once more and kissed her cheek.

His words were haunted with sadness.

"You didn't," she lied, but the blood on her leg told the truth.

They lay in the sun for a long while, their bodies warm and wet with sweat. Finally, she stretched against him, shoving her damp hair out of her face.

"I guess we both could use a bath." He stood and reached for her. "We'd best be getting back to town."

"A bath sounds wonderful." She laughed, coming awake in an instant. When his hand touched hers, she shoved him backward into the stream.

Adam sank beneath the water with a mighty splash. When he surfaced, he was laughing and spitting water. "Help," he shouted. "I can't swim."

She didn't believe his cry for a moment, but she offered her assistance knowing he'd pull her into the water that ran crystal clear three feet above sparkling rocks.

It was two hours before they stopped splashing and fighting enough to declare a truce and dress. As she dressed, he undressed her, loving the way she played as wholeheartedly as she made love. By the time they were respectable looking, he was already hungry for her beneath him again and her eyes spoke of the same longing.

He took a step.

"No," she held up a hand, "we have to get back. Everyone will be looking for us."

Adam pulled his passion in check. "I can wait."

"I'll not come to your bed tonight. I'll sleep in my own," she teased.

"Then I'll come to you, but you'll not sleep." He offered his hand. "Until tonight."

She accepted his hand. "Until tonight."

They rode back to town in a comfortable silence.

The afternoon was bright with spring and all the world seemed right for Adam for the first time in years. Since they may have caught the men who robbed and burned the stage, there was no reason for Nichole to hide. He was looking forward to seeing the expression on Bergette's face when she discovered a woman had been hiding out in his room. If the news didn't send her packing, Nichole had suggested several ways to encourage her to go, one more outrageous than the next.

He wanted to do the everyday things with Nick, like sit on the porch at sundown or drink coffee at the kitchen table without worrying that someone might come in. He wanted to go for rides at sunrise and sleep in a bed with her nude body wrapped around him.

Adam was still laughing when he opened his office door and found Sister Celestine sitting at his desk with a rifle across her lap.

"Sister?" he asked as Nichole followed him inside.

The nun stood slowly, cradling the rifle in her arms as though she'd done so many times. "Doctor," she announced without emotion, "we've got an outbreak of trouble around the place."

Nichole lowered her gun belt from her shoulder.

Rose entered at full run from the examining room. She held a butcher knife in each hand. Her thick curly hair had fallen from its bun, making her look very much like a pirate. "Who—"

She froze when she saw Adam and Nichole. Slowly lowering her knives, she whispered, "Thank the Lord, you're back."

"You may say that again, Sister Rose." The nun raised her chin to attention. "Reinforcements have arrived."

TWENTY-TWO

GLANCING AT THE WOMAN HE HAD JUST SPENT THE MORNING MAK-ing passionate love to, Adam tried to adjust his mood and his eyes to the muted light of his office. Little remained of the beautiful, funny, sexy woman he'd held only an hour ago. She'd been replaced by a warrior he hardly recognized. Her body had hardened to stone, her wonderful green eyes darkened with purpose. The holster she'd carried lightly over her shoulder was strapped around her waist. The transformation was complete.

"Stay away from the windows," Rose whispered as though someone outside might hear her. "We've been shot at several times since noon."

"What is going on?" Adam looked directly at Sister Cel, knowing she'd be miserly with the answers.

"Charles and Lily are covering the back. Nance boarded up the windows in your rooms. Bergette and Mrs. Jamison are safe upstairs judging from the crying." Even Sister Cel was adopting Nichole's stance. Only she looked more like heaven's warrior than one on earth. "We've secured the perimeters as much as possible, Doctor."

"Start at the beginning and tell me what happened." Adam kept his voice calm though panic spread across his brain like bindweed as he moved around the room counting bullet holes in his window-panes.

"I'll tell you what happened." Rose bobbed up and down between the windows as she crossed the room, following the doctor like some crazed jack-in-the-box pull toy. "All hell's done broke loose, that's what's happened. But don't you worry none, we're going to fight to win. Remember the Alamo!"

"They all died at the Alamo," Adam stated, wondering if Rose and the nun had downed all his supply of medicinal whiskey.

Rose reached him trying to stare him down from her foot shorter disadvantage. "Well, it's the only battle cry I know. I say we fight to the death if we have to just like old Davy Jones did."

"It was Davy Crockett, Rose," Sister Cel interrupted. "I remember someone saying he was the oldest Texan to die at the mission. Old Davy."

"He wasn't a Texan." Rose waved a knife to make her point.

"He was if he died at the Alamo," Sister Cel raised her nose in the air as if ending the argument.

"Forget the Alamo!" Adam shouted. "That was thirty years ago. What is happening now?"

The door to the hallway creaked. Everyone swung at once and aimed.

No one breathed.

The door opened wider, then Nance crawled around it, smiling with excitement. "Hello, Doc."

Adam bent down to the child. "Maybe you can tell me what is going on."

"You bet." Nance sat crossing his legs in front of him on the floor. "About noon, Harry from the stage office came over to tell Lily that some men on a trail drive caught the raiders who burned his stage. He was real happy. He swung Lily around like they was dancing. He said word was there was a woman who could identify them as the stage robbers and as cattle rustlers and murderers."

Nance shrugged his shoulders as if he doubted such a statement. "Then, a few minutes later, he comes running back to tell Lily . . . he likes to talk to her and I just listen . . . that two of the men escaped from the deputy and Mole who rode out to bring them in. Then," Nance looked as though he were putting everything in order in his mind, "somebody started shooting at the house." He shrugged again. "Nothing much happened after that." He put his chin on his palms and his elbows on his knees, looking bored with the game. "Except every time I stand up more than two feet high, someone yells at me."

"One shot came from the roof across the street," Nichole announced as she studied the bullet holes. "Another from the second floor, back room of the house next door."

"That's Mole's room." Rose bit her knuckles.

"I know," Nichole answered, not missing the quick turn of Adam's stare. But there was no time for questions.

"Has the back or sides of the house taken any shots?" she asked, hoping Adam would forget about how and why she might know where Mole's room was located.

"No," Sister Cel said. "Only the front. And I'm thinking it's one shooter, maybe two, no more. Every now and then they seem to have to take a break and we don't hear anything for a while."

Nichole looked out the windows. There were a dozen places where someone could wait with a rifle. The windows were wide and tall, but the porch shadowed some of the view. From twenty feet away she imagined someone could see no more than movement inside the house. That might account for the several shots and no hits. The collapsing shacks across the street would make perfect places to hide.

"They're after me," Nichole whispered. "There's no need for me to put the rest of you in danger. The men who escaped the deputy have nothing to lose and everything to gain by killing me. I'm the only witness to both crimes. They have to have seen me ride in with you, Adam. So they are setting out there just waiting for a clear shot."

"No," Rose argued. "It could be Mole after me. He's not a good shot, but if he drinks enough he thinks he is. He told me once that if I ever walked out on him, he'd see me dead. You already said one of the shots came from his room, and we all know he's too much of a coward to come right up to the door again."

"The shooter could be after me," Sister Cel added softly, as if it were her turn at a quilting bee and she had to add another patch. "I was the only one in the room when the first shot was fired." She cleared her throat. "And I've a few things I haven't told you, Doc, about my life."

Adam looked closely at her. "Now seems like a good time." For a woman of the Church, she had her secrets. Her knowledge of words like perimeter and shooter made him wonder about her past. She also showed no sign of releasing her grip on his rifle.

"Well, he's not gunning for me," Nance volunteered. "I ain't done nothing."

"Quiet, all of you," Adam ordered. "It doesn't matter who he's after, he's not getting anyone." He looked at Sister Cel. "There's no time to hear all the whys. Later. Right now, we've got to get out of this mess."

A shot shattered the glass on the front door. Adam grabbed his Colt and leaned against the wall. Rose screamed so loud he thought she was hit until he saw her dart across the room toward the kitchen. Sister Cel and Nick each took post beside a window.

Another shot echoed in the hall as the front door flew open as if it had been rammed. All weapons turned to the entrance.

A leather-dressed body rolled into the office like a huge cannonball and slammed into a bookcase, sending books flying.

"Wes!" Adam and Nick shouted at once.

Wes came out of his roll with his gun ready. After a moment, he cut his gaze to the others in the room. "Hell of a doorbell, brother."

"Someone's shooting at us." Rose repeated her bobbing motion between each window until she reached Wes. "They're trying to kill us all."

"No lie. Couldn't you tell them I don't live here, I'm just visiting?" He glanced at Adam and sobered. "Everyone all right?"

Another shot hit the wall between two windows. Everyone in the room took cover once more. This time Rose didn't run from the room, but found her cover behind Wes.

Wes checked his guns to see that they were fully loaded. He couldn't help the smile of excitement that reached all the way to his scar. "I heard about the deputy losing the raiders we caught. One of my men was late leaving town this morning and rode back with the story. So a few of the boys and I rode in. I told them to meet me here, but they'll hear the shots and take cover."

Another bullet splintered wood on the porch as footsteps thundered down the stairs.

"This can't be happening! I can't stand it!" Bergette screamed as she entered the room in a cloud of peach lace and silk. "Someone simply can*not* be shooting at this house."

"All right, darlin'," Wes volunteered. "It isn't happening. Happy now?"

Bergette twirled around to look at Wes and pressed her lips together so hard they disappeared completely. "This is your fault," she decided, staring at the newest arrival. "What are you doing here?"

"I followed you, darlin'. I couldn't stand being parted. When I heard you were going to marry my brother, there was nowhere else for my heart to go but Texas." His words were as false as a two-bit actor playing to an empty hall. "I was just praying I got here in time to change your mind." Wes turned his scarred cheek directly toward her and winked.

"Stop calling me darling, Wes McLain, and go stand in front of the window!" Bergette shot him a look that plainly wished him dead as he laughed at her.

"Adam, can't you do something?" Bergette whined as she turned to the younger brother.

Adam looked bothered. "About which request, the shooting, Wes calling you darling, or getting him to stand in front of the window?"

"About the shooting, you fool." Bergette looked around her as if she'd been forced into a cage with monkeys. "This is the middle of town. How can someone be firing shots at us and no one be doing anything about it? I ordered Charles to stop it, but he's proven himself a coward. He said he'd work as a cook on a cattle drive before he'd leave this house in a rain of bullets." She stomped her foot. "I've had it with the lot of you men."

Another shot rang out. Wes raised a hand and jerked Bergette to her knees. "Stay down," he ordered as he moved to the side of the window, "or you'll have a bullet in that powdered chest of yours."

She squealed in embarrassment and crawled to cover beneath the desk.

Adam watched the street closely. When the next shot was fired, both he and Nichole returned the volley.

Several blasts bombarded the porch in answer. When the ringing stopped, a loud voice shouted, "Send the woman out by sunset, or you're all dead!"

"What woman?" Adam yelled back.

"Figure it out, Doc, or you'll be worm meat by dark." The shooter punctuated his sentence with a bullet.

For several minutes everyone in the room was still, not even breathing.

"I'll go," Sister Cel said quietly.

"No." Adam shook his head. "They don't want just anyone."

"But what I've done was a terrible crime." She stood proudly as she confessed her sin. "My brother was Nance's father's partner. When I visited him in prison, he told me they killed Jamison and he'd be next. I brought him a weapon. He killed a guard escaping."

Everyone in the room looked surprised by her words except Nance.

"I'm responsible for a man dying," she admitted. "I've been part of a crime."

Adam let out a long breath. "Dead men don't come back to shoot at you, Sister. And if the law wanted you, they'd knock, not fire."

"They want Nichole," Wes whispered, "but they'll have to go through me to get her."

"And me," Adam added.

"And me." Nance nodded once as he joined the men.

"Who's Nichole?" Bergette looked around the room and noticed the tall woman in men's clothing for the first time.

Wes couldn't resist. "She's the woman who slept in my arms just before dawn."

Bergette opened her mouth in shock that he'd say such a thing in mixed company, and that it might be true.

"I'm the woman who didn't sleep while in Adam's arms all morning." Nichole looked directly at Bergette, making sure the lady got her point.

Adam closed the distance between them and spread his hand around Nichole's waist. His smile told much more than any words.

Bergette let out another little cry of horror.

"You've all lost your minds!" Bergette shouted. "I'm getting out of here. I'm sure whoever is shooting at us will listen when money talks."

She stood, shoving away Wes's offer to help. "You disgust me." She slapped his offered hand away. "And you, Adam. I never expected you to behave so. I no longer believe you to be a gentleman."

Adam moved his nose softly over Nichole's hair without looking at Bergette. "It really doesn't matter what you think of me, Bergette. I can't live my life in fear of rumors you might spread. There are some things in life you can't buy at any price."

Nichole smiled and spread her hand over his at her waist.

Bergette turned and ran up the stairs. Five minutes later, she placed a white flag at her window and screamed continually while it was shot down.

Before the echoing from the bullets stopped, she thundered down the stairs, shouting, "Send her out before they kill us all! Send her out!"

No one even bothered to answer her.

Time passed slowly through the afternoon. Rose couldn't sit still and finally left her knives in favor of cooking. Lily abandoned her post at the back to take care of Bergette. But Charles stood his ground. Everyone else took a shift in the office watching the front of the house.

Nichole walked around, checking each opening, hoping to catch sight of the shooter. She and Wes discussed all the options. Everyone in town must have heard the shots. Surely they'd come. But as the day passed and no relief showed up, Nichole knew there was only one way to ensure the others' safety.

She crossed into her little corner of the study off Adam's bedroom and dressed in black. With the windows boarded, she had to light the lamp to find her way back through Adam's room. Carefully, she lifted his scissors from his shaving tray and stepped in front of the tiny mirror where he shaved. Silently, she pulled the curls from her neckline and began to cut.

Ebony locks fell like tears around her. "It'll be a long time before I wear the ribbons," she whispered as she prepared for what she must do.

TWENTY-THREE

ADAM STOOD AT THE DOORWAY OF HIS ROOM AND STARED AT THE circle of light around Nichole. She was dressed in black again, as she had been the night he'd first kissed her so wildly. Had it only been a few nights ago? It seemed a lifetime.

"You're beautiful," he whispered as he moved behind her. "As beautiful as moonlight and as fiery as the sun."

When she looked up into the mirror and saw his face, her hand glided along the short hair close against her scalp and neck. "There isn't enough left to curl around your fingers," she whispered.

"It doesn't matter," he answered as he brushed his cheek against her head.

His arms slid slowly around her waist and gently pulled her to the length of him as he closed his eyes and breathed deep of the fragrance that was only Nichole, wild and warm with passion. "I know what you are planning is the only way but I'm not sure I can let you go," he whispered. "One morning in the sun won't last me a lifetime. I thought we'd have tonight to talk of all that needs to be said between us."

She turned in his embrace and framed his face in her hands. "I know," she whispered. For a moment this morning she'd believed there might be a forever for them.

His lips brushed lightly over her cheek, not kissing, but just feeling her skin. "I'd keep you here if I could." His jaw tightened against her cheek. "I'd stop you from going if I knew how."

"You can't." She closed her eyes loving the way he seemed to breathe her in with each breath. "I have to do this. It's the only way."

"I know. I'd be less of a man if I bound you to me. And you'd be less my Nick if you let me. If you stayed, I'd keep you safe with my life." He raised his hand to the back of her hair, moving his fingers down the short strands.

She could feel his heart pounding against hers and knew if he gave his life to save her, hers would end.

"You've never said you loved me," she whispered, needing to hear the words no one had ever said to her.

"I don't think about saying it. Loving you is a part of me like breathing. I knew the night we met that I'd always love you and miss you beside me even though we only had that few hours in that old run-down farmhouse together." He hugged her, rocking her slightly from side to side. "I want to hold you forever. Freeze you against me so that no one could ever pull us apart. I'm not sure after this morning that I can let you go this time."

"We know it's the only way," she whispered as he buried his face against her throat. "The others need you and Wes to protect them."

"I'll come after you when it's safe," he promised. "I'll find you."

Nichole laughed with tears in her eyes. "Why do all the men in my life keep saying that to me?" Kissing his ear, she promised, "I'll find you when it's safe. If there ever is a time such as safe. It doesn't seem to be on my map in this life."

Wes bumped his way around the door and into the room. He took one look at them, and said, "You're not thinking of really letting her go, Adam? Her plan is insane. She's staying here with us and that's final. The sheriff is due back in a day or two. This will all get straightened out by then."

"Someone is shooting at us now," Nick reminded.

"We've enough guns to hold the whole town at bay," Wes answered. "Eventually my men will find a way to take out the shooter. You can't go, kid, and that's final."

Adam raised his head but didn't lessen his hold on her. "We've talked it out. Nick thinks she should go and her chances are better alone than with one of us following trying to help. She's got to find a sanctuary until the sheriff returns and the men are behind bars. Any faith we have in the law vanishes with our deputy around. She has to be out of harm's way, Wes."

"Well, I don't like the idea of sending her out in the dark all alone," Wes grumbled. "I'll go with her."

"No," Nichole argued. "I've already told Adam. Both of you have to stay here and keep firing until I'm safe."

Nichole raised her head from Adam's shoulder. "Besides, where else would I be safe but in the night?'' she asked. ''You're putting a fish back in water.''

Wes made a face, but didn't argue anymore. Nick had a way, like no other woman, of looking at a man as though she thought herself an equal. And damned if he hadn't started believing it. ''All right. We'll cover you.'' He moved closer. ''If you'll turn loose of my brother, I'd like to show you a map I drew. It should get you to Daniel at the settlement near Dallas. I figure it will take you most of the night. If you run into trouble there's a place about halfway there called Emery's Post. It's not more than an old drifter with a shack who makes his living selling half-wild horses. But he'll help you for a price. Tell him I'll be along in a day or two and settle up if you owe him anything.''

Wes raised an eyebrow as he saw her better in the poor light. ''Cut your hair, I see.'' His comment was a statement, not a judgment.

''It's short.'' She touched her head once more. ''But it was getting so long I was starting to look like a woman.''

Wes laughed. ''You could shave it off, kid, and this fool of a brother of mine would still look at you with cow eyes. What makes a woman beautiful is a lot more than curls and ruffles.'' He looked up toward the second floor. ''At least in most cases.''

Nichole reached for her hat. ''It's almost dark. I have to be going. I have to make it through the passage Nance told me about and out the shack across the street just at sunset. The shooter won't be able to see me then.''

Wes opened his arms. ''Take care, kid.'' Nichole moved into his hug. ''Keep an angel on your shoulder and your fist drawn till I'm there to cover your back.''

The old saying the McLain boys had never used except for a brother told Adam how dearly Wes cared for Nick.

''I'll get everything ready while you two have a moment alone,'' Wes called over his shoulder. ''I don't like the idea, but if Adam was willing to let you try it, I'll not go against both of you. Besides, Sister Cel has told me more than once another will be watching you.''

Adam didn't say a word. It was too late for words. He simply pulled Nichole close and held her as tightly as he could against him. For one morning of his life he'd known paradise. He'd held passion and wild beauty in his arms. For a few nights he'd slept next to someone whose heartbeat matched his own. He wanted a hundred more passion-filled mornings, thousands more days holding her, and ten thousand more nights. But if they never had them, at least he knew of their existence. And he'd go to his grave remembering every smell, every taste, every feel, every heartbeat of the little time he had with her.

Nichole pulled away. "I have to go," she whispered. "Don't worry about me."

Adam couldn't force any words past his throat. The very air he breathed was vanishing. He was suffocating. But he couldn't say more. She read his mind, she knew his heart. She'd return, he told himself. If she didn't, he'd find her.

When she reached the door, she turned and tried to memorize him.

"I love you," he whispered his thoughts.

She turned unable to say the words she'd so longed for him to say. Opening the door, she melted away.

At the end of the hall, Wes handed her Adam's medical saddlebags. "The doc wants his bag back," he mumbled. "Rose packed food for you in it." He saluted as he moved away in a hurry to be back at his post. They'd all agreed that if something happened and she made a sound while in the passage, or in the shack, they'd make enough noise in the house to keep the shooter busy.

"Ready?" Nance asked, proud to man a station in her escape.

"Ready." Nichole bent and kissed him on the cheek. "Tell the others I'll see them soon."

Nance wiped his face as if to wipe off the kiss as he opened the trapdoor beneath the rug in the corner of the foyer. "It drops down a bit to a kind of cellar. I think the troops who stayed here used it to store supplies, but Mom never let me go down there except one time with my dad." Nance repeated what he'd told her several times before. "Feel the wall and keep to the side and you'll find a tunnel about my height. Follow it and you'll come out in the cellar of the shack across the street. My dad says the cavalry built it as an escape from Indian attack. If nothing's fallen on that trapdoor, you should be able to push it open. I haven't been down there since I went with my dad and he carried a light, but you'll have to go through in the dark. Adam says any light from the tunnel might show through across the street."

"I'll find my way." She slipped into the trapdoor. If this worked, all the hours of listening to Nance tell of the mazes in this house would have paid off. "Thanks, General Ears."

He saluted as he'd seen Wes do.

The drop was not far, not more than eight feet, but for a boy it must have seemed long. She hit soft dirt, uneven beneath her feet.

As Nance closed the trapdoor, the world turned black. Not night like she was used to, but total, absolute black.

She reached out and touched the soft earthen wall of the cellar. Move along the wall to an opening, she said to herself as she slowly felt her way. The room was so silent she could hear her own heart pounding. As she slid her fingers along the wall dirt dribbled off in her hand.

Something scurried behind her. Rats! She clenched her teeth, forcing herself to stay calm. Of all the animals on this earth, rats were the only ones that made her shiver. She'd face a wolf, or a bear, or even an angry porcupine before getting close to a rat.

Another movement, rattling something near her feet. Two rats. Maybe she hated them so much because they thought they owned the night.

Probably a tiny one, she thought, only traveling over broken bottles or bits of trash. The rats weren't interested in her, she reasoned. Keep moving! Find the tunnel.

A weight scurried across the toe of her boot. Not a tiny mouse, but a long fat rat that widened as it moved until the body covered her boot and pressed against her leg.

Nichole couldn't stand still. She twisted, kicking the varmint off her foot. It hit a wall and let out a cry, causing the floor to liquify with movement. They were everywhere. Not one or a dozen, but a hundred running past her boots, sniffing up her legs almost to the knee, pushing other rats into her shins.

She kicked again, almost losing her balance. Her hand reached out to steady her. She touched a shelf in the blackness. A moment later something ran across her fingers and jumped from the shelf. Reacting, before thinking, she stepped away and bumped into another shelf. It toppled, sending rats squealing as they fell to the floor.

Panic climbed up her spine on tiny feet. It took all her willpower not to scream or run. But if she ran, she was sure to step on one and in the blackness she might fall or they might bite through the thin leather of her boot. If she fell, they'd be all over her in victory.

She'd lost her bearing in the blackness. She no longer knew where the wall was. If she took the wrong step, she could trip and fall, or bump into something, or feel another rat. There was as great a chance of her moving away from the wall as toward it.

Nothing, not a single beam of light pointed the way. Not even a smell or sound to follow. If she made the wrong choice and fell . . . Oh, God, if she fell she'd die of fright.

"Help me," she whispered to the stale air as a rat tried to climb her leg. "Help me!"

Adam and Wes were only a matter of feet above her, but with the trapdoor and rug, she knew they wouldn't hear her cries even if she screamed. She couldn't force herself to reach out again and try to find the wall. She couldn't scream. She couldn't breathe in the heavy musty air.

"Help me," she whispered in panic to no one.

Something shifted to her left. A shuffling sound unlike that a rodent would make.

"Easy, now," someone said to her as the shuffling sound came again. "Don't lose control of your senses. And don't be afraid of me. I was told to help if needed."

For a moment, she thought she was imagining a voice. Nichole forced herself to remain perfectly still, not even breathing.

"Who are you?"

Movement came again. "I'm Celestine's brother. She said we had to help you, even if it meant my getting caught and being sent back to prison. She said I had to do what I could to see you safely away."

"You killed a guard." Nichole remembered the nun's confession.

"I did. I killed the man who murdered my partner, Nance's father."

Nick didn't say a word. She was trapped in a cellar with a killer and a hundred rats. There was no light to point her way. If she hoped to get out, she had to trust a murderer.

"Hold your hand out," the voice commanded so softly she still wasn't sure she heard it. "Stay real still, I'll find you and see you out."

Nick slowly raised her hand out in front of her, ready to pull back the moment she encountered anything.

"I'm not going to harm you," the voice moved closer. "I'm only going to touch your hand."

She breathed. The voice had anchored her in the blackness. Panic began to recede. This man in the cellar with her was making the world return and her fears move back to nightmares.

A wrinkled hand, not much larger than her own, grasped hers. "I'll show you the way," he whispered in a voice rusted with age. "I've walked this tunnel many a night. I've seen you travel the darkness also. Only you do good, I only want to disappear."

Slowly, one step at a time, she followed as they moved across the room. She could still hear the rats running about, but they no longer crossed her path.

"Lower your head," he mumbled as he pulled her down into a crouch. "The tunnel's free of rats mostly, but when it rains the walls get muddy. Be careful of the uneven ground. My sister, Cel, will have my hide if I let anything happen to you."

She followed as they shuffled through the tunnel slowly. A dozen questions came to mind, but she didn't speak. This guardian angel was risking his life and his freedom to help her.

The air was a little easier to breathe as they came out of the tunnel and into what must be the cellar across the street from the boarding-house. Here a few cracks in the trapdoor provided enough light to get a vague view of the room.

The man turned loose of her hand and slid a box between them. "All you have to do is stand on this box and push the door gently. I checked to see that it was unblocked when I heard Nance tell you about the secret passage. I guessed you'd choose this way out."

"Thanks." She waited, hoping he'd tell her his name. "You saved my life."

"No," he stepped away. "I've watched you in action. You would have found your own path. I just helped out a bit. We all need help now and then."

Before she could say more, he was gone. She could hear him moving back through the tunnel, brushing the wall with his hand. The rats scurrying to get out of his path. Someday, maybe they'd meet again. She'd always remember the feel of his old hand.

Straightening her stance, she touched her Colt and took a deep breath. It was time to do what she had to do, she thought. It was sunset.

TWENTY-FOUR

Wɪᴛʜ ᴀ sʜᴏᴠᴇ, ɴɪᴄʜᴏʟᴇ ᴘᴜsʜᴇᴅ ᴛʜᴇ ᴛʀᴀᴘᴅᴏᴏʀ ᴏᴘᴇɴ ᴀɴᴅ ᴘᴜʟʟᴇᴅ herself into the remains of what once had been a building. The roof was half caved in and the last glow from the sun could still be seen lighting the sky. The air felt good on her face and in her lungs.

Sister Cel's brother had saved her life in the tunnel and when everything settled down, she planned to see what she could do to help him.

She walked silently across the cluttered floor, careful not to step on a loose board that might make a sound. Slipping out the back where a door had once stood, Nichole moved down the alley toward the stables.

No one was in sight. If the shooter were near, he couldn't see her in the dying light. She slipped through the skeleton of what once had been a settlement. The town might be growing, but it seemed content to allow the quickly erected old fort to die.

The fine black stallion Wes had bragged of trading for at Emery's Post was tied by the door of the barn, still saddled. Wes said it had been trained to respond to a touch or a tug on the bridle.

A gunshot sounded from behind her. She glanced at the prairie beyond the stables. She could be away and free before full dark.

Another gun fired from the direction of the boardinghouse. They should be safe once it was dark, she reasoned. Unless they lit a lamp. Unless they tried to come out. Unless the shooter managed to crawl through the night and get to a window of the house. If he shot Wes or Adam, there wouldn't be anyone left to cover all the sides. It would only be a matter of time before he'd be in the house. Everyone might be dead before the shooter figured out Nichole wasn't in the house.

She swung into the saddle and turned Wes's horse toward the boardinghouse. She couldn't leave without helping them.

At full gallop she rode between Adam and the shooter. The dusty, deserted street made a perfect racetrack and Wes's stallion was all Wes promised he would be.

Shots came from the second floor of an old building and from a corner beside the very shack she'd escaped through. The bullets flew past her and Nick leaned low over the horse, blending into the midnight mane. Answering shots came from the boardinghouse, splintering off the walls where the shots were fired. She thought she heard the shooter yell an oath as she passed from range.

Turning at the corner, she reined her horse and began crossing back and forth through the town, staying out of sight, leaving no trail. By full darkness, she was riding slowly out of town to the east, slumping in the saddle providing a silhouette of a tired hand heading home for the night. She'd learned years ago no one would look at her twice if she moved at an easy pace, but if she hurried, all would remember seeing her leave.

She knew the shooter would follow her as best he could. She also knew that he'd never find her. As soon as she was away from the lights, she'd find the stage trail and follow it. Here she could travel twice as fast without near the danger and uncertainty of the land. By dawn they'd be circling Fort Worth looking in every bush and she'd be at Daniel's settlement.

Nick's wild ride between the shooters and the house was the break Wes's men had been waiting for. In all the excitement, they closed in on the two outlaws and overpowered them.

A few minutes later when they hauled the shooters into Adam's office, everyone in the house was surprised to see Harry from the stage line leading the posse. As soon as Wes's men made plans to help, Harry and several other merchants joined in the fight. They'd been waiting patiently for their chance.

Suddenly the boardinghouse rivaled any saloon for noise. Everyone was talking at once and hugging except, of course, for the nun. Adam didn't miss the way she stood quietly in the corner, her arms still folded around the rifle.

When she thought no one was watching, Adam saw her walk past the two prisoners tied in chairs and ''accidentally'' thump the butt of her rifle against both men's knees. Then she went to the kitchen, put the gun down, and began serving everyone raisin bread and coffee.

Adam smiled and shook his head. She was the kind of saint Nick would probably turn to. There was something ornery about the old lady who looked like an angel.

"She made it." Wes lifted his cup toward Adam. "The kid made it."

"I know." Adam smiled. "But I wanted to strangle her for riding past us. She should have headed right out of town from the barn. She had a clear shot there with little danger."

Wes took a drink. "She knew what she was doing. She had to make sure the men firing at us knew she was no longer in the house." He took another drink. "And she damn well better take care of my horse. I thought we told her to steal a mount."

Adam laughed. "She did."

Shaking his head, Wes added, "You need to marry that girl if we ever find her again. Maybe if you kept her pregnant, she'd slow down to a gallop."

"Before I think of marriage, I've got to make sure we have all of the gang. The deputy managed to lose two of the three you caught this morning before he got back to town. I just heard the third escaped an hour ago. Once we have them in our sight I don't aim to look away until the sheriff gets back to town. I want Nick safe away until I know they will stay behind bars."

Wes looked at the two prisoners. "The third won't be hard to find. Nick cut a line across his throat just deep enough to bleed last night. He was shorter than average and thick bodied. I've got until my partner shows up to help you find him. Even if Vincent shows up, I might have him start moving and I'll catch up. I wouldn't want to leave with someone still gunning for Nick. I haven't had this much fun in years."

"Captain McLain?" Charles interrupted.

Both Wes and Adam turned around, but Wes answered, "Yes?"

Charles straightened. "I've been informed that you need a cook for the trail drive. I feel my qualifications are adequate though I know nothing about driving a herd. My first position was as assistant cook at a hunting lodge. I can prepare any game and am familiar with cooking on a campfire. I'll make the drive with you as cook on the condition that you buy me a train ticket back to Indiana when we reach the rail station."

The little man wasn't friendly even when applying for a job, but Wes and Adam didn't make fun of him. They'd both been raised by a strong working-class foreman who'd taught his sons to respect a man's right to work no matter what rank the job.

"You believe your position is over here?" Wes asked.

"I was told so today," Charles answered. "I have enough funds to secure the proper clothing and personal supplies needed for such a trip.'' The cold little bully of a man who'd tried to put them both in their place stood proudly before them as he awaited their answer. He wasn't asking for a handout, only employment.

Wes offered his hand. "The job's yours if you want it, Charlie. And a share of the profit at trail's end to go along with your ticket."

"Thank you, sir, but it's Charles." The man lifted his nose. "I'll be ready within the hour." He walked away without another word.

Adam smiled at his brother. "You figure he'll survive out there with the cowhands?"

"If he can cook half as well as I'm betting he can, they'll allow him his room and even call him Charles. Besides, it would be worth the train ticket to know how happy I'm making Bergette."

"Speak of the devil." Adam pointed with a nod of his head.

Bergette floated down the stairs looking all fresh and powdered, as if she'd been bathing and sleeping while all the trouble was going on. Lily followed, mirroring the other side of the coin. The poor maid looked like she'd been trapped in a cage of screaming monkeys. Her normally orderly hair was a shambles, her dress wet and her hands red from hauling water up and down the stairs.

"Lily!" Harry pushed Bergette aside, breaking her featherlike descent into the room. "Lily! Are you all right?"

The poor girl melted into the young man's arms. "Harry!" she cried. "You saved me."

"You knew I'd come." Harry looked a little embarrassed by all the folks staring at him, but he didn't push Lily from his embrace.

Several cowhands cheered and shouted comments like, "She's all right now."

Harry smiled nervously.

Bergette opened her fan loudly and continued into the room, allowing her face to show anger for only a moment at the young man's attention toward her maid. She cared nothing of Lily and her beau, but she bitterly hated having an entrance spoiled.

Adam watched her move into the room. Every step seemed calculated, every movement planned to provide the best advantage to her figure and dress. She was as perfect as always, her golden hair curling down her back to her waist, her face powdered and brushed with just the right touch of rouge, her tiny hands and waist, her startling blue eyes she knew how to use almost like a language.

Wes leaned close to Adam. "Being around Nick for a day sure does tend to ugly Bergette up, don't it?"

Adam watched her closely as he answered Wes. "You notice it, too."

"When the genuine item walks in the room, even in trousers, she makes the porcelain dolls come in a poor second." Wes raised his coffee cup as he whispered, "But since you have the lady's heart, mind if I harass the doll?"

"With my blessing. But remember, she is my house-guest, uninvited or not." Adam leaned closer. "Which reminds me, how did you know Bergette's breasts were powdered?"

"Lucky guess," Wes answered a bit too quickly.

Bergette reached them before Adam could say more.

"I understand the soldiers from Fort Griffin have been wired to come get the prisoners." She waved her fan with a graceful movement that seemed to brush Wes's presence from her sight.

"Correct," Adam acknowledged. "They should be here in a day or two. Some of the men from town have agreed to help the deputy guard the prisoners around the clock until the army arrives. We don't want them getting lost on the way to the jail again."

Bergette glanced about. "Where is that woman in the awful clothes?"

"She's gone." Adam set his jaw. "But she'll be back."

"That's comforting," Bergette said sarcastically. "I'm afraid I'll have to miss her return. I've decided to go back to Fort Griffin with the cavalry. From there I can find a stage easily. I can endure this town no longer. Fort Griffin may be just as harsh, but at least I'll have men in uniform to protect me." She left no doubt that she felt Wes and Adam had failed.

Looking around, she added, "Have you seen Charles? I must tell him to begin the packing."

Wes bowed before Bergette as though he were trying hard to reform and prove himself a gentleman. "My dear Bergette, may I have a word with you?"

She hesitated, then followed him into the kitchen. A few minutes later Adam heard her screaming all the way through the house. Wes must have told her of Charles's change in employment.

He was thankful he wouldn't have to get used to the sound of her screams. Bergette was a woman accustomed to having everything one way, her way.

Suddenly, he was impatient for everyone to leave. He wanted to be alone so that he could think of Nichole . . . if just for a few minutes before he began walking the streets looking for the third man.

TWENTY-FIVE

Every muscle in her body ached from trying to stay in the saddle and not fall asleep. Finally she saw the tiny lights of Daniel's settlement flickering on the horizon like ghost fires in the Smoky Mountains.

The homes ran along one side of a broad stream while a church and school had been built on the other side. Wes's map had been accurate, allowing her to use natural landmarks and stay away from civilization.

She'd even avoided Emery's Post halfway between Fort Worth and Dan's home, not wanting to awaken Emery. Wes might trust the man, but in her experience, horse traders had never been overly honest. If he'd help her for a price, he'd help anyone looking for her for the same price.

Nichole climbed off her mount, deciding to walk the last mile. Wes had told her that this settlement, like many others in Texas, was a small religious group who thought they'd tame the frontier with their plows and Bibles. Like Parker's Fort on the banks of the Navasota some thirty years ago, Wes assured her these people, for all their religion, were fighters.

She walked through a freshly plowed field, knowing she'd never ask them to fight to protect her. As she walked, she studied the land looking for routes of escape should the raiders have followed. But they couldn't have, she reasoned, she'd left no trail.

Wes also told her the house near the edge of the settlement next to the livery would be Daniel's. The youngest McLain had joined the group as a blacksmith, not a preacher, though both his brothers thought he'd go back into the ministry in time.

Nichole tied her horse and moved up the three steps to the front door of a small, well-built home. Lights were already on in the place so, she hoped she wouldn't frighten anyone by calling so early. She knocked lightly.

Someone shuffled about inside the house before a young woman opened the door.

"Yes?" she inquired with a shy smile. "Can I help you?"

"Willow?" Nichole couldn't believe the change. The barefoot little wet nurse stood before her in a dress, not the shift she had worn months ago. Her hair was clean and combed back from her face and she had on shoes. "Willow, is that you?"

The girl tilted her head in confusion. "It's me, but who are you? I know ever'body in the settlement."

"I'm a friend of Daniel's. You only saw me once—you might not remember me. My name's Nichole Hayward. I was there at the McLain farm the day you first saw the babies."

"I don't remember you, but if you're Daniel's friend, come on in. He says all are welcome."

Nichole stepped into a neat little two-room cabin. A loft lowered the ceiling on one side where the kitchen stood. The floor was wood and the furnishings almost stark—a table, a few chairs, a rocker by the fire. In the center of the floor was a huge rug made from scraps of material crocheted in a circle. Two babies sat in the middle of the rug. They both had golden curls, angel faces, and clean nightshirts.

"Me and the twins were just having our morning snack. We sometimes get up earlier than Mr. Daniel." Willow folded down on the rug. "You want one?" She handed Nichole a slice of bread covered with jelly.

Nichole lowered her empty saddlebag to the floor and removed her hat. She sat at the table and watched Willow and the babies. "This is good," she said as she tasted the bread.

Willow shared her piece with first one twin, then the other. "I remember you now," she grinned. "You told me the twins' ma was a good cook. I remember that and I tell it to the twins sometimes. But Mrs. March from next door made this jelly and bread. She's a widow with five kids. Mr. Daniel takes care of her stock in exchange for fresh bread twice a week and a meal every night for us. She brings it over, and all I have to do is wash the pot and give it back to her come morning after Mr. Daniel cooks breakfast." Willow smiled. "He cooks whatever I like, unless he's in a hurry."

Nichole watched Willow. She couldn't help but notice that not only were the twins healthy and happy, Willow seemed to be also.

Willow stood and moved to the neat little kitchen. "Want some milk? We got lots of milk. All the milk I can drink. Mr. Daniel's got a cow just so we don't run out." She poured two cups of milk and handed one to Nichole, then sat down and offered the twins each a drink from her cup.

"Mr. Daniel is good to you?"

Willow smiled. "Ever'body is here. Most of the women come by to check on me ever' day, and sometimes they invite me and the twins to their house. Then I don't have to watch the twins so close because the older girls want to hold them." Willow grinned. "Us women make butter and soap and important things like that together. I bring my share home and give some to Mr. Daniel, and he says I'm priceless."

Nichole smiled and leaned back in the chair. She knew Adam and Wes had feared how Daniel, being widowed with two babies, might survive. He seemed to be doing just fine.

"What are the twins' names?" Nichole smiled at the girls.

"Twin," Willow answered. "That's all, just twin. Mr. Daniel calls them angel or dear one, but I just call them twin. They both look up at me when I do."

"Where is Daniel?" Nick asked.

"I don't know. He didn't talk much at supper or play with the girls as long as he usually does." Willow lifted one of the twins. "Some nights he sleeps in the loft, but some nights he leaves and don't come back until morning. He says he has work to do."

Moving toward the only other room, the bedroom, Willow added, "I got to nurse the babies. Mrs. March told me I can only feed them twice a day now 'cause it's time they were drinking from a cup." She looked around as if unsure what to do with a guest in the house.

"I have to be going." Nichole stood. "Thank you for the bread and milk."

Willow smiled, seeing that she'd done right.

"Good morning, Willow." Nichole moved to the door. "I'll see you later."

Relieved that her problem was solved, Willow nodded her good-bye.

Nichole walked outside, wondering where she would bed down for a few hours. She had thought to be welcome at Daniel's house, but couldn't blame Willow for barely remembering her. The girl had only met Nick one day when her world was changing. Nick couldn't help but smile at the memory of how Wes had reacted to Willow showing her breasts. After his comment about Bergette's powdered chest, she knew she'd have enough ammunition to tease him when next they met.

Strolling over to the livery, Nichole decided to at least give her horse a roof. She unsaddled him and was rubbing him down when someone stepped between her and the lantern she'd lit.

"That's my brother's mount." The low voice startled her with its less than friendly words.

She turned around to find Daniel standing behind her. He was thinner than she remembered and there was a hardness about him that removed all the boy she'd met less than a year ago. He wore a sleeveless shirt and his arms were powerful from the work he did as blacksmith. So much of his face was cut like Adam's, strong and handsome, but his sandy blond hair was very different.

"I know," she answered. "Wes and Adam sent me to find you. You may not remember me, but I was there the night the twins were born. I'm Nick."

Daniel limped a few steps closer. "I remember," he said with pain. "It was also the night my wife died."

For a moment he stared at her, letting the pain of the memory hit her full as it must hit him every hour of every day. "What can I do for you?" he finally asked in a formal voice.

Nick thought of saying nothing. Daniel had his own life, his own pain, he didn't need her. But if she left, Adam might not be able to find her.

"I need a place to stay for a few days." She watched him closely. "You see, I—"

"All right," he answered. "You can sleep in the loft in the house. I bunk out here half the time anyway."

"Don't you want to know why?"

Daniel shook his head. "It doesn't matter. You're welcome in my house for as long as you want to stay."

Nichole watched him move away. The sadness that cocooned him made her want to cry. He seemed to have aged years in the months since his wife's death.

She finished with her horse and followed the light to where she could hear him working. The sun hadn't yet broken through but his work fire was already hot. She wondered if he'd worked all night. He sat at a bench twisting leather around metal, creating a harness.

"That's fine work." She moved closer, studying his excellent craftsmanship.

"Thanks," he mumbled without looking up.

"You do a lot of these?"

"Some."

She glanced about, trying to think of something else to say. The workshop was orderly. He was far more than a blacksmith. She saw all matter of smith work, including a few pieces of silver. "You're up early, Daniel."

He didn't answer. He didn't even look at her. If she hadn't understood his sorrow, she would have given up. But she did know the source of his pain, and she'd seen tonight how well he'd taken on the responsibility of the twins. He probably wasn't yet twenty-one, yet he'd taken the load of a man.

She had never had time to learn the subtleties of conversation or how to give comfort. In her world a loss was a loss and no one spoke of it. But when she thought that she might never hold Adam again, she caught a glimpse of what Daniel must feel now.

Silently, she knelt in front of him and began straightening the leather straps he worked with. This she knew. Within minutes they were working together, making the tedious chore fly.

An hour passed. Nichole was so tired she could hardly stand, but she didn't know how else to help him. He said only what was necessary and never smiled, but she could feel him relaxing at her side.

When the work was done he walked her back to the house without saying a word except thank you as she passed through the door. He silently cooked breakfast for Willow and her, but by the time the coffee boiled Nichole was curled into a ball sound asleep on the rug in front of the fire.

For three days his work pattern didn't change. She awoke in the loft with Daniel already cooking breakfast. He ate very little, but played with the twins while Willow took her time eating and telling him every detail of her day's plans. Then he'd leave, always asking if Willow needed anything. Nichole didn't miss the kindness he showed the girl, and he'd never raised his voice at her. There seemed to be one hard rule. Willow never left the house without telling Daniel where she was going.

Since she had no dress, or desire to be with the women, Nichole followed Daniel to the barn each morning. Folks came by, but she noticed no one stopped to visit. After three days, Nichole had no trouble guessing why. Daniel never said more than a few words. Sometimes she'd help him, sometimes she'd just watch, but never did he make any effort to start a conversation with her.

On the fourth night of her stay a spring storm blew in from the west. Willow went to bed early with a twin nestled on either side of her, and Nichole was left alone in the house. She passed the time for a while listening to the wind, then glanced out to see the light still on in the livery. With the coffeepot half-full and two mugs in her hand, she ran through the rain to the side door of the barn.

At first, she didn't see Daniel when she went inside. He was sitting in a corner of his workroom with his head on his knees like a child afraid of the rain.

When she entered, the storm slammed the door closed behind her and Daniel looked up with pain-filled eyes.

Nichole set the pot down and ran to him, thinking that he must somehow be hurt. "Daniel!" She knelt beside him. "Are you all right?"

Slowly he raised his head. "I hate the rain and the wind," he whispered. "God, how I hate storms."

"You've been drinking," she said as she brushed the blond hair back from his damp face. His brown eyes were floating in tears.

"Not enough." He turned away from her as if trying to curl inside a ball.

Nichole wasn't sure what to do as she lifted the bottle beside him. The loneliness surrounding him was so thick she could taste it in the air, hear his screams in his very breath. She could feel his pain as real as one feels the fire when standing too close to the flames.

All she could think to do was to crawl inside the pain with him so he would at least have company in his sorrow. "Then let's drink until we have drunk enough."

She bit the cork off as she'd seen Wolf do a few times and took a swallow, then handed it to Daniel. He looked surprised but downed his share.

The liquor fired down her throat and exploded in her stomach. Nick opened her mouth wide trying to breathe, but she didn't say a word. She'd made a decision to drink with him and drink with him she would.

An hour later the bottle was empty and the world looked fuzzy. "Come on." She pulled Daniel up. "I'll put you to bed."

He'd downed twice his share and was in no shape to navigate the stairs to a pile of hay he used as a bedroom. "If I leave you down here, the good people of this settlement might find you. They seem nice enough, but Bible thumping and whiskey bottles don't mix. I'd best hide you away."

After several tries, they finally made it up the ladder. He fell in the hay, mumbling his wife's name.

Nichole covered him with a blanket. "I wish I could help," she whispered, realizing that helping him drink had not been one of her brighter ideas.

As she stood, he caught her hand. He didn't say a word. Even drunk, he wouldn't allow himself to ask, but she read his gaze in the flashes of lightning. He was asking her to stay.

Nichole wrapped another blanket around her shoulders and sat down beside him. Without a word, without touching her, he fell asleep.

For a long while, she listened to his breathing. He had a kind of loneliness inside him too deep for words. Leaning into the hay, she decided to rest a few minutes before heading back through the storm to the house. She couldn't blame him for hating the storm, May had died during a storm. Nichole closed her eyes wishing it were Adam next to her and not his brother.

The storm continued to rage. Finally, Nichole scooted close enough to use Daniel's arm for a pillow. She fell asleep swearing she'd never drink a drop of liquor again as long as she lived. If she lived to get over this headache.

In what seemed like only minutes, gray morning fought its way through the rain. Nichole rubbed her eyes and stretched, waking her headache up along with her body.

Something moved in the shadows, footsteps muffled by faraway thunder still grumbling. Nick came awake in an instant. She reached for her knife as her gaze focused on the outline of a man.

"Adam," she whispered at the man too angry to speak standing over her and Daniel.

TWENTY-SIX

"ALL RIGHT, ADAM, STOP YELLING! I'LL MARRY HER!" DANIEL SHOUTED as he shook himself awake and tried to stand in the hay.

"Like hell you will!" Adam jumped toward his brother like a lion in full rage. The sound of the rain on the roof seemed to echo his fury.

Wes, unable to control his laughter, stepped between the two, trying to referee and maintain his balance in the shifting straw. "Hold on, now, Adam," Wes protested. "If Danny says he only slept beside her, then nothing happened last night worth your getting riled about. Hell, we've all slept with her."

Suddenly, like angry children, the three brothers were shouting and swinging at one another. Daniel's emotions, which he'd kept so locked away for months, exploded. Adam took his anger out on them both. Wes, well, Wes just loved a good fight and never wasted time looking for reasons.

Nichole watched from the loft ladder as hay and fists flew in the shadowy light of early morning. The storm outside was nothing compared to the one going on in the barn. These three men she'd grown to love and think highly of were scrapping like wild wolves.

"Stop it!" she yelled as they all three tumbled into the back of the loft and began to roll into one huge ball of arms and legs. "Stop it!" she shouted again as the ball slammed into one wall and changed direction. Dust from the rafters sifted down like fine wheat flour over everything.

Thank goodness no one was around. Willow had said, if the rain continued, she and the women would be loading wagons at first light for Sunday service. They didn't want to trudge through the mud and across the bridge to the church in their Sunday best. These three wild McLains would probably frighten poor Willow to death.

Nichole thought of firing her Colt, but she didn't want the entire community to hear the shot from the church and come running. She looked around the neat workroom below the loft. The pot of cold coffee was the only thing on the table.

Dropping a few rungs down the ladder, she grabbed the pot and hauled it back up. With one mighty swing, she flung the cold liquid through the air toward the pile of men she once thought reasonable.

They broke apart yelling as the cold, grounds-thickened liquid splattered them all.

"I said stop it!" Nichole stood in front of them like an angry parent as she fought down a smile. "What do you think you are doing? Wiping out the McLain family from within?"

To her shock, all three men broke into laughter.

Adam stood and wiped his face on his sleeve. "You sound just like our mother used to," he said as he moved toward her. "We wouldn't have hurt one another. Honest, Nick."

The other two joined Adam. Wes rubbed his jaw. "I'm not so sure. Little Danny boy's got a real wallop of a right. Maybe one of us should show him how to pull his punches now that he's finally grown."

Daniel shoved him with a massive shoulder, and Wes shoved back.

"Stop it," Nick warned, "or I'll throw the pot next time. I don't even know what you're fighting over. If it's me, I'm not for the winning by the whole lot of you. I've always thought Yankees a little slow-witted with their fast talk, but you three are downright vacant brained."

Adam took a step toward Nichole, but she raised the pot like a weapon.

Wes raised an eyebrow as if to argue, but Daniel motioned with his head toward the door.

Wes nodded. "We'll go wash up by the horse trough in the barn," he offered as they both moved toward the ladder. "Even brainless, we can tell when we're not wanted. You two need to talk . . . or something."

At the opening, he turned and added, "Kid, if Adam gets too hard to deal with, shoot him."

"Don't tempt me," she whispered as the brothers disappeared, leaving Adam and her alone in the dusty hayloft with only the watered-down morning sun for light.

He stood facing her, still rubbing coffee off his three-day growth of beard. "Must I always find you sleeping in my brothers' arms?" he snapped, still angry. His brown eyes were almost black with smoldering rage.

Without knowing how to answer, she doubled up her fist and swung, but he saw the punch coming this time. He blocked and pulled her to him as he tumbled backward onto the hay.

He held her close, letting her struggle, feeling her anger. Dear God, he loved her. He loved her more than he'd ever loved anything or anyone in his life, but the harder he tried to hold her the more she struggled. She was a fighter to the core. He might have the advantage now, but she wouldn't stop and eventually she'd find freedom, or he'd make a mistake and she'd break from his hold.

It would take a strong man to hold Nichole, but not this kind of strength, he realized.

He opened his arms and she jumped to her knees, whirling to face him, ready to fight. Her clothes were wrinkled and dusty. Her hair, cut short against her head, made her eyes seem even larger. Her entire body was tense with the spirit of a survivor. She'd never looked more beautiful to him, more desirable.

Adam lifted his hands in surrender and lowered his head. He couldn't even look at her without wanting her so dearly all other thought left him. Maybe she was right, maybe he was brainless. He could never fight and keep her, yet he wasn't sure he had the strength to let go and allow her freedom.

Nichole relaxed when she saw he wasn't going to grab her. "Don't ever try to hold me like that again or I'll . . ."

"You'll what?" Adam's head snapped up and brown eyes challenged green. "You'll shoot me for wanting to protect you? You'll cut me deep for helping you? Tell me, dearest Shadow, how do you kill someone who loves you?"

"I don't need you to protect me." She saw her words slice him like a knife. "I can take care of myself." Couldn't he see by offering to protect her, he was telling her he didn't believe she could take care of herself? He was silently calling her weak, something no one had done in years. His words of assistance were an insult, not an endearment. But he couldn't see it.

Adam rose to one knee. "That's right. You don't need my help. You've proven it over and over. You don't need anyone or anything, do you, Nick? You can't even think you might, because if you did that would be a weakness and there are no weaknesses in you. You're the finest, the best, the strongest, the fastest. . . ."

She stood and checked her Colt's strap. "That's right," she said, wishing his words hadn't sounded so hard. How could something she'd always been proud of sound so wrong when he voiced it?

Adam stared at her, wanting to scream that she'd learned to be everything but a woman, and all he wanted, needed, was that woman somewhere inside her to be his woman . . . his love . . . his other half. But he couldn't hurt her, no matter how angry he was, by voicing his thoughts.

"We caught the two shooters just after you left." He broke the silence between them. "Thanks to one talking, we rounded up the third outlaw. He wasn't hard to identify with a cut across his throat."

There was so much more he wanted to say, but he stayed with the facts. "Wes and I stood guard over all three until the sheriff arrived yesterday. The sheriff thinks Mole and the deputy might be involved somehow, but he can't prove it, so he's having both of them watched.

"I guess there's no reason for you to stay here with Daniel. Fort Worth will be safe." Adam stood, but turned away from her as he added, "Wolf wired that he's on his way, so by the time we get back there'll be no reason for you to stay in Texas."

Adam watched her out of the corner of his gaze. "Wolf didn't say your fiancé, Tyler, was coming with him."

Nichole lifted her chin. "Tyler wasn't my fiancé. I just didn't want you to think nobody wanted me."

"I see." He couldn't add that he wanted her . . . wanted her so badly his entire body shook. She'd made it plain she didn't need him, and pride wouldn't allow him to admit that he might need her. He'd even told her of his love without her saying the words in return.

"I'll be glad to get back to Tennessee," she lied again. "I've had enough of you crazy McLains."

"Well, I haven't exactly been void of trouble since you came to visit. Half the time I think I'm losing my mind. The other half I'm sure it's already long gone."

Nichole raised her chin a little higher. "I could never be what you want."

"No," Adam countered. "You don't even know who that is." She was doing it again, he thought, plowing through his heart before it had time to heal. His loving her didn't matter. He wasn't sure what she needed, but he knew he wasn't it. Maybe no man would ever be.

"I'll be fine alone." She closed her eyes. She'd rather be alone than have someone constantly protecting and pampering her. At least Wolf let her do her job and had respected her for that.

"So will I," Adam echoed with his back turned to her.

The silence in the air was thick, almost liquid. The rain had slowed to a depressing rhythm, drumming, adding to the silence with its monotony.

He wouldn't reach for her again, no matter how dearly he wanted to hold her.

And she couldn't reveal her need for him. The years of being silent and standing alone were drilled too deeply into her. Her survival had depended on it. Now it blocked her from any happiness in the future.

"Adam!" Daniel yelled from below. "Come quick! There's been an accident!"

Adam turned away from her, unable to say another word. She'd said she didn't need him. At least someone below did. All he'd ever wanted was to help others, even if he couldn't help himself.

"I'm coming!" He dropped down the ladder, leaving Nichole standing in the loft alone.

Closing his heart away, Adam ran with his brother into the rain. Daniel didn't need to talk, his few words had said it all. No matter how Adam hurt inside, he had a job he was born to do and it had to come first.

As he sloshed through the mud, Adam realized no woman would ever understand him. She'd have to always be willing to step back and be second to what he must do. He had no right to ask any woman to do that, especially not one like Nichole, who deserved a full-time man.

Daniel led him past several houses to the bridge that crossed the creek in town. Most of the homes lay on one side while the school and church were on the other. Through the sheets of rain, Adam saw Wes standing beside the bridge. A few feet behind him men helped women and children climb from the canvas shelter of a wagon into the rain. They may have boarded the wagon to keep their Sunday best dry, but now something had happened that made their clothes unimportant.

Adam pushed past the people to the bridge.

"They're pulling one boy up now!" Wes shouted as he signaled Adam near. "He looks to be hurt bad from a blow to the head."

Adam looked below at the river that had been only a stream the last time he'd seen it. Now the water whirled and turned and pounded an overturned wagon with raging force. Through the gray light he could see four, maybe more, children fighting to hold on to the remains of an old Conestoga.

Men were lowering ropes to the stranded, but the rain and the wind were swinging the ropes off course. All the children were screaming for help. Cries from parents on the bridge echoed in answer.

"We have to go down to them!" Adam shouted as he grabbed a rope and began circling it around his waist. "They'll never have the strength to hold to a rope while we pull them up."

Wes nodded and began organizing the men.

"No." Nichole stepped in front of Adam. "I'll go down." She tried to pull the rope from Adam's hand. "I weigh less so I'll be easier to pull up, and I'm strong enough to hold a child while I climb."

"No!" Adam tugged the rope away.

A hundred replies came to her mind. Didn't he think her capable? Was he afraid of losing her? What of losing him? But only one answer would make him stay on shore. "You're needed here." Nichole knew him well. "I can do this, but I can't do the doctoring."

There wasn't time for him to think. He glanced at the boy lying in Daniel's arms a few feet away, his head covered with blood. She was right.

As he turned loose of the rope she pulled it around her. For a second their eyes met. Adam saw something he'd never expected to see, gratitude in their green depths. In that one moment he knew what she needed, more than being loved or protected. She needed to be accepted for what she was, an equal. Not better, or less, but equal.

His hand passed along the rope now anchored around her waist. "Nick?" he whispered against her hair, but there was no time for more.

Adam turned from her and ran to the boy as she began her descent down the bank to the wagon. Wes was only a step behind her, but his footing was not as light as hers. Within seconds she was yards ahead of him.

Adam carefully lifted the bleeding child in his arms and moved toward the nearest house. As he passed the women, a few turned with him, knowing they could help more inside than watching from the bank.

As Adam left the bridge, Nichole reached the wagon. She grabbed the first child and swung back into the water. The men on the bank began pulling her in. There was no time for Adam to watch more, he had a boy to worry about.

An elderly woman answered the door when Adam kicked it with his foot. She took one glance and held the door wide.

"I need bandages and warm water," Adam fired. "Have you someone to send to the barn for my medical bag?"

An old man unfolded himself from the rocker. "I thought I'd miss church what with the rain, but I guess the Lord means me to get wet this day.'' He pulled on his coat and headed out the door without another word. Several other women passed him on his way out, all heading directly to Adam to await orders.

Adam laid the child on the table and examined the wound along the side of his face. ''Clear the furniture near the fire and make beds. All the children will need to be dried and kept warm until I can get to them.''

Before he could finish with the stitches on the first boy, another child arrived with a broken arm, then another badly bruised, then another in shock from fright and cold. In the back of his mind, as he worked, Adam realized Nichole was doing her part. One by one, she saved the children.

Adam issued orders to everyone who walked through the door as only a man who'd lived through countless emergencies could. There was no time to waste. He cared for each child with skill and practiced swiftness he'd learned from his years in the army.

When Daniel entered, Adam asked without stopping working, ''How many more?''

Daniel carried a child toward Adam. ''This is the last and he's in fine shape, only cold. The women with babies were in the first wagon. It made it across the bridge. The second had mostly school-age children. It missed the corner of the bridge and broke the pole acting as a guardrail. The third wagon had these women in it.'' He looked around at all the women moving about, busy working. A few were already gathering up their children to take home.

''Where's Willow?'' he asked almost softly as he passed the child to Adam. ''I thought she'd be in the last wagon.''

''She was in the first wagon,'' someone answered. ''She's safe across the river with the babies.''

Daniel bolted, but two of the men caught him at the door. ''She's all right,'' one said. ''And so are your twins. They made it across the bridge.''

''I have to go,'' he pulled at where they held him. ''I have to know.''

''Let him go,'' Adam ordered as he handed the frightened child he held to her mother.

The men lowered their grip and Adam added, ''Danny, be careful.''

Daniel nodded. ''I'll be back as soon as I get them home safely.''

Adam glanced around the crowded room. ''Stay with them. Everything seems to be under control here. Not nearly as bad as it could have been. I'll probably be back at your place before you return with Willow and the twins.''

Daniel opened the door to leave. He seemed suddenly in a hurry to have the twins close to him.

Adam glanced out into the rain. One lone man splashed through the mud toward Dan's house. Wes! His head was low against the rain and he cradled a body, limp and lifeless in his arms.

''Nichole!'' Adam whispered the word, but it seemed to silence the room.

He grabbed his bag and ran to catch Wes. Adam knew she must be hurt and Wes was taking her where all three brothers knew she belonged. Beneath a McLain roof.

A scene from months ago flashed through Adam's mind. Only Wes had been carrying May, Daniel's wife, in the rain. And May had died.

TWENTY-SEVEN

ADAM LEANED HIS KNEE ON THE BED AND SLOWLY UNBUCKLED NI-chole's gun belt. The leather was soaked, the Colt covered in mud as he unwrapped it from around her.

"She handed me the last kid," Wes mumbled, "and I turned to pass the child along. In that moment, her foot must have slipped and no one was holding the rope tight. We were all laughing and hooting, because it was over and all the children were safe. She fell back hard before I could grab the other end of the line and start pulling her up."

At the bedroom door, Daniel held one of his twins on his arm. "Is she all right, Adam?"

Adam ran his hand along her ribs and felt her slow, steady breathing. "I think she'll be fine," he answered. "Both of you get into dry clothes. I'll take care of her. I'll call if I need anything."

Wes raised an eyebrow, but he didn't argue. He left Adam and Nichole in Daniel's bedroom and closed the door behind him.

Slowly, Adam began undressing her, checking for any bumps or cuts as he worked. Her breathing was normal, even her body temperature was not unduly low considering she'd been in cold water for the past hour. When he'd lifted her from Wes and carried her through the rain to Daniel's house, she'd held to him tightly. Silently her embrace told him that maybe she was in need of a very special kind of care.

He opened her shirt, feeling slightly like a Peeping Tom as she laid unaware. He moved his hands to her waist and began unbuttoning her trousers. She was so beautiful, not like an untouchable statue or doll as he used to think of women, but like a real flesh-and-blood woman.

He slid down beside her and felt her curl against the length of his body. Raising his hand to her throat, he spread his fingers wide as he moved down the length of her with enough pressure to let her know that he was touching her. His hand stopped below her waist. He shoved her wet clothes aside.

When she didn't respond, he repeated his cure, pressing her flesh with his bold action as he moved downward from throat to below waist. Holding her breast as his fingers passed over her, feeling her ribs, pressing into the soft valley where a child would someday grow within her.

His touch was not light like an admirer, but bold and demanding as a seasoned lover's.

She rocked slightly with pleasure, but didn't open her eyes.

He repeated his action, bolder, feeling her fully as she lay beside him, imprinting his hand upon her skin, warming her with his gentle branding.

Finally, he could wait no longer to taste her half-opened mouth. He lowered his lips and kissed hers lightly. When she didn't move, the kiss deepened, forcing her mouth wide with its plundering, taking fully while demanding a response.

Her eyes opened.

Adam didn't move. He stared into the bottomless depths of her fiery green eyes as she lay so close against him. Her shirt barely covered her shoulders, but she made no effort to pull it closed. Without breaking his stare, his hand spread out across her abdomen. There could be no doubt what he'd been doing while she'd been unconscious. The only question was how she'd react.

Without a word, she raised her lips to his once more, offering her mouth. As he kissed her, she stretched beneath his hand, offering her body as well.

Silently, he made love to her. Gently worshipping with a touch what she willingly surrendered. Unlike the first time that had been wild and free, loving now was deep and sweet with tenderness.

She gave herself easily to his every embrace, and he lost his very soul in the depths of her. They were not two people mating, but one being intertwining around and around itself until there was no place where one began and the other ended. He entered her again and again, pulling out before completion so that he could continue to hold her and touch her as she strained for more. Her breathing quickened with need for him, but he held her away, forcing her to endure more of his endless pleasing, allowing himself all he wanted of the feel of her.

And he took his fill, turning her on first her side and then her stomach, so that his hands could caress every part of her. When she cried out in pleasure, he pulled her back against him and cupped her breasts tightly as she felt his need for her pressing against her.

He held her there, denying her the fulfillment she wanted until she relaxed once more in his embrace. When she leaned her head back on his shoulder in truce, he tasted her throat hungrily as his fingers explored her now soft, waiting body.

She was pure joy in his arms, responding to his every touch now. Her body was warm and wet and shaking with need for him. For a moment he'd tamed the wild spirit and caught the fire in his hand. She responded to his needs, be they bold or slight.

As he moved across her, she welcomed his every advance. He closed his fingers around her breasts, gently tugging them again and again until they felt swollen and ripe. His mouth made her senses explode as he kissed her with the hunger of starvation. He gave her the sanctuary of his arms, and the warmth of his nearness and all life's passion.

When she could stand his sweet caresses no longer, she turned to face him, opening to allow him inside her once more. Wrapping her arms around him, she drew him close, welcoming him fully.

All the control he'd so carefully practiced vanished as she melted against him, her heartbeat matching his. There was nothing for either of them to do but ride the fire of passion, holding tightly to one another as their hearts melted together.

He thought he heard her whisper his name as she shuddered and fell back to reality. For a long time he could only hold her, marveling at the way she moved him. Even with passion spent, he still hungered for the taste of her, the feel of her, the smell of her.

Then, just before they fell asleep he said the words he swore he'd never say again until he'd heard them from her.

He whispered, "I love you."

It was almost noon when he awoke. The rain had stopped and the sun blinked between the broadcloth curtains in the bedroom. Nick was gone from his side, but the taste of her was still on his lips and the feel of her against his skin. He could hear muffled voices from beyond the door and knew they must be preparing lunch.

Adam dressed quickly. He needed to check on the children before eating. He should have done it two hours ago. Smiling, he told himself that he'd have to remember his work in the future no matter how inviting Nichole was in bed. And she'd understand, he knew she would. No matter how many times he had to leave her, he'd always come back, hungry for her once more.

When he stepped into the kitchen, Willow and the twins were alone at the table. Willow smiled up at Adam as if she were surprised anyone was still in the house.

"I forgot about you." She giggled. "I think I was to wake you."

"Where are the others?" Adam asked as he poured himself a cup of milk.

"The man with the scar and Nichole left about an hour ago. I heard Nichole say her brother was coming to Fort Worth and she wanted to be there." Willow seemed happy to have someone to talk to so she related every detail. "Mr. Daniel tried to talk her into waking you, but she said she was in a hurry to see her brother and get back home."

Adam fought down the anger. She'd left him again. After the way they'd made love, he'd believed that they could find a middle ground somewhere. To him, loving someone meant more than just wanting that person for a night. It meant wanting someone for a lifetime. She was his. How could she have any doubt after this morning?

He'd been a fool, he realized. She'd never said she loved him. For her, he was just one more adventure. Well, this adventure was going to last a little longer than she may have planned, for he wasn't going to give up.

He forced his voice to sound calm. "Where's Daniel?"

"He's in the barn getting your horse saddled," Willow answered. "He says he wants to ride over with you and pay his respects to Nichole's brother."

Adam didn't hear the last few words. He was out the door and heading to the barn. An hour later, Adam had made a final check on the children and Daniel had arranged for Mrs. March to keep a close watch on Willow and the twins. The brothers rode toward Fort Worth.

Halfway across the open land, they crossed near Emery's Post. The half-Indian, half-Frenchman's farm could hardly be called a trading post, but it had served as one in this country for almost twenty years. Emery welcomed travelers with a free cup of coffee and sold them spirits if they were willing to stay and share. He considered himself more a trader than a salesman and was always looking to make a deal for a horse or a few weeks' rations if the traveler had something to barter.

Adam hadn't planned to stop on the return trip, but when he saw

Wes's horse in the corral, his interest was piqued. Wes's animal was ten times the worth of any horse Emery owned.

"Maybe Wes traded that stallion back to Emery," Daniel offered as they rode in. "I thought when Wes told me of buying it from the old man that Emery must be losing his eyesight to allow such an animal to go."

"Maybe." Adam shook his head. There wasn't a better horse in Texas. "He didn't say anything about wanting the horse back when Wes and I stopped to water our horses yesterday on our way to your place. But looks like he's got the horse back now."

Something didn't feel right around Emery's cabin. Adam couldn't shake the feeling. The place had not only a look of neglect about it, but also one of abandonment.

Atop the dugout cabin rose a flagpole as fine as any found in a fort. Emery might not have fought in the war, but he considered himself a patriot. During the war he'd flown both the Union and the rebel flag and would raise a glass to either side, some said.

Daniel glanced up at the pole as they rode near Emery's home. "Do you see it?" he whispered.

"I see it," Adam answered as he moved his coat away from the handle of his gun. The Stars and Stripes were flying upside down, a sign of distress. "You got another weapon besides that rifle?"

"No," Daniel answered. "Maybe he was just hungover this morning when he raised the flag."

Adam shook his head. "A man who takes the time to post a flag every morning takes the time to do it right. That pole is the only thing around this place Emery seems to take any pride in."

Adam remembered having the same uneasy feeling the night he rode into Wes's camp. Nichole had said he hadn't trusted his feelings. Well, he planned to trust them now. Something was wrong.

Emery appeared at the door of his cabin. His smile was friendly enough, but he didn't call them in.

"Welcome," Emery said as they stopped. "You strangers just passing through?"

Now Adam knew there was trouble. Emery wouldn't have forgotten him. Before, he'd offered a drink, now he seemed to be just waiting for them to leave.

Adam played along. "We thought to water our horses."

Emery nodded. "Help yourself," he said, and waved them away as he walked back inside.

Daniel watered the horses while Adam lifted his Colt and followed Emery into the house.

As he stepped inside, he blinked, trying to pull the shadowy cave of a room into focus. Just as he made out Emery sitting at the table with his head in his hands, the cold barrel of a gun pressed into his left ear.

"Move," a man whispered, "and you're a dead man. We don't mean you no harm, mister, we just don't want you in the way."

Adam lifted his Colt and the stranger grabbed it away without decreasing the pressure of the barrel at the side of his head.

"In the way of what?" Adam straightened.

"Soon as our boss gets here, we're going to have a trial. We caught us a horse thief a few hours back. But don't you worry, we'll let you and your friend go after the hanging." The man's voice bore no malice. "If you'd just watered them horses and moved on, we wouldn't be slowing you up none."

"But—"

"No more questions. Walk!" The stranger shoved Adam toward the back of the room where a small door lead to a dugout. "You just think of the next few hours as a rest time on your trip."

When they reached a doorway leading to the back room, the stranger encouraged him with the barrel of his gun. Adam stumbled down the steps into a room dug out of the earth. It was full of supplies and built with only the roof aboveground. The cool room smelled of dirt and apples and spices.

"Got another one for you and the boys, Charlie." The stranger shoved Adam hard, sending him tumbling into a man twice his width.

Adam was surrounded by men who looked to be more like ranch hands than thieves.

Before he could react, his hands were tied behind him and his feet strapped with something that felt like a belt. He was pushed into a corner. A minute later, Daniel landed on top of him. Charlie and his boys left the room, closing the only door. The room darkened to musty gray. Their corner was completely without light.

Adam shuffled to a sitting position as Daniel leaned against the wall beside him.

"I was right about the flag warning." Daniel sounded proud of himself. "You should have taken heed. I knew there was trouble."

"Well." Adam kicked, trying to free his feet. "I figured my little brother would come to my aid if I got into trouble. So I thought I'd take a look."

"So did I," a voice said from only a few feet away in the shadows, making both Adam and Daniel halt all struggling.

"Wes?" Adam whispered.

"It's me, little brothers. I've been waiting for you to come to my rescue. You did a good job of finding me, but the rescue part is a little lacking."

"But I thought you were with Nick." Adam asked.

"He is," Nick answered. "In fact he's the reason we're in this mess. It seems that fine horse he bought didn't belong to Emery."

"That's a horse trader for you," Wes mumbled. "Only sold me the animal because he thought I'd be in Kansas before the real owner came back."

Nichole continued as if he had only been talking to himself. "These men are from a spread south of here and have been waiting for Wes to come back so they can hang him as a horse thief. It seems the boss man only left his mount here for a few days. When he came back, Emery claimed the animal had been stolen."

"We're going to be hung as horse thieves?" Daniel shouted.

"Only me," Wes answered. "I'm the fool who told Emery when we rode by earlier that I'd be back before nightfall to share a bottle with him. I deserve to be hung. Mom always said my drinking would get me in trouble. They just tied you three up to keep you out of the way."

"I've been in nothing but hot water since I came to Texas and found you all." Nichole's voice was laced with anger. "Your mother should have drowned the whole litter of you McLains. I'm getting out of here before Charlie and the boys discover I'm a woman."

She struggled and Adam guessed she was on the other side of Wes. He didn't blame her for being mad. For a Shadow, getting caught and tied was a great punishment.

"Between the three of you, I can't figure out how the South could have possibly lost." She continued to swear as she struggled. "It's hard to believe that a handful of cowhands could have hog-tied three McLains without one bullet being fired."

"And one Shadow," Adam added teasing her. "Isn't that why you're angry, Nichole? Not because we were stupid enough to ride into a trap, but because you were."

"Who you calling stupid?" Wes grumbled.

"Quiet!" Nick snapped at Wes. "Your wanting to stop for a drink got us into this mess. And Daniel, you'd be wise to learn from your older brother about drinking. Stop drowning your troubles in a bottle and start thinking of names for those twins."

"Are you finished?" Adam said in the general direction of her voice. "I don't care about this mess. We'll explain our way out when the boss gets here. What I want to know is why you left in such a hurry this morning? Were you afraid of being tied down to me?''

"She—''

"Hush, Wes. I want to hear it from her.'' Adam ordered. "In fact, you two stop listening. This is none of your business. As far as I'm concerned you aren't even here.''

"Do we have to talk about it?'' she whispered. "*Now?*''

"Yes,'' Adam answered. "There's never time for words with you. Having you tied up seems as good a chance as I'll ever get. I know you feel the same way I do. This morning proved it even if you won't talk about it.''

"We're not right for one another.'' Her voice shook a little. "You've never even seen me in a dress. You need a wife who—''

"Who can be as worthless as Bergette? I never needed that kind of wife. I was a fool to even think I did,'' Adam answered. "As for seeing you in a dress, you couldn't be more beautiful to me. Nick, I don't care about that. What I care about is how you sleep so close beside me, and how you stand up to me when you think I'm wrong. And how you fight for my brothers as if they were your family.

"I know I'll never have all of you. A part will always be free, but I can't let you go.''

"You can't stop me,'' she whispered. "I'll be out of here in ten minutes. You'll never find me.''

He could hear her struggling with her ropes.

"In Tennessee, six-year-old children can tie better knots,'' she complained.

"Daniel!'' Adam shouted in anger, knowing his time was short. He had no doubt that she'd be untied and gone in a matter of minutes.

"I'm not listening,'' Daniel answered. "I'm not even sure I'm here. How about you, Wes?''

"I think I left five minutes ago. I'd check if I was listening but Adam told me not to.''

"Are you still ordained?'' Adam asked without playing into their joke. "Can you still marry folks, Dan?''

"Yes.'' Daniel now sounded interested. "Providing both the parties are willing.''

"Then marry us,'' Adam said. "Right here, right now. She's not leaving me again without knowing she belongs to me as truly as I belong to her.''

"B-but—'' Daniel stammered.

"Hold on, Adam!'' Wes jumped in. "I want the kid in the family too, but she don't seem all that willing.''

"I love her," Adam said. "And she loves me, too. She can run from me, but she can't deny it any longer. We're one, we always have been since that first night. There will never be another for me or her. At least this time when she runs, she'll know how I feel about her."

"Nick," Wes whispered. "Do you agree with Adam? Do you love him?"

"I don't want to." She sighed. "He's the most frustrating man that ever walked the earth. Half the time I want to shoot him for what he does, and the other half stab him for what he refuses to do. There's no understanding the man."

"That's not the question. Do you love me?" Adam asked.

"Love's something for the weak-minded who don't have anything better to think about." She kicked in the darkness and Wes groaned. "You'll fit in here, Wes."

"Like hell," he mumbled. "I'm never riding close to love again as long as I live. Stop trying to change the subject, kid. Do you love my brother or not?" Wes repeated.

There was a long silence. "I do," she finally whispered. "But—"

"Daniel, start at the beginning," Adam interrupted her. "She's already said the end."

"Dearly beloved, we are gathered here together in this dusty dugout, while awaiting our brother's hanging, to join this woman and this man in . . ."

TWENTY-EIGHT

WOLF SLOWED HIS HORSE FOR THE TENTH TIME AND ALLOWED THE boy to catch up with him. Three hours ago he'd arrived in Fort Worth on the stage. Wolf had no trouble finding Doc McLain's place, but everyone in the house was crazier than bedbugs on a hot skillet.

A nun kept insisting she'd never seen any woman named Nichole and tried to push him off the porch. Once he finally got inside the house, a cute little cook flirted with him as if he'd been freshly washed. When he asked her about Nick, she didn't lie any better than the nun.

Finally, a pale woman came downstairs. She claimed to be the widow who owned the place, but insisted he was mistaken about Nichole. She told him several times that nothing happened in the house without her knowledge, so his sister had never been under her roof.

Wolf believed her and was about to leave and look for Nick somewhere else when he collided with a tiny ball of lace and curls he remembered as Bergette. He smiled his best smile and offered a handshake. She screamed as if she were under full attack and started throwing things at him.

He was obliged to put his arm around Bergette and lift her off the ground a few feet to settle her down and give her a better look at his face so she'd remember seeing him. But she didn't take well to settling.

The more she screamed and kicked and threw things, the more everyone else in the house seemed to take pity on him. At first he had the feeling the little princess didn't like him, but with what happened next, he realized she'd done him a great favor.

The nun and the cook finally got him down to the kitchen and out of Bergette's way. Before leaving her range of fire, he promised to come by for another visit with the little lady some other day.

Suddenly, the nun and the cook couldn't say enough about Nick and all that had been happening. Bergette had convinced them that Wolf must truly be Nichole's brother. The trouble they described didn't seem like anything Nick couldn't handle, till the little boy piped up about how Nick was hiding out by sleeping in Adam's room.

Wolf stood and asked where to rent a horse. He'd heard enough.

Before he knew it, the kid named Nance was riding beside him talking like a magpie. All Wolf wanted to do was plot how to kill Adam, but the boy wouldn't give him time. He'd sent Nick to Texas so she would be safe. He'd even convinced Tyler there was no need for him to come along to fetch Nick. But when he heard Adam had been sleeping with his sister, he knew he'd be killing a McLain. Wolf liked the family, but a duty was a duty.

As Nance caught up to him again, Wolf couldn't help but smile. He liked kids. Back before the war, he used to dream of finding a woman and settling down with more children around than they could keep up with. But the closest he'd been to a woman in years was when he held Bergette back at the boardinghouse while she was trying to kill him. Wolf couldn't hold back a laugh. She felt good, he thought. Real good. Like fire all wrapped in powder and lace. Maybe he'd even think of shaving before he paid her another call.

"Captain Hayward?" Nance asked. "Did you ever have to kill anyone in the war?"

"Not if I could help it," Wolf answered.

"I bet you just scared them, didn't you?" Nance held his reins tight. Like most boys his age, he could ride a good trailing horse. As long as he didn't have to take the lead, he had no trouble riding.

"Hold them reins like this, boy." Wolf put his fists in front of the saddle horn about six inches apart. "Run the right rein through first your right hand, then the left. Then thread the left rein through your left hand, then the right. That way both hands hold both reins."

The boy closed his fists in front of him with his reins in place.

"Now, all you have to do is turn one fist down and you turn the horse." Wolf pulled his right fist thumb up and the horse moved to the command. "But remember, you control a horse more with your legs than with the reins. The bit's a guide. No sense tearing a horse's mouth up by jerking on it."

Nance sat up proud in the saddle, enjoying the lesson. It had been a long time since he'd gone with a man on a real adventure. But the nun said she'd square it with his mother cause the doc would look after him on the way home. Sister said he needed to get out of the house and get some air, like there was none left inside.

Wolf smiled. The boy had forgotten his questions of war.

An hour later, they came upon a place the stable hand had said would be Emery's Post. Wolf slowed as he noticed several men gathered about a tree. The closer he got, the more his hand itched for the feel of his Colt. But he'd learned, never go in like you're in a hurry and never offer help until you know which side right stands on.

"Stay well behind me, boy," he ordered with no room for argument. "And don't say a word, no matter what you see."

"Yes, sir," Nance whispered. "I can do that. I've been practicing most of my life."

"I'm going to play a game, but it's just an act. Do you understand?" Wolf was close enough to smell trouble, and he wanted to know the boy would follow orders and stay out of harm's way.

"Yes," Nance answered, his voice shaking slightly. "No matter what, you can count on me."

"Good," Wolf whispered. "Follow me."

Nichole looked up and saw Wolf riding in. She lowered her head, not wanting to give away her joy at seeing him. She'd been near panic when they'd been hauled out of the dugout. The trial had lasted about five minutes and now it was time for Wes's hanging. Only Wolf was here. Wolf would know what to do.

"Afternoon," Wolf said casually to the ranch hands standing about. "Mind if I watch?"

An older man who was obviously the leader shook his head. "It'll be good for your boy to see a horse thief hang. Keep him on the straight and narrow."

"Much obliged." Wolf's Southern accent marked him as a friend. He smoothly introduced himself as a captain with the Tennessee regulars.

The ranch boss smiled and identified himself as Colonel Wilcox, formerly with Terry's Rangers.

Wolf pointed with his head. "You hanging them all?" He glanced at the cowhands' stained leather chaps and knew these were working men, not drifters or troublemakers. If they were hanging a man, they probably thought they had good reason.

Colonel Wilcox pointed toward Wes. "The other three are just friends of his come to watch. We'll let them go when the hanging's over. I don't have no quarrel with them. Only with this Yank with the scar on his face. He stole my horse while I left it here for Emery to keep an eye on. My place is a few hours north of here, so my men have been waiting for the stranger to pass by. We don't look kindly on horse thieves in these parts.''

Slowly lowering himself from his horse, Wolf walked over to Wes. ''He looks like a mean one, all right.'' Wolf leaned closer. ''Evil eyes,'' he added as he stood within an inch of Wes. ''Worst I've ever seen. And that scar would frighten most women and children.''

Growling like a trapped animal, Wes shoved Wolf with his shoulder.

Wolf's arm went around Wes for only an instant as he tried to right himself.

In that moment, Wes felt the blade of a knife slide between his wrists and slice the rope binding his hands.

Leaning back, Wolf took a good look at the prisoner. ''Yep. Evil eyes.'' He winked at Wes. ''Good thing you got him tied.''

When Wolf moved away, Wes kept his hands crossed behind him.

''But I think you're hanging the wrong one of these fellows.'' Wolf rubbed his hairy chin as he addressed the ranch boss. ''You see, one of them slept with my sister while he was guarding her from harm. Now, a man who'll do that is worse than a horse thief.''

Colonel Wilcox nodded. ''But it was a fine horse.''

''It was my *only* sister,'' Wolf countered.

''Get another rope ready, boys!'' Colonel Wilcox yelled, then turned to the McLains. ''Which one of you low-life, no-good snakes slept with this man's sister?''

They all three looked guilty, and Wolf had to fight for control to keep from heading straight into them with fists flying.

''I did.'' Adam stepped forward facing Wolf squarely.

Years of playing the game of control, like an actor on a stage, snapped in Wolf. His mighty fist swung, catching Adam hard on the jaw.

Adam staggered and spat blood.

''I thought you were an honorable man!'' Wolf growled like a wild animal. ''I thought she'd be safe in your care.''

''I am an honorable man, and she's not the easiest woman to keep safe,'' Adam defended. ''But I slept with her, and I plan to again if I get out of this mess.''

Wolf hit him with another right, hard and full with a blow that would have knocked most men down.

Adam staggered once more.

The ranch hands stood back, cheering the huge man on. It wasn't a fair fight, but it was more fun than a hanging. They all seemed to think that a man so foolish as to admit he wanted to sleep with a girl in front of her brother deserved to have some sense knocked into him.

Nichole held her tongue. She guessed Wolf was just playing a game, getting the men off guard. But when she saw blood dripping from Adam's lip, she wasn't so sure.

"Untie him!" Wolf raged. "Let him try and defend himself. Hanging's too easy for him."

Someone cut Adam's ropes, and Wolf hit him again before he had time to lift his hands in defense.

When Adam raised his head, with blood streaming from his nose and his left eye swelling closed, Nichole had enough. She charged her brother. "Stop it!" she shouted, shoving him hard with her shoulder. "Stop trying to kill my husband!"

All the cowhands froze in sudden silence.

Nichole closed her eyes in dread. She'd given herself away. In one moment of anger, she'd foiled any plan Wolf had. After all the years of training and drilling, she'd failed him. There could be no doubt of her gender now.

Wolf placed his hand on her back and smiled at her as the blade of a knife cut her ropes. "It's all right," he whispered, knowing she expected him to yell at her for breaking her disguise. "It's time to stop pretending to be something you're not."

When she looked up at him, he added, "Now I know you must love this Yank. I think I knew it from the first. If you married him, it's time for me to step aside."

Then he lifted her up in his arms and gave her the big bear hug she'd waited for all her life. To her horror, tears welled in her eyes. She shoved them away. Right here in front of her brother and all the McLains, she was starting to act like a woman.

The ranch hands couldn't have been more enthralled if they'd been at a grand opera house in the city. They all stood around waiting like the curtain would be coming up any minute on the second act.

While Nichole ran to Adam, Wolf faced the ranch boss. "I changed my mind," he said with a smile. "I don't want to hang him. Not now that I know he's in the family. In fact, if we had whiskey, we'd all need to drink a round to celebrate my little sister's marriage." He patted Nance on the head, letting the boy know the game was over.

Emery answered the call. Within minutes everyone was lifting a cup of whiskey to the bride and groom, and Emery filled to the brim as long as he knew the big man was paying. No one seemed to notice that Wes had removed the rope from around his neck and was toasting with the rest.

Wolf told the story of how Adam and Nick met as the sun lowered. Eventually he told of Wes and Daniel and May and of the night they all felt like family. Emery was so touched by the story that he admitted he might have been mistaken about the stolen horse. Since it was back in the corral, maybe it had been borrowed and not stolen. His memory didn't extend to Wes paying for the horse. For even with Wes's encouragement, he could remember no money exchanging hands.

Then Colonel Wilcox lost any anger in his whiskey. Like many, North and South, he'd had too few reasons to celebrate. A marriage outranked a hanging any day. He cornered the youngest McLain, asking if Daniel might consider riding out to his ranch some Sunday to marry several of the couples.

Adam walked over to the well and used his handkerchief to wipe the blood from his mouth. The shadows spread night over the prairie, making the earth seem peaceful in sleep. He noticed Nance already curled up on the porch asleep with Wolf's bedroll tucked around him.

"How many times were you planning to let Wolf hit you before you hit back?" Nick asked from behind him. She was in her world now, the shadows, but she was no less beautiful.

"I told you once I was through with fighting." Adam faced her. "I figured he had a right. I not only slept with you, I forced you into marrying me. If I'd been your brother, I'd have probably killed me."

"But you're not my brother. You're my husband." Nichole touched his arm lightly, letting her fingers slowly move up to his shoulder. "No one forced me into anything today."

He studied her closely, knowing she was right. He might love every ounce of her, but he controlled none. She was her own woman, but she was also his wife. And she was looking at him with those beautiful green eyes that promised a lifetime of passion.

Adam put his hands on her waist gently, testing. When she didn't pull away, he drew her close, loving the way she fit against him. "Nichole Hayward, will you marry me?"

She laughed. "You're a little late in asking, Doc."

"I know, but I don't want my wife to say someday that I didn't ask her properly. I love you more than I've one lifetime to show. I want you by my side, no matter what happens. Be my wife, Nick. Be the mother of my children. Be my partner in everything I do."

"Do your brothers come with the deal?"

"I'm afraid so." Adam grinned. "Though I'm the one who should be asking that question."

She smiled into the warmest brown eyes she'd ever seen. "Someone's got to keep you out of trouble. This is a wild country, this Texas." She gently kissed his busted lip. "It'll be a full-time job just keeping my brother and brother-in-laws from killing you." He was a man of peace in her world. She'd known it the night they'd met. He alone could heal her inner scars with his love. "I'll marry you, Adam."

He kissed her tenderly. "I have a feeling with you as my wife, I'll probably die in bed." He moved his hands over her hips and pressed her close. "Say it," he whispered against her ear. "Say you love me."

"I love you, Doc, I always have." She rocked against him, kissing him lightly as she whispered, "From now on, I'm no longer a Shadow. I'll be beside you in day and night."

"In day and night," he echoed as he kissed her fully. "Until death do us part."